“Not m

“No, not married.”

“Never?” It would’ve been better if she’d gotten married, Cam thought. At least then he’d have an answer, even if the answer was that she’d fallen in love with some other guy.

She shook her head.

“Too busy saving the world, huh?” Cam gazed into Nicole’s eyes.

“There’s no point going into all of that now. Why don’t we order and then talk about your son? That’s why we’re here, isn’t it?”

“Sure.”

“So, as Michael’s teacher, what can I do?”

He gave a hopeless shrug. “I don’t know, Nic. I guess I thought that, as his teacher, you might see something I’ve missed.” With an ironic grin, he added, “I didn’t know the teacher would turn out to be an old friend.”

An old friend.

Yes, they were old friends. They’d been other things, too. But if she could manage to think of him as only a friend…

A flicker of indecision flashed in his eyes, and then he reached out, his touch achingly familiar as his hand covered hers. “I need help with Michael, Nic. Will you help me?”

Dear Reader,

Courage is usually associated with dangerous situations and with saving lives. But many times, just facing the daily challenges thrust upon us requires great courage, too, sometimes more than we think we have.

In *Slow Dance with a Cowboy*, I wanted to explore the challenges confronting Nicole Weston, who was given an unchangeable set of circumstances that affect her whole life. Cameron Colter is dealing with his own challenges when his son brings him face-to-face with yet another—the woman he couldn't forget. And soon love becomes the greatest challenge of all.

I like writing stories that are reflective of life, stories with lots of gray areas. I like writing about heroes and heroines who have their flaws but when faced with seemingly insurmountable odds, triumph and go on to make better lives for themselves and for the people they care about. They're able to do this through their courage and through the strength of their love. My heroes and heroines don't always make the right decisions; they don't always know what's best. But whatever their flaws, they learn from their mistakes and go the distance. Nicole Weston and Cam Colter are such people. I hope you enjoy reading their story as much as I enjoyed writing it.

I'm always thrilled to hear from readers and would love to hear from you. You can write to me at P.O. Box 2292, Mesa, AZ 85214 or by e-mail at LindaStyle@lindastyle.com and through my Web site at http://www.LindaStyle.com. Best wishes and happy reading!

Linda Style

Books by Linda Style

HARLEQUIN SUPERROMANCE

923—HER SISTER'S SECRET
977—DADDY IN THE HOUSE

Slow Dance with a Cowboy

Linda Style

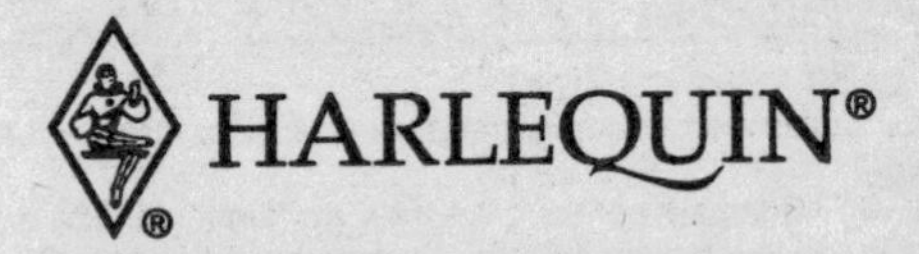

TORONTO • NEW YORK • LONDON
AMSTERDAM • PARIS • SYDNEY • HAMBURG
STOCKHOLM • ATHENS • TOKYO • MILAN • MADRID
PRAGUE • WARSAW • BUDAPEST • AUCKLAND

ISBN 0-373-71062-3

SLOW DANCE WITH A COWBOY

This edition published by arrangement with Harlequin Books S.A.

Visit us at www.eHarlequin.com

Printed in U.S.A.

DEDICATION

To the "Girls."
Mogie (Margaret), Pat, Fran, Alice, Geri, Diane and Sharon.
When I write about friendship, I think of ours.

ACKNOWLEDGMENTS

My deep appreciation to Sue Davis, Executive Director of the Arizona Alliance for the Mentally Ill (AAMI) and to the National Alliance for the Mentally Ill (NAMI) for the wealth of information made available to me—and to the professionals in the field of mental health, many of whom were my co-workers over the past ten years. Without you, my understanding of mental-health issues would not be as complete. Many thanks also to the Gilbert, Arizona, Police Department and the Citizens' Police Academy, especially the program's facilitator, Officer Joe Gilligan, for insights about police procedure. Since this is a work of fiction, I have taken liberties in some areas for the sake of the story. Any errors are mine. Additional thanks to my friend Eve Paludan, who read this book in its first incarnation, and to my family for your love and support and, most of all, for the fruitful brainstorming sessions. Great teamwork, guys!

CHAPTER ONE

FOR ONE FRACTION OF A SECOND, she thought the crimson letters dripping down the wall might have been painted in blood.

Nicole Weston stood in her classroom doorway, staring in stunned disbelief.

Graffiti covered every surface—desktops, walls, blackboards, the wastebaskets, even the corkboards with her students' brightly colored drawings thumbtacked to them.

With a quick, sharp breath, she reached for the phone on the wall near the door and called the office. No answer. She glanced at the clock. 7:00 a.m. The principal was usually here by this time. Where *was* he?

If the creeps who did this were still around, she wasn't going to go looking for Roy or anyone else. She punched in 911. *Ten weeks before school's out for the summer and my room gets trashed.*

Keeping her voice low, she said, "I'm a teacher at Barton Elementary and my classroom's been vandalized." She gave her name and the school's address.

"Are you hurt?"

"No. I just got here. Will you please send someone?"

"Are you alone?"

"As far as I can tell." She looked over her shoulder, newly aware of all the dark stairwells, closet doors, niches and shadowed corners in the hallway of the old building. "Can you please send someone right now?"

"They're on the way."

The operator had barely uttered the words when the faint wail of sirens echoed in the distance. A moment later, the high-pitched squalls amplified, and as help neared, a sense of relief shot through her. But too soon.

A shadow crested at the end of the hallway. She caught her breath but then released it as she saw Roy Sipowitz rounding the corner. The short, balding principal strutted toward her like a banty rooster checking out his domain. She'd only been there a week and she had his number.

Within seconds, blue-uniformed officers swarmed into the building. Sipowitz turned, glancing to the right and the left, confusion on his face. Then, one by one, Barton's administrative staff and a half-dozen teachers filtered in, eyes wide and shocked.

The children. They'd be here soon and shouldn't see the room like this. If it was a disturbing sight to her, it would be that much more upsetting to a child. She waved the principal over.

When Roy reached her—and before he had a chance to mouth a syllable—she shoved the phone into his hand. "My room's a mess, and when I couldn't get hold of you, I called 911. I'm going to catch the children before they come in and see the damage."

As she headed toward the double-door entry, a police officer pulled her aside and bombarded her with questions.

The police weren't taking any chances, she knew, because in the past three months, two schools in the Phoenix metropolitan area had been involved in shootings, and in one, five students and a teacher had been held hostage.

She had no answers, and with each question her nerves stretched tighter. "Can I go now? I really need to stop my first-graders before they come in."

The officer nodded.

Roy, who'd sidled up while the man questioned her, said, "Use the conference space in the library for the day. I'll have one of the aides redirect the students and also have Bob bring more chairs if you need them."

While Roy commandeered an aide, she went to the conference room and set up shop. Bob hadn't bothered to bring the extra chairs, so instead of half the class sitting on the floor, they all did. Once the children had settled down, she explained the change of room as an adventure. Most took it in stride, but a few students used the opportunity to act out. When noon arrived and her aide led the children to the lunchroom, she was relieved to have a few minutes to herself.

Still sitting at the long oak table, she rested her head in her hands and closed her eyes. *Just for a minute or two.*

"My dad's coming to see you," a small voice said.

Her eyes snapped open. One of her students, a blond boy, smaller than most of the children in the class, stood at her side. He had big blue eyes. Sad eyes.

"That's great...um, Michael." She pulled his name from the list at her elbow.

"Are you gonna tell him I'm bad?"

She gave him her full attention. "Did you do something bad?"

"I did when the other teacher was here."

"Well, Michael. You've been perfect since I got here, so let's just forget whatever happened before this week and call it a new beginning."

The boy beamed—until he saw the scowling aide in the doorway waiting for him to join the rest of the class. He left, and Nicole tried to relax again.

There were no scheduled parent-teacher conferences she was aware of, but she made a mental note to go through the departing teacher's records as soon as possible. She might be just a sub, but she was going to do the job right.

If only she could get her hands to stop trembling. The graffiti incident had shaken her more than she realized. Later, when the long day was finally over, she heaved a sigh of relief, packed up her things and went back to her classroom to assess the damage.

Surprisingly the room looked much the same as always. She skirted the knee-high tables on the way to her desk, then fell wearily into the chair. The strong turpentine-like scent of cleaning solution burned her nostrils and cloaked the odor of sweaty children and pungent sneakers.

Spotting a piece of chalk on the floor, she leaned down to pick it up. As she did, her gaze caught something scrawled on the side of her desk. *What in the world…* She crouched for a closer look.

Warning number 1!

Her pulse raced. Had someone done this today, after the cleanup? Or had it been missed? Was it meant for her?

It couldn't be. She hadn't been at Barton long enough for anyone to know anything about her. She tried to remember. Had there been any other messages like this scrawled around the room? None had registered at the time. She'd been too shocked.

Kids, usually teens, do this kind of thing for a thrill, or for effect, one officer had said. She wanted to believe that. She *had* to believe it.

Still… A deep sense of personal violation lodged in her chest.

Gritting her teeth, she grabbed a paper towel and started rubbing at the thick white letters.

"Guess one of your students didn't like his homework assignment, huh?"

She jerked around. Bob, the janitor, was standing in the doorway. Annoyed because she knew what students he meant, she said, "Well... Someone didn't like something."

He meant the teens in the At Risk program she taught two evenings a week and Saturday mornings in the portables out back, a special tutoring job she'd taken on before she'd been hired to sub full-time. Her A.R. students were on the verge of dropping out of high school, but if they could pass the two courses she taught, they would graduate with their class.

One final swipe got the last of the graffiti.

Bob waved and continued on down the hall. Even though she had no patience with people so quick to place blame without knowing the facts, she smiled and waved back. This morning, the officer had implied the same thing as Bob about her A.R. students, and her skin prickled just thinking about it.

They knew nothing except that the class was geared to students who had trouble learning. How that translated into one or all of them being guilty now, she had no idea. Or maybe, unfortunately, she did. She hated to call the police again, but she had to—in case they hadn't seen the cryptic message.

A few minutes later, tired, ready for a hot bath and a cold beer, she stuffed the remaining papers in her briefcase and hurried out the door. The sooner she got to the hospital to see her mother, the sooner she could relax and indulge herself.

The halls were silent, the fluorescent lights eerily dim. She locked the door, then slumped against it.

The week from hell was over. Thank God.

What else could possibly happen?

"Excuse me, ma'am." A man's deep voice penetrated the silence.

Nicole jumped, and suddenly aware of her vulnerability, she felt a wave of apprehension sweep over her.

"I'm here for the conference about my son."

A parent. She expelled a breath of relief and whirled around. "I'm sorry. The regular teacher is out for the rest of the year and—"

"Nicci?"

Oh, God. Her first instinct was to bolt.

But she couldn't.

She couldn't be rude to a parent—even if the parent was Cameron Colter.

"Nicole. I can't believe it!"

His startled expression said his surprise was as great as hers, and he looked as if he felt just as unsure about what to do next.

Okay. She took in a deep breath. She could handle surprise. She'd had plenty of experience there. And it was a heck of a lot easier to deal with than the awful note on which their relationship had ended.

"Hello, Cam."

His brilliant blue eyes narrowed. "Hello? That's it? Ten years and that's it?"

She forced a smile and tried for casual, but her tongue felt as if it was glued to the roof of her mouth. "Well, yes," she finally managed. "I'm surprised to see you, too—here, I mean."

Lips pressed into a firm line, Cameron stared at her, and in this strange lighting, she couldn't discern the emotion. Disapproval? Anger?

She hadn't recognized him right away because he wore a dark navy suit, a light blue button-down Oxford shirt and a crimson tie, a look vastly different from the way he'd dressed back when they were together.

Back when he'd always worn faded Wranglers, western-style shirts and battered Roper boots.

Back when she'd thought he was the sexiest man alive. He crossed his arms and rocked on his heels, still studying her face. "You haven't changed, Nicci. Not even a freckle. Amazing. Absolutely amazing."

His broad white smile caught her off guard, and her pulse skittered out of control. She gazed at his tanned face, evidence of his father's Native American heritage, and the sky-blue eyes, a tribute to his mother's Scandinavian genes that had oddly won out over the dominant brown.

Eyes that used to send her into instant meltdown…

She hesitated, drew in another breath. "You haven't changed much either, except…" As she glanced up, he raised a hand, combing long fingers through hair that barely skimmed his collar, hair that ten years ago had trailed in shiny, ebony waves down his back, or was sometimes pulled into a ponytail at the nape of his neck.

"Times change. I'm a taxpaying citizen now," he said with a grin. A beat later, he added, "Hard to believe, isn't it?"

Oh, yes. Hard to believe for more reasons than one. She made herself look at him, instantly recalling the dissident college student with bronc-busting in his blood. But right now, he was more the corporate executive than the rugged ranch kid with whom she'd once been so in love.

So in love she'd gone to every rodeo competition he'd entered. Lord, she remembered… The earthy scents of leather and sweat, the reckless lovemaking afterward…

She remembered it all as clearly as if it were yesterday.

But he was there for a conference, he'd said. Only it

couldn't be with her, because even though she hadn't memorized all her students' names yet, she knew she *didn't* have any boys in her class with the Colter surname. She'd have noticed it immediately.

He pulled a scrap of paper from his pocket and held it out, squinting to read. "I thought you were Mrs. Jessup, since this is my son's room." As he crumpled the paper in his fist, his eyes came back to hers.

She looked away. "Mrs. Jessup is very ill, and I'm taking her place for the remainder of the year. The school sent out notices at the beginning of the week."

He shrugged. "Not to me."

"Maybe your son is in the other class? I don't recall a student with your last name."

"Ah," he said. "Michael's registered under his mother's name. I've just had it legally changed. Guess I need to update the school records, too. Michael Hale. Is he in your class?"

Oh dear. All she could do was nod—and wonder why the child had his mother's last name and not his father's. Maybe the boy was his stepson? The man she'd known ten years ago would never have allowed a child of his to be born out of wedlock.

He gave her a puzzled look. "So *you're* Michael's teacher. Y'know, that's hard to believe, too."

Nicole straightened. "Really. Why is that?"

"Well, I guess I figured you'd be long gone, off saving lives somewhere."

Ah, there it was. The bitterness in his voice was unmistakable; and *that* was the reaction she'd always expected if she ever saw him again. The reaction she deserved.

Expecting it, she should've been prepared.

But she wasn't. She didn't know how to respond. Certainly not with the truth. Not here. Not now.

It didn't matter, anyway. Nothing had changed, and it never would.

"I decided teaching suited me better."

He jammed two fingers into the knot of his tie to loosen it. "Yeah. I see that. Kinda strange you being my son's teacher and all, don't you think?" His rancher's drawl was still with him, despite the new image.

Yeah…strange, all right. A bizarre twist of fate, as her friend Risa was fond of saying. "Will that be a problem?"

He frowned at her quizzically. "A problem? In what way?"

She turned and started down the hall again, but he kept in step with her. "In the way that our personal history might interfere with the parent-teacher relationship. If you think it's a problem, I can request a transfer for Michael to the other first-grade class."

"Whoa!" He swung around in front of her so she had to stop walking. "No more transfers. Another change would be the worst thing for him."

"Okay. I just thought—"

"He's got enough problems already. That's why I arranged for this conference."

She cut around him and started walking again. "I'm terribly sorry about the mix-up. No one gave me any information about this conference, and I've got another appointment, for which I'm already late. I'll be happy to reschedule the conference for you."

She wished *someone* had let her know. With a message. A phone call. Anything. Anything but seeing him so suddenly like this. Wham, out of nowhere, he was there—the man who'd affected her life in ways she could never have imagined.

"If you or your wife would like to call me tomorrow, we can set another time."

"Great. But since there is no wife, you'll have to put up with me."

No wife. Her heart skipped a beat.

"Fine, just give me a call," she said, then checked her watch. "I've got to go now." It was true, not a lie just to get away, even though the urge was almost overwhelming.

If she didn't leave right this minute, she might remember how wonderful his arms felt around her at the end of the day. How gently he could kiss when he wanted. Of course, neither of them had wanted gentle back then.

Young love and lust went hand in hand, and just thinking about it made her blood rush and her breath come short. But so what? A relationship between them was no more plausible now than it was before. She was his son's teacher. Period. End of story.

Cam reached inside his suit jacket and took out a business card and pen. "Okay, what's your number and when's a good time to call?"

Her number? "The usual procedure is to call the school."

He raised his eyebrows. "Will someone be in the office tomorrow? It's Saturday."

Heat climbed her cheeks. Good Lord. She was blushing—even after all these years. "Then call me on Monday."

"Okay. But just so you know, I *would* like to reschedule as soon as possible because I have some real concerns about Michael."

She squared her shoulders. She had concerns, too, and they had nothing to do with Michael. Michael, in fact, seemed like a normal, healthy, well-mannered little boy.

But Cam *had* made an appointment and it wasn't his fault she couldn't keep it. "Sure. I'll do what I can."

"I'll walk you to your car." He locked a hand on her elbow and guided her through the door and outside to the parking lot, just as if nothing bad had ever happened between them.

And all she could think of was that he'd said, "*No wife.*" *Incorrect, Nicole.* All she could think of was his touch. Even through her white cotton sweater, it felt hotter than fire.

And did he have to walk so close? So close she couldn't help inhaling his clean masculine scent—and found herself responding with the same gut-level excitement she'd felt so many years before.

"I'm right there." She gestured toward her ancient Volvo and picked up her pace. Escape was imminent. She swiped at a wild clump of hair and thrust it behind her ear as she barreled ahead, hoping he hadn't noticed how much he'd unnerved her.

As they approached the car, she fished for keys in her backpack and finding them, reached for the handle. His big hand closed over hers. *Oh, man.* She eased away, allowing him to open the door for her. A gentleman to the bone.

She immediately slid into the driver's seat, and tucked her broomstick skirt under her legs, impatient to leave.

"Y'know," he drawled, still standing in the opening between the door and the car.

Apparently her escape *wasn't* going to be as fast as she wanted.

"I'd like to call before Monday if I could. I'm *very* concerned about Michael, and I was hoping his teacher could help me." He leaned down, his face so close she could smell spearmint on his breath. ‘‘Why don’t we have lunch tomorrow? Two old friends…’’

Oh, jeez. That was *not* what she wanted to hear. ‘‘I’ll have to check my schedule,’’ she answered, then jammed the key into the ignition and started the car, her need to flee even more urgent now.

‘‘Okay. I’ll call you later. Are you in the book?’’

She shook her head. ‘‘No, and I won’t be home till late. I really have to go now.’’ She shoved the manual shift into gear.

Check her schedule? Good grief. Had those words actually come out of her mouth?

‘‘So, you call me in the morning then.’’ He handed her his card, stepped back and shut the door.

As soon as he was far enough from the car door so she wouldn’t clip him, she backed out and sped to the exit, tires squealing all the way. Embarrassed at the noise, she shot a quick glance at the rearview mirror. He was still standing in the same spot.

His feet were planted apart, his arms crossed and plastered on his face was that…that damned cowboy grin.

And then he waved.

‘‘MUST BE SOMETHING special goin’ on today?’’ Risa puckered her fuchsia lips into an enthusiastic whistle as she stood at Nicole’s condo door early Saturday morning, examining Nichole’s red pantsuit.

‘‘A little different from your usual hippy-dippy retro look, eh?’’ Risa nodded, as if absorbing every last detail. ‘‘Nice touch.’’ She tapped a sculptured scarlet nail to the silver pin on the lapel of Nicole’s jacket.

‘‘C’mon in.’’ Nicole gave an exaggerated sweep of one arm, but her neighbor was inside before the words had left Nicole’s lips. In the two years since Risa Beaumont had moved into the condo across the hall with her brother, she and Nicole had become close friends—despite the fact that they had nothing in common. Risa's brother had moved out the previous year, but she'd stayed on.

Nicole went to the kitchen and her friend followed, dropping into a chair while Nicole brought the coffeepot and two mugs to the round pedestal table.

"No appointments today?" Nicole asked.

Risa worked as a manicurist and massage therapist and managed to escape the tedium of nine-to-five by working for herself. She jokingly called herself "the mobile massager" and traveled with her portable table wherever needed. She also rented space in a nail salon to do manicures, but she set her own hours, working only when she wanted, which was usually when she needed the extra money. "Nope, I'm free today."

"Well, I've got to be at school by eight," Nicole said, filling their cups. The aroma itself was almost strong enough to get her revved for the day. Black and strong, that was how she liked it.

"Oh yeah, I forgot. You're the living time clock."

"Only on school days."

"Which is every day but Sunday. Right?" Risa snapped her fingers. "Okay, gimme the poop. I know you don't get dressed like this for those dropouts of yours."

Nicole shrugged casually. "Nothing special. Just a conference lunch with a parent. It's business." She ran her fingertips over the seat of the garage-sale chair, checking the wood for rough edges before she sat.

"Since when do teachers hold conferences with parents over lunch?" Risa pulled an incredulous expression. "Puh-leeze."

"He had an appointment with the other teacher for yesterday afternoon and I couldn't do it then. And he just happens to be an old friend."

"Uh-huh. Well, at least that makes *some* kind of sense. So, did you say he's a single dad?" Risa arched a perfectly contoured brow as she added liberal doses of milk and sugar to the earthenware mug.

"No, I didn't say."

"Anyone I know?"

It was a facetious question, because she dated infrequently and never long enough to make introductions to anyone. "It was so many years ago that I don't know if *I* even know him anymore."

The penciled brows arched again. "But what you *do* know is enough to get you into something that shows your figure for a change."

"My intent is to look professional, Risa."

"Uh-huh. Is he married?"

Nicole sighed. "He's not married."

Risa said nothing, but Nicole knew she wouldn't be satisfied until she had all the details. "He showed up last night for a conference with the teacher I replaced, but I wasn't apprised of that, and I had to visit my mom. He said it was important because his son has problems. He called last night before I got home and left a message. Since it wasn't his fault the conference was canceled, I called him back and we decided to do it over lunch."

"And?"

"I'm meeting him at Sam's at the Arizona Center."

"Which explains the outfit?"

"Right."

Risa leaned forward, settling both hands on her ample thighs. Bleached, spiked hair on anyone else of Risa's age might've seemed odd, but forty-something Risa, Brooklyn-born-and-bred, carried it off with a confidence all her own. Brash, outspoken and downright rude were the usual adjectives Nicole heard from others about her friend, and Risa was always ready to give an Oscar-winning performance to prove them right.

Nicole was probably the only person in the world who knew that her friend was a truly caring person underneath the brazen facade.

"And does mystery man have a name?"

"Yes, he does." Nicole grinned.

Raising her cup, Risa peered over the rim at Nicole. Waiting.

"Cameron Colter."

More waiting.

"That's it, Risa. Just lunch with an old friend." Nicole shrugged again, palms up.

"So he's an old boyfriend, he's single and his kid's in your class. Is that, like fate, or what?"

"It's business."

"Sure. Okay. That's cool." Despite her words, Risa's doubtful expression lingered.

"I have to go." Nicole pushed to her feet. On Saturdays, she had to be at the school before her students arrived. There were only four of them, but given their backgrounds, the school board insisted someone be there at all times.

She'd originally had five students in the class, but one of them, after a fight with his peers and disagreement over the work required, had quickly decided the program wasn't for him and dropped out. Failing before she'd even started wasn't the way she wanted to begin her new career, even if the A.R. class was a temporary position. She'd vowed then and there that she'd do everything she could to ensure that no student of hers ever dropped out again.

But right now, she had other concerns—like getting used to the idea of having Cameron's son in her first-grade class. Seeing her old love again, even on a professional basis, wasn't going to be easy.

"Okay. You can tell me the rest later."

Apparently satisfied for the moment, her friend got up to leave and Nicole followed her out. Risa stopped abruptly in the hallway, sniffed the air and inched closer to Nicole. "You smell that? *Something* smells a lot like one of those fancy seduction perfumes." She frowned. "Nah. Can't be. No one would wear that stuff to a business meeting."

"Will you get out of here? I'm going to be late." Nicole shooed her friend off.

Certain that her face now matched the color of her suit, Nicole marched back into her apartment, heading for the bathroom and a bar of soap.

Ten minutes later, she was urging her old car up the mountain, downshifted into second and then coasted through the Dreamy Draw Pass. The road cut a southwesterly path through the curving contours of Squaw Peak, one mountain in the ancient volcanic caldera encircling Phoenix.

Coming down she picked up speed, exited onto the Squaw Peak Expressway and drove toward the Central Corridor, her thoughts on Cameron Colter. Was he still a tease? Could he still make her laugh?

She smiled at the memory. She'd adored his teasing, sometimes dry sense of humor, and when they'd parted, she'd felt that loss more than anything. He'd brought laughter into her too-serious life.

With him, her world had gone from black-and-white to Technicolor.

She reached into the side pocket of her backpack where

she'd slid Cameron's business card. Raising it, she read, Cameron J. Colter, President, Colter Construction. That he owned a company wasn't a huge surprise; he'd majored in business, after all. But a construction company in the city? It was as far from what he'd wanted to do as becoming an astrophysicist.

Ranching had been his lifeblood, and he'd been adamant about going back to it after college. What had happened to change his focus so significantly?

She'd heard a few years ago from a college friend that Cam had moved back home after being away for a time, and she'd wondered then how she'd react if she ever ran into him again. But she'd figured there wasn't much chance of that happening. Patterson, a small mountain town near Payson, was a hundred miles or so northeast of Phoenix, and she had no reason whatever to go there.

Now she knew exactly how she'd react. *Stupidly.* She'd acted really, *really* stupid.

So much for thinking she'd adjusted. So much for believing she'd snuffed out all those old dreams and desires—dreams that had included a husband and a family of her own. Dreams that would never come true.

An ache of regret settled in her chest. Time hadn't changed a thing. Not for her.

Well… She hauled in a lungful of air. Enough. *Life goes on.* She should know that better than anyone. She'd made a conscious decision. The only decision she could make.

The question was, could she help Cameron with his son and not get caught up in old emotions?

"Yes, I can," she said out loud. She was an educator, a professional. She needed to remember that—no matter how much she'd once loved him.

CHAPTER TWO

CAMERON STORMED into his office with hard work on his mind. Anything to keep busy until noon when he met Nicole for lunch. He couldn't stop thinking about her surprise that he'd given up ranching and moved to Phoenix. Did she think he wasn't cut out for anything else?

Why did he even care what she thought? Nicole didn't know his reasons for making the move to Phoenix, and he had no reason to tell her.

He loved the ranch. His dad had worked long and hard to build something substantial to pass on to his sons, and the Colter brothers had been committed to continuing the legacy. Cameron had planned on it since he was a kid.

But after falling out with his brothers, he simply couldn't be part of it anymore. For a while, he'd tried living in Patterson without working on the ranch but that was like having potatoes without the meat.

When Michael's problems surfaced at school, the decision to move seemed a good one. He wasn't going to let his son be taunted and bullied because of his dad's reputation, and if that meant moving away, then so be it.

Cameron found the coffeepot, filled the reservoir and dumped two scoops of coffee into the filter. He needed an extra-strong jolt today. If only he could find a cup….

Glancing around, he saw a stack of dirty dishes in the small sink; he went over and rinsed out a mug. He made a mental note to call a temp service to get another secretary.

He didn't need the place to be spotless, just a bit more orderly. This was a working man's office, comfortable not fancy. That was the way he liked it.

On one side, a huge picture window allowed him to see South Mountain, and while there were saguaros on it instead of pine trees, it made Phoenix feel a little more like home. The window at the other end faced the construction yard, giving him a clear view of the trucks and large equipment. A good reminder that there was always work to be done.

He went to the filing cabinet for his latest job contract. After a cursory look, he shoved the papers back into the drawer. Preparing a multi-faceted bid like that would take more concentration than he could muster today.

Cameron stalked over to his dad's old, beat-up desk and ran a hand over the rough oak on the front edge. His fingers stopped on the little nicks his dad had made with his hunting knife. *Sorry, Dad.*

His father had wanted his personal effects to remain on the ranch, in the hope of keeping his sons there after he was gone. Removing the desk had been another contentious issue between Cam and his older brothers since he'd decided not to be a working partner at Morning Star Ranch. Harry was the only one who'd understood.

But his disagreement with Jack and Ransom wasn't about moving the desk from the ranch—it went deeper than that. After the split with Nicole, his desire to stay on the ranch dissolved, and family expectations felt like a yoke around his neck. He'd decided that maybe he needed a life of his own, not one his parents had planned for him. But in that decision he was a disappointment to everyone, especially his mom and dad. After his father's sudden death, he'd gone to California and his older brothers stayed on at the ranch, like the good sons they were. They figured he should've stayed, too.

As payback, they hadn't told him how serious his mother's illness was. If he'd known, he would've had a chance to come home before she died. Instead, his mother had gone to her grave thinking he didn't care. His chest ached every time he thought about it.

His older brothers had paid him back for leaving, all right. And there was no forgiveness in him for that.

He pulled out a plat given to him by a client who wanted an estimate on a warehouse. Cameron rested his feet on the desk and began to review the site. But try as he might to focus, all he saw was Nicole's face, which, since yesterday, seemed permanently etched in his brain.

He'd even dreamed about her last night.

Man, oh, man. He was one sick puppy.

No way was he going down that road again. After their breakup, he'd spent far too many hours trying to figure out what had gone wrong. Wondering where he'd failed again.

He no longer cared about that. He had a new life in a new place, and if he could get Michael's problems straightened out, everything would be great.

But he needed Nicole's help. He was at his wits' end with Michael, and she was the only professional the boy had responded to.

If he had to use her to help his son, he had no qualms about doing it. None whatsoever.

But it would be a hell of a lot easier if they didn't have all that history between them.

REACHING THE SCHOOL, Nicole steered her mustard-colored Volvo into the principal's parking spot, cut the engine and got out. As the only teacher there on Saturdays, she had the place to herself.

The old adobe building was too small to house all the students whose parents had chosen Barton Elementary, a private alternative school. So two portable buildings had been constructed in the back. One of those rented out for ten hours a week to a charter high school in another neighborhood and was used for her part-time class with the high school's At Risk students.

Her class supplemented the high school program and, if successful, might be implemented throughout the system.

Hurrying, she cut around the pink stucco building, noting how the secluded area where the steel-gray portables were located would have been much easier to vandalize than her regular classroom. That alone had convinced her the act hadn't been perpetrated by one of her A.R. students.

But what bothered her the most was the nature of the graffiti she'd discovered on her desk. Had the vandals simply done it for effect, as one of the officers said? Was it a random incident? Or was someone sending her a message? If so, a message about what? With everything that had happened yesterday, she hadn't had time to dwell on it. Lord knows, she didn't have time now.

Well, intimidation, if that was what it was meant to be, didn't work on her. She'd learned to take care of herself years ago.

As she neared the portable, she saw Dylan McGinnis making his way across the playground, his bad-ass strut conveying the attitude he wanted the world to see. She waved, then hurried inside, hoping he'd wait on the field for the others.

She needed a minute to organize and put up assignments for the next three days. The class wouldn't meet again until Tuesday afternoon when her regular class ended.

At the board, she reached for the chalk, but it wasn't in its usual spot on the ledge. She glanced around. The erasers weren't there, either. Maybe Bob had gotten carried away with his cleaning and put everything in the supply drawer.

Or… She cast about for signs that someone might have been in the room. No, everything looked fine, which made her feel a little foolish. Besides, if someone was going to steal, why choose something so inconsequential.

She pulled open the supply drawer. Empty. Except for a single scrap of paper on the bottom. *What the heck…*

She reached inside, picked up the paper and turned it over. Her nerves coiled as she read the cut-and-paste message.

Warning number 2!

"Lookin' for something?"

She jumped, dropping the paper. Then she slammed the drawer and spun around, her heart racing as if on fast forward. Dylan stood in the doorway, his right shoulder propped against the frame.

The intensity of his gaze bored through her. Between his body language and the black clothes he wore, he was the epitome of teen rebellion. And she had to admit that right now, he made her nervous.

"Just the chalk. I guess someone misplaced it."

Dylan cocked his head, eyelids at half-mast. "Want some help?" His tone was sarcastic.

"Nope. I'll get what I need from the other classroom." She brushed past him and went outside to the portable next to hers. As she walked, she wondered how she might get through to this boy.

He was only seventeen, but his deep-set brown eyes reflected knowledge of hardships far greater than anyone his age should have. His records had verified her assessment—abandoment by his mother and physical abuse by an alcoholic stepfather, until a run-in with the law had landed his so-called guardian in jail. After Dylan spent a few years in foster homes and experienced a few legal problems of his own, a social worker had finally located a great-aunt, who'd agreed to take Dylan in.

No wonder he'd had problems and ended up at the Black Canyon Detention Center.

No wonder she'd felt such a need to help him.

In the three months since she'd been teaching the class, Dylan was the one she hadn't been able to reach. Initially, she'd taken the part-time tutoring job with the charter school because it was the only one available. She'd graduated midyear and couldn't wait six months for a regular position.

Certified K–6 she'd put herself on the city's sub list for the elementary grades, as well, hoping that would lead to a full-time position. When she'd learned that secondary certification wasn't mandatory to teach in a charter school, she'd put herself on that list, as well.

After one day with the A.R. students, she'd seen their need. Each boy was so desperately in crisis, none of them willing to admit it or ask for help. In that finite moment, she was committed. Getting them over the hump had become her goal—her mission.

If she'd had a teacher willing to help when she needed it, she might not have been so traumatized by her own school experience. Caring for her mom had taken its toll. With little sleep some nights, her ability to do her schoolwork plummeted. She missed classes, and when she did make it, often she fell asleep at her desk. If even one teacher had taken an interest, it might not have made a difference to her work, but at least she wouldn't have felt so desperately alone.

Helping these kids was something *she* needed to do.

When she found the chalk, she returned to her room. Dylan was still leaning against the doorjamb. He was still standing there when she went to her desk. She thumbed through the stack of papers for the next assignment to copy on the board. After a moment, she looked up. "If you've got nothing to do, c'mon in. You can get started early."

At the invitation, he sauntered inside and dropped into a chair at the desk in front of hers, legs extended. "Sure, Teach. You gonna help me?"

"I'll be happy to give you all the help you need," she said as she continued her search. "But first, you've got to do the work." Because if he didn't shape up quickly, he wouldn't graduate.

And graduation was the whole purpose of this class.

When he gave no response, she shrugged. Still concentrating on the papers, Nicole said casually, "But that's up to you. It's your future that's at stake, not mine. If you want to jeopardize it, you're not as smart as I thought you were."

There was a moment of silence, then…"I'm not wasting nothin' except time."

She glanced up.

He thrust out his chin. "And I've got lots of that."

Interesting. Very interesting. Maybe she *had* made a tiny dent in his armor. At least enough to cause a reaction. He'd never bothered saying anything before.

She came around, stopped directly in front of him and leaned down, palms flat on the desk where he sat. They locked eyes. "Well, I know better. And I think you do, too."

He stared at her, teeth clenched, eyes narrowed in resistance. He wasn't going to allow himself to communicate with her on any level other than the one he'd already established.

Understandable. How else could he protect his tough-guy image? How else could he show he was immune to being hurt?

Some things about Dylan reminded her so much of herself at that age. Only she'd taken the wallflower route. Instead of acting tough, she shrank into the background so no one would notice her. She'd learned a lot since then and doubted anyone would accuse her of fading into the background anymore.

She started back to her desk.

"If you know so much, then I guess you know who trashed your room."

She froze midstep. Did *he* know? Or was this a test of some kind? She turned to face him again. "No, I don't. But I know it wasn't any of my students."

Surprise registered, then his gaze drifted beyond her to the door. Justin and Mitchell entered. Dylan raised his chin to acknowledge the two as they walked past. "Hey."

Justin tapped Dylan's arm on his way to the back of the room.

She took a breath and dusted her hands together. "Okay. Let's get to work."

SITTING ON THE PATIO at Sam's, the trendy Southwestern café at the Arizona Center where he'd had lunch a few times before, Cameron studied Nicole as she read the menu.

Just looking at her awakened desires he didn't want to

acknowledge. Desires that puzzled him. Irritated him. He'd gotten over her. His life was different now. And he needed to keep it that way.

So what was wrong with him?

The only thing he could figure was that a certain part of his anatomy wasn't connected to his brain. Because if it was, he wouldn't be having this problem. "The fish tacos are good. So are the fajitas."

"I should've known you'd pick a Mexican restaurant," she said, looking up.

She smiled wide. A smile that lit up the space around her, as a jumble of all-too-vivid memories slammed him back into the past. Memories that, even now, after all this time, twisted his belly into knots.

Everything had been perfect until she'd given him some cockamamy story about being too young to get serious. Truth was, she had bigger plans and didn't want to be stuck on a ranch somewhere in the boondocks with some *half-breed* cowboy. She hadn't said those exact words, but he knew it was what she'd meant.

He'd known all along that there was more to their breakup than she'd let on. But the bottom line was, if she didn't want him, she didn't. He wasn't going to grovel and ask why—not then and not now.

He ground his teeth.

"Something wrong?"

"Nope. Just thinking about old times." He forced a smile. "Thinking about old times and how much fun it was back then."

"It was, wasn't it?" She leaned forward with both elbows on the table, and cupped her chin in her hands. Her face was framed by a wild tangle of auburn curls, her easy white smile accented by dimples on both sides.

"But," she added, "I suspect, as we get older, it's easier to remember only the good stuff."

Her eyes, an unusual amber, had tiny flecks of gold in the brown. Sparklers he used to call them. And if it was possible, she was even more beautiful than he remembered. "Or maybe we just wise up and don't think about the rest of it because there's no point."

The bitterness he'd thought long forgotten rose up like bile in his throat. He shifted in his chair. This meeting was to talk about his son. That they'd once had a relationship had nothing to do with anything.

He didn't need to know what she'd been doing, how she'd been, or even if she'd missed him just a little. He didn't *want* to know any of it. Ten years had passed, for God's sake.

But those were his rational thoughts. And his body didn't seem to understand the logic. His body said he wanted her. Now.

Still.

He reached out and drew her left hand down to rest in the palm of his, then stared at the slender fingers, the perfectly manicured nails bare of polish.

"Not married?"

She retracted her hand. "No, not married. And you obviously were. Any other children?"

"No. No other children."

"Oh." She looked as if she didn't know what to say. "Divorced?"

He nodded. "The marriage lasted twenty minutes. It was a bad choice. You?"

She shook her head. "No. Never."

"Never?" It would've been better if she'd gotten married. At least then he'd have an answer, even if the answer was that she'd fallen in love with some other guy.

"Too busy saving the world, huh?" He locked his gaze with hers.

"What do you mean?"

"That's the reason you gave when you left, wasn't it? You were too young to settle down, had too many things to do, too many people to help. A husband and family weren't in the plan."

"It wasn't exactly like that."

"No? What *exactly* was it like?" He felt a rush of adrenaline.

Nicole was aware of the tension radiating across the table and lowered her eyes to the menu. "It wasn't that simple."

After their relationship ended, she'd vowed never to let herself be so vulnerable again. "And there's no point in going into all that now, anyway. Why don't we order and then talk about Michael? That's why we're here, isn't it?"

His eyes went dark. Cameron had never been able to mask his feelings. He was the most open, honest person she'd ever known. And the most proud.

"Sure." He gestured to the waiter.

He'd been deeply hurt ten years ago, but she couldn't do anything about it. Not then, not now. Even so, a wave of guilt washed over her.

Yet it didn't change a thing. He'd always been committed to having a large family, the one thing she couldn't give him. Besides, how could she bring anyone into her life on a permanent basis when she didn't have a clue what her future might hold? She couldn't handle her mother's illness back then, and she could barely handle it now.

She'd been young and scared that he'd find out. So scared she'd bolted. She'd ended it because that was better than the alternative. If he found out, he'd start looking at her the way everyone else did when they learned about her mother.

He'd watch and listen, thinking every little lapse, every silent moment or angry outburst was a sign that she'd follow in her mother's footsteps. Hell, she worried about it herself.

All the time.

All she could've offered him was a life of uncertainty and pain. And eventually, he would hate her and leave. Just as her father had done.

She'd rather die than put someone she loved through the agony she'd experienced. She'd rather die than watch love disappear.

So she'd run away from Cameron. She'd run from the only man she'd ever loved, and there wasn't a day that her heart didn't ache with regret.

But she'd never doubted for a minute that it was the right decision.

The waiter came and took their orders, and when he'd finished she said, "I haven't had time to get to know your son since I just came on board at the beginning of the week. But he seems like a wonderful little boy."

With conversation about his son, Cam's shoulders relaxed, and he seemed less tense. He forgot the other subject and smiled. But he didn't take his eyes off her, not for a second.

"He is a great kid. And he likes you a lot. All this week, every other sentence has been, 'my teacher' this, or 'my teacher' that."

She wasn't used to such compliments and let a smile emerge. "I'm sure it was only because I'm new. Or maybe because it was such an eventful week."

"Hmm. Michael didn't mention any events. Can you fill me in?"

"Oh, boy. I'm afraid it would take more than a lunch hour to cover it all."

"How about the condensed version?" He smiled in the same lopsided way that had always made her willing to do just about anything. Almost.

"Okay, but remember, you asked for it."

"I usually do."

Her face went hot. Ignoring the comment, she launched into her explanation, which she'd rehearsed more than once so the experience wouldn't sound as awful as it had actually been. "Well, on Monday, the call to sub came as a huge surprise. I wasn't prepared, and when I got to the school, I discovered the other teacher hadn't completed a single lesson plan. It was pretty obvious to the class that I wasn't in total control and within the first hour, one of the boys popped open the door on the hamster cage and a half-dozen furry creatures darted out, immediately sending twenty-three screaming six-year-olds scrambling. I called for a rodent rescue, but the janitor was busy and only a few boys participated—the rest of the class was scared to death." She sighed. "It was chaos. And later, when I thought things had settled down, someone set off the fire alarm—twice.

"The next day was a little better," she went on, now able to see the humor in it all. "Just an irate parent who did a slice-and-dice job on me in front of the class, then two sweet little girls had a slug match, and to top it all off, yesterday my classroom was vandalized."

She shrugged and smiled. "Nice week, huh?"

"Whoo-ee!" Cam let out a whoop of laughter, which was more like the Cameron of old, and she laughed right along with him. It felt good to do that.

"I can't believe Michael didn't mention any of it."

"Nope, he didn't say a thing. He hasn't mentioned any

of his teachers all year until this past week. I figured it was some kind of breakthrough and any teacher who'd made such an impression might be able to help.''

''In what way?''

He pulled out a leather wallet and a half-dozen photos flipped out from a plastic accordion case. Proudly, he held it out to her.

She took the wallet in hand and looked through the photos. ''I would never have guessed he was your son,'' she said softly. ''He's so blond. Not at all like you.''

Just knowing that this adorable little boy was Cameron's son rekindled every maternal instinct she'd ever had. She swallowed back the emotion and cleared her throat. ''His mother must be very beautiful.''

''Michael is rambunctious,'' Cam said earnestly, ignoring her comment. ''Full of piss and vinegar.''

''Uh-huh.'' She smiled again. ''Then I guess he *is* like you.''

Tilting his chair back on two legs, Cam grinned. ''Hey… I've matured some over the years. I'm not nearly as rowdy as I used to be, and if I'm full of anything, it's redneck opinions and bad jokes.''

''Like I said, you haven't changed.''

At that, he cracked another smile. Then, very pointedly changing gears, he set the chair flat and fixed his gaze on hers. ''My son lived with his mother until a year ago, so I'm trying to make up for lost time. I'm also trying to bring some stability into his life. Michael's mom had some problems and because of that, he has some emotional scars.''

''Oh, Cameron. I'm so sorry.''

He took a deep breath and looked away. ''Yeah. Me, too. The thing is, I haven't been able to make a connection with him. On the surface, we seem okay—we joke around and all that. But whenever I think we're set, he gets into trouble. Then I don't know what to do.''

He raked a hand through his hair. ''I've got to get some help, Nic. I'm worried about him and it's tearing me up.''

His heartfelt plea melted any resistance she might have felt about getting too close. How could she keep an emotional distance after hearing the pain in his voice, after seeing it in his eyes? He loved his son, and if she could help in any way, she had to do it.

''What kind of trouble are you talking about? Children do a lot of things that might seem strange to someone who hasn't been around kids much, and those behaviors might be perfectly normal for a six-year-old.''

''He gets into fights, lies, steals, and when I find out, he won't talk to me or tell me why. I had to take him out of the public school because of it. I thought an alternative school like Barton would be better, but I didn't have a chance to talk to his teacher to discuss any of this.''

''How long has he been enrolled at Barton?''

''Two weeks. I made the conference appointment because I wanted to make sure the teacher and I were working together. If this school isn't the answer for Michael, I'm out of ideas. Sometimes I feel like he's testing me to see how long it's going to take before I give up. Hell, I wonder about it myself. Maybe I just suck at being a dad and maybe he would be better off elsewhere.''

How could he even say that? Especially since he'd been such a hellion himself. ''Where on earth could be better than being with his father?''

He shook his head. ''I don't know. He needs a mom. I know that. He needs a mom and a dad. Family is important to a kid.''

She knew that all too well. ''How about professional help, like counseling?''

"Tried that. It was a disaster. Each time before we went, he'd throw a fit. Then we'd get there, and he'd sulk and keep his mouth shut for the whole hour. Later at home, he'd give me the same silent treatment because he was mad at me for taking him to the shrink in the first place. Finally it was easier not to go. I thought if I gave him a sense of security that would do it. But it hasn't."

"So, you think he's acting out because he's insecure?"

"His mother abandoned him several times. What kid wouldn't have problems after that?"

She heard the frustration in his voice, the anger. And she knew exactly how he felt. She knew how frustrating it was to be unable to help someone you loved. But where had Cameron been when the boy's mother abandoned the child?

"A child shouldn't have to deal with his parents' baggage. It isn't fair," she said. "But then, kids don't get a choice. All you can do is love him and go from there, Cam."

She wanted to ask why, if Michael's mother had been so terrible, he hadn't tried for custody before now. But, somehow, it didn't seem appropriate. He might think she was blaming him for not jumping in sooner. But whatever the reason for Michael's situation, it didn't matter. The child was the one who needed her support.

"So, as Michael's teacher, what can I do?"

He gave a hopeless shrug. "I don't know, Nic. I just don't know. I guess I thought his teacher might see something I've missed. Maybe offer some insight that would help me make a connection."

He met her eyes, then said with an ironic grin. "I didn't know the teacher would turn out to be an old friend."

An old friend.

Yes, they were old friends. And if she could think of him in only that way…

A flicker of indecision flashed in his eyes, and then he reached out, his touch achingly familiar as his large hand covered hers. "I need help, Nic. Will you help me?"

CHAPTER THREE

THE BELL RANG, sending Nicole's students scrambling to their seats. Most of the students, anyway. Michael hung back, just outside the door.

A week had passed since Cam had come to see her at school and even though she'd promised to call him to discuss Michael's behavior, there had been nothing to report. She hadn't had contact with Cameron since then, not even the day he'd been in to change his son's last name on the school records.

Class was ready to start, but Michael hadn't budged. "C'mon in, Michael, and shut the door."

"He's scared you're going to send him to the principal's office," one of the other boys piped up.

"And why would I do that?"

"'Cause he was fighting on the playground."

The playground aide hadn't said anything about a fight. She glanced up to tell Michael to come in again, but he was gone.

"Okay, everyone, eyes to the front and look at what I've written on the board. Print your name on your papers, plus the day of the week and the calendar date just as I've printed it." While the children worked, she walked to the door and peered down the hall.

Michael was nowhere in sight. She went back inside and called the office. "Hi, Kara. One of my students didn't come in when the bell rang. Can someone track him down? His name is Michael Colter."

"Sure. What's he look like?"

"He's six, about three feet tall and blond. He was here just a minute ago, but now he's gone. Could you have Bob check the lavatories?"

"I would if I knew where he was. I'll send an aide instead."

When Josie arrived, Nicole had her sit with the children while she went to look for Michael herself. She stepped into the hallway and stood there for a moment, wondering which way to go, when she noticed the toe of a black sneaker poking out from under the stairwell.

She walked over and checked underneath. Michael sat huddled in the corner, knees tucked into his chest. His lip was bloodied and when he saw her, he scrunched down even further.

"Hi there, Michael. Looks like you had a little problem."

Silence. "I didn't have no problem," he muttered. "I got punched."

She nodded solemnly. "I can see that, but I'd like you to come out here and tell me about it." She squatted to sit on her heels.

He shook his head.

"Okay. Then I'll come and visit you." Staying low, she duck-walked to where he sat. Light shone through the risers and she could see that his clothes were grass stained and one knee of his blue jeans ripped. Telltale evidence of a playground fight.

On closer inspection, she saw tear tracks down his dirt-stained cheeks. "You okay, buddy?"

He nodded, sniffled a couple of times and then wiped his face against his sleeve. Nicole pulled a tissue from her shirt pocket and handed it to him. ''Here. This might work a little better.'' She waited a second before she asked, ''Who punched you?''

He shrugged. ''I can't tell you.''

Oh, yeah. She'd forgotten. A six-year-old boy would rather eat nails than be called a snitch.

''Okay. What *can* you tell me? Was it your fault?''

He looked up at her, uncertainty in his round blue eyes.

''Are you gonna send me to the principal's office and call my dad?''

''Well, we need to talk about this. If you started the fight and got punched, it's probably what you deserved. In that case yes, I would send you to the principal's office. If you didn't start the fight, and the other boy punched you, then *he* should go to the office. But, if both of you were fighting, regardless of who threw the first punch, then it's both of you to see Mr. Sipowitz.''

She reached out, gently lifting his chin so she could view the cut lip. ''And from the looks of you, your dad's going to know, whether I tell him or not.''

Michael's chin dropped to his chest, bottom lip protruding. Talking into his knees, he asked, ''Are you mad at me?''

She smiled. He was hurting and yet he was worried that she might be mad at him. ''No, Michael, I'm not. I'm concerned and I'm sorry to see you got hurt. That's all. But as your teacher, I need to know what happened. It's my job.''

He hesitated, as if deciding, then said, ''I didn't start it, but I don't want to say who did.'' He paused for a few seconds. ''You don't have to tell my dad, do you?''

''I think he'll know by looking at you.''

''No. I mean…you don't have to tell him I didn't start it. Do you?''

An odd question. ‘‘Why not? Wouldn’t he be happy that you didn’t start the fight?’’

‘‘I guess. But he doesn’t need to know.’’

What a strange twist. Why *wouldn’t* Michael want his dad to know he wasn’t to blame? ‘‘C’mon, let’s get you cleaned up.’’

‘‘Aren’t you going to send me to the principal’s office?’’

‘‘You said you didn’t start it, right?’’

He nodded.

‘‘Did you punch him back?’’

When he hesitated, she could see his little-boy mind sorting through the options. To lie or not to lie, that was the question. Finally, his voice dropping, he said, ‘‘Yeah. But I missed and didn’t hit him.’’

‘‘Well, then. Why would I punish you for something you didn’t do?’’

Michael seemed genuinely surprised. ‘‘’Cause we’re not supposed to fight?’’

‘‘And it takes two to make a fight. You know that, don’t you?’’

He nodded again.

‘‘So, I think you learned a lesson, and I’m going to give you another chance. Everyone deserves a second chance once in a while. Okay?’’

He rubbed his nose with the tissue, and his eyes glistened with what looked like relief. ‘‘Okay,’’ he managed through a muffled sniff.

‘‘Fine. And now that it’s settled, let’s get out of here. I’m a lot bigger than you and I’m all twisted up like a pretzel.’’

Nicole didn’t call Cameron to relay what had happened until after her students had gone home. She was confused by Michael’s insistence on *not* telling his dad that he wasn't to blame. When she called, Cam was out on a job and the background noise was too loud for him to hear well, so he told her he'd call her back that evening.

All day she'd wondered about Michael's motives. All day she looked forward to talking with Cam. Maybe he had an answer.

But later that night she wasn't sure she'd heard him right. She glanced at the clock on her kitchen wall. It was after eight o'clock. Maybe he'd wanted her to call him instead?

Or maybe his son's problems weren't as important to him as he'd said. No, that wasn't it. Cameron was a devoted father. She knew that much already. And she would have expected no less.

After making some tea, she went into the living room and curled up in the big easy chair with the latest Grisham book. As a teacher, she'd done all she could. It was Cameron's responsibility to take it from here.

And thinking about responsibility, where were the other people in Michael's life who could provide support? Grandparents? The boy's mother's family? His father's family? Why hadn't Cam mentioned anyone but his youngest brother.

Unable to concentrate on the book, she put it down. Why couldn't she stop thinking about Cam? She had her life on track, was happy with what she'd accomplished and satisfied with the status quo. Because he'd asked for her help, that's why.

Restlessly, Nicole went to the window, parted the miniblinds and gazed out at the street below. In the silvery light of dusk, the parked cars and worn low-rise buildings were muted, softened. Nicole saw no one outside; the street seemed uncharacteristically quiet.

Just then a silver BMW convertible cruised into a spot

behind another car. The vehicle looked out of place because people who drove BMWs didn't live in her neighborhood; they lived in Scottsdale or Paradise Valley.

As she watched, the car door slowly opened and the driver climbed out—and her mouth dropped open.

Cameron.

What was he doing here? He couldn't be coming to see her; she hadn't told him where she lived, and she wasn't listed in the directory.

He took a moment to look around, then pulled himself straight and tall. Cameron Colter was still the most striking man she'd ever met.

With his dark good looks and a lean muscular body, Cameron exuded an innate self-confidence that few men possessed. As he walked across the street, his long fluid strides suggested a man in total control. He was boldly attractive, and the scar directly below his right eyebrow only added to his aura.

Nicole smiled, remembering. He had more than one scar from his rodeo days, and she'd located and kissed every one.

Souvenirs of life, he'd called them, and he'd worn them proudly. He was a man who wanted to experience life, not watch it from the sidelines.

Ten years ago, she'd admired his fearlessness, his bravado, his passion for life—the way he embraced everything he did. It had been exciting just to be around him.

Even after all this time, even knowing there could never be anything between them, she was not immune.

The doorbell rang and, for one microsecond, she thought about pretending she wasn't home. But since she'd called him and said she wanted to talk, it seemed silly to avoid him.

Yet inviting him into her home implied a closeness, an intimacy she couldn't allow.

A loud knock followed the ring. She hurried to the foyer, and on the way, smoothed out her baggy blue sweats. Stopping in front of the mirror above a half-moon table, she shoved a few stray curls into her ponytail, drew a breath, then turned and swung open the door.

Cameron stood in the arch of the doorway like a cowboy waiting for a showdown. Before Nicole could utter a word, Risa's door flew open. Cam pivoted, his eyes skipping from one woman to the other.

"Sorry, guys," Risa said, adjusting the front of her pink chenille robe. "I heard someone makin' a lot of racket out here. I got worried."

Nicole grinned. Risa wanted to know who was knocking on her friend's door. Plain and simple. "Cam, meet Risa Beaumont, friend and neighbor. Risa...Cameron Colter."

"Hi, Risa." Cam smiled and extended a hand.

"Hi, pleased to meet you." After a quick handshake, Risa retreated. "Gotta go. You guys have fun now." She gave them a singsong, "Bye," and shut the door as abruptly as she'd opened it.

Cameron's amused gaze caught Nicole's. "She always so timid?"

"Always." Nicole motioned him inside. Her place was small and it took only a couple of steps for Cam to be standing in the middle of her living room.

She turned to face him, crossing her arms. "I'm confused. Did I ask you to come over and then develop a case of amnesia?"

He shoved his hands in his pockets and with a sheepish expression said, "I thought it would be easier to talk in person." He looked directly at her. "And I figured it'd be harder for you to turn me away if I was on your doorstep."

He was wrong about the first part. It would've been much easier for her to talk on the phone rather than in person. But he'd pegged the second part. She'd have met him anywhere before inviting him here, and it *would* be hard to tell him to go since she'd said she wanted to talk to him about Michael.

"How did you know where I live?"

"You left your phone number, so I looked up your address in my reverse directory." He rubbed the back of his neck. "Sorry. I thought it'd be okay, but I see I was wrong. Should I go out and start all over again by calling first?"

"No. I wanted to talk about Michael, so we might as well." She gestured toward the couch.

"I really appreciate this," he said, glancing around for a spot to sit.

"Oh. Sorry." She shoved aside the newspapers and magazines on the couch to clear a spot for him.

He maneuvered his long legs into the small space between the sofa and an old trunk that served as a coffee table, then studied the room. "Lived here long?"

"A couple of years." She sat opposite him, more aware than ever that her condo was far from sumptuous. Filled with an eclectic assortment of used furniture and mementos, her place would never grace the pages of *Home and Garden*. But it was hers and she was proud of it.

Proud because this was the first permanent home she'd had. After an itinerant childhood—stealing away in the middle of the night, ducking out on irate landlords because her mom hadn't paid the rent—she finally had a semblance of security, an important commodity in a life marked by upheaval.

She had a lease on the condo with an option to buy, and she planned to do exactly that once she'd saved enough money.

"Would you like something to drink? Water...soda...a beer? I have Red Dog." *His favorite.*

Cameron's eyes glinted, as if he knew she remembered. As if remembering might mean something.

"I also have Corona."

The quirky grin emerged. "Yeah. Red Dog would be good."

His voice sounded a little husky.

Nicole hurried into the kitchen, relieved to be out of his sight.

Through the opening that served as a pass-through between the kitchen and the combination living-dining room, she saw Cam examine the bookshelves on the opposite wall.

He wore a light blue chambray shirt and, from the back, his shoulders seemed broader than before. Her attention was drawn downward to trim hips, his trademark blue jeans and weathered boots. Just looking at him called up all manner of memories.

Memories that tapped into yearnings she'd chosen to ignore. How long had it been since she'd felt a man's arms around her? Two years? Three?

After Cameron, she'd had only one physical relationship and it had been a sorry one at that. Since then, she'd been abstinent and *thought* she'd gotten used to it.

Nicole closed her eyes and recited what might as well be her mantra. This too shall pass.

Removing two bottles of beer from the fridge, she popped the caps, then took a couple of frosty pilsner glasses from the freezer. As she started to pour, she remembered how particular he used to be about the way it was done.

Engrossed in her task, she was startled to find him standing next to her. His arm grazed hers as he eased the cold bottle from her hand. She moved to the side and leaned an elbow on the counter while he brought both glasses to frothy perfection.

"I never could get that right," she said.

He turned to face her and gave her one of the chilled glasses. With his own glass in hand, he leaned against the counter beside her. "You did some things perfectly."

Her senses sprang to life, and she was acutely aware of the color of his shirt and how it brought out the brilliant blue of his eyes. She noticed how the white T-shirt visible at his throat accented his bronzed skin. He seemed more muscular, his presence even more imposing than she recalled.

He'd been in great shape ten years ago, long and lean, all sinew and muscle. Over the years he'd filled out—deliciously so. Despite her resolve, an ache of want unfurled deep in her belly, then instantly spread....

"Who's watching Michael?" she asked, grasping for a topic to take her mind off her sudden physical awareness of him. "Do you have a regular sitter?"

He rubbed a hand over his chin. Eyeing one of the rickety ice-cream parlor chairs, he reached out and swung the chair around, straddling it with the back against his chest, his arms resting on top. He grabbed his glass, indulging in a long drink before answering her question.

"I have a housekeeper who does double duty as a nanny sometimes. But right now Michael is at Harry's." He took another slow swallow. "He likes to stay at the ranch on weekends."

She nodded, listening but not hearing. Her eyes focused on his mouth. His lips. His well-defined lips. Kissable lips.

"Remember Harry?"

"Oh…of course." She returned her attention to the moment. "I can't believe you'd leave a little boy with Harry."

Cameron chuckled. "I can't believe it either. But my little renegade brother's turned into a regular homebody."

"That's incredible," was all she could think to say. Two years younger than Cam, Harrison Colter had been the most rebellious of all the brothers, and Cameron had bailed him out of trouble time and again. Now Cam was saying that Harry, little rebellious Harry, was a homebody and settled enough to have a child stay with him.

That was a major turnaround. She leaned against the counter, feet bare, legs crossed in front of her.

"Yep. One day Harry just straightened up, found a wonderful girl, built a place on his section of the ranch and had a passel of kids. Now they're living happily ever after—like in one of those romance novels."

He took another long swig of beer and reflected a moment before adding, "It's been great for Michael to have close family nearby. Somewhere he can be with people who care about him."

"But he has that here, too. With you, I mean."

"Oh, yeah. I know he does, but it's not the same as growing up with family around. Brothers and sisters. A kid needs that."

"Of course. Well…what about his mother's side, grandparents and all?"

"There's no contact," he said. "They're out of the country and not interested. It's their loss."

"And your older brothers?"

"He sees them when he's at Harry's."

"I still can't imagine Harry with a wife, much less with children."

Cam nodded. "I know. At first I couldn't believe Harry was serious about getting married. Even harder to believe is that the two of us get along now. No more knock-down, drag-out fights."

He paused, staring at the glass in his hand. "But then, a lot of things are different now." As he spoke, his gaze drifted from the bottle and landed by her feet. Then he slowly looked upward till he'd covered the entire length of her. His eyes locked with hers.

Nicole recognized the sultry expression. Heard the unspoken words and felt his desire. She knew exactly what was on his mind. Because, Lord help her, it was on hers, too.

She rolled the cool glass between her hands and took another sip. Eyes still locked, they stayed quiet for what seemed an eternity. Then, Cam suddenly polished off the last of his beer and rose. He flipped the chair around with one hand and slid it under the pedestal table.

"Shall we talk about Michael?" he asked.

She fingered the slender silver chain at her neck, and could actually feel her pulse throbbing at the base of her throat. "Yes, of course." *The sooner the better.*

They headed back into the living room where she claimed the well-worn easy chair opposite the couch. She wasn't going to get any closer than necessary. "The reason I called was to talk over what happened in class today. But I'd prefer this to remain just between us, okay?"

"Okay. Shoot."

"Michael was involved in a playground fight today. It wasn't his fault and we straightened it out. I told him I wouldn't send him to the principal's office—this time."

He nodded for her to go on.

"Even though anyone would know just by looking at him that he'd been in a fight, he made a strange request. He asked me *not* to tell you the fight wasn't his fault."

Cam frowned. "What do you suppose that was about?"

"I thought you might have an idea. It seems odd that he didn't want you to know the fight wasn't his fault, doesn't it?"

He shrugged. "Odd, yeah. But it doesn't seem like a big deal, though. Do you think it is?"

"A big deal, no. But I wondered if it had some significance. Usually kids want their parents to think they've done no wrong. This is just the opposite."

Cam let out his breath, obviously perplexed. "I'm the last person to ask. I don't have a clue what's going on with him, no more than my dad knew what was going on with me." He grinned. "But that's normal, isn't it?"

"Normal, as in parent-child normal. Or do you mean it's a guy thing?"

"Maybe both. Perhaps he wants me to think he's tough and if he told me he didn't stand up for himself, I'd think he was a sissy."

She wasn't convinced of that, but the male of the species was a mystery to her; most of her understanding was confined to what she'd learned in psychology classes.

"He's small, like I was. I regularly got the stuffing kicked out of me, and I'd never tell my dad because then he'd give me this whole big lecture about standing up for myself and how 'Only sissies back down. A Colter never does.' No kid wants his dad to think he's a sissy."

The explanation made sense and he might be more on target than any she'd come up with—and it gave her a little insight about Cameron that she hadn't had before. "Sounds reasonable. I don't want to make problems where there are none, but since I said I'd let you know, I wanted to fulfill my promise.''

He smiled widely, and his eyes warmed when he looked at her. ''I appreciate it. More than you know.''

With the earlier tenseness gone, they segued into friendly conversation, the kind only old friends could have. Before she knew it, they were laughing about some of the good times, and purposely ignoring others. Cam said his parents had both died, first his father after being thrown from a horse, and then his mother after losing her battle with cancer.

Although Nicole had only met his parents a few times, she knew how close the family was. Cam had always talked about his parents with pride, love and admiration. And now, hearing the pain in his voice, she knew he must've been devastated by their deaths.

The Colter family had operated a large spread on the outskirts of Patterson, a small ranching community near Payson an hour and a half northeast of Phoenix. Cam had spent his early years learning how to run the ranch with his brothers, and he'd always said there was no place he'd rather raise his family.

The fact that he'd tossed his dreams aside and moved to Phoenix still baffled her. The man she'd known would never have lived in town—no more than he'd be an accountant chained to a desk all day.

What had happened to make him do such a one-eighty? She remembered a particular visit to the ranch; one of the hands had told her about Cam's dad, Jackson Colter, aka Black Jack. He'd been a maverick, a skilled rodeo champ before he'd been tamed by Cam's mother.

Winona Ransom Colter's staid family had opposed the marriage because of Jack Colter's Apache blood, but the family's resistance hadn't stopped Cam's parents. After the wedding, Black Jack quit the rodeo circuit to build the ranch into something he could leave his children. But he never got the rodeo out of his system and taught each of his sons how to ride before they could walk.

That stubborn Colter determination was evident in everything Cam did. Whether it was roping, riding or ranching, Cameron Colter did it with a vengeance. Looking at him now, she wasn't convinced he'd changed all that much.

"And your older brothers? You haven't mentioned them."

"Nothin' to tell," he said quickly. "I spent a few years in L.A. When I got bored, I moved back to Patterson."

"After you and your wife—"

"After we divorced." Cam's mouth tightened.

"I'm sorry it didn't work out for you."

He shook his head. "The marriage was a mistake. We barely knew each other, we weren't in love and we didn't want the same things. It was a whole lifetime ago and not worth talking about."

"But you have a son to consider. How can you dismiss it so easily?"

"Michael…well, that's another story altogether. To make a long story short, she never told me she was pregnant and I didn't find out about Michael until last year, when his mother died."

"Oh." How awful. How could any mother deprive a child of his father? And *that* was why he didn't know how to deal with his own son—why he hadn't stepped in sooner—why he didn't care about the child's mother. He hadn't been there for the boy's first five years because he hadn't even *known* about his son. That explained a lot.

She'd mistakenly assumed that even though Michael

had lived with his mom, Cam had been seeing him. Good grief. "That's terrible, Cam! How could she do such a—"

He cut her off. "The important thing is that I know now, and I have him with me. He's given my life a new purpose."

His ex-wife was obviously a taboo subject for him and she knew when to quit. Why should he tell her, anyway?

"So then what? How did you get into the construction business? I remember the summer you spent on the circuit," Nicole said. "I figured you must've continued with that after we broke up."

Cam eased back against the couch pillows. "I worked construction while I was in California," he said. "When I returned home. I wasn't interested in ranching anymore, so I tried construction. With the population growth in and around Patterson, business was booming, and I realized I could be working for myself rather than someone else. I started small, it went well, and eventually, I opened the place in Phoenix."

"And what exactly does Colter Construction do?"

"Commercial jobs, the big stuff. Walls, foundations, footings, slab and concrete. Hard work in the summer when temperatures soar to triple digits."

"So what do you do then? Shut down?"

He raised an eyebrow. "The men start at 3:00 a.m. and they're finished by noon."

Cam didn't go into further detail. Instead he said, "That's my life in a nutshell. Now it's your turn."

Nicole's pulse raced as she wondered if she should tell him about her mom. *Could* she tell him? If she did, she'd just be bringing up things that had no bearing on the present.

Wouldn't she then have to explain why she left—and reveal her deepest fears?

CHAPTER FOUR

"I MOVED, TOO. I had to drop out of school for a while because my mom was sick," she said. "I got a secretarial job, but money was tight, so going to school full-time was out of the question. I fit in a few classes whenever I could, but doing it that way, it took forever to finish. The time lag gave me the opportunity to reassess my career goals, and I decided on elementary education."

She stopped for a breath then went on, hoping to get it all out without going into detail.

"I received my degree midyear and for some extra cash until I could find a full-time position, started working with the At Risk program almost immediately. It's part of a charter high school that's using Barton's facilities for this particular class. And because I was at the school when Mrs. Jessup got sick, the principal knew I was available. I'm hoping it'll lead to a contract for the fall."

Cam frowned. "Charter? The one that's been in the news lately?"

"Yes. There's been a little discussion in the news, mostly about the structure and concept of the school itself, not the program I teach. I think the whole concept is great. But I'm a little biased on that, and as you probably read in the papers, not everyone agrees with me. Frankly, I don't understand how anyone can have a problem with a program that gives kids a chance they wouldn't otherwise have had."

At his third nod, she realized she was going on too much. "Sorry. Guess I get a little involved."

Cam sent her a warm smile. "I remember."

He broke eye contact first. "So, tell me about your mom? You said she'd been sick."

Her heart raced.

"She live nearby?"

"Not too far. Close enough for me to stop by a couple of times a week."

"And your neighbor, Risa? You two good friends?"

Grateful for the change of subject, Nicole grinned. "Yes, as a matter of fact we are."

Cam glanced at her oddly.

"What? Don't we look like we could be friends?"

"Something like that."

"Something like *what?*"

He shifted in his chair, and she remembered how he hated being put on the spot.

"Well, you're not the same type. That's all. She's a lot older than you. And there's that whole punk-rocker thing with the hair. And you're so—"

She arched a brow.

He hesitated, apparently searching for the appropriate word. "So...down-to-earth." His smile widened as if he felt relieved that he'd finally found the right description.

Not how she saw herself, but it wasn't the worst thing one could be, either. "Well, you're right about us being different, but we've become good friends nonetheless." She waved a hand toward him. "Like you and Harry."

Cam threw back his head and chortled. "Yeah. Me and my little brother—we're different all right."

"So, what made you *really* decide to move from Patterson?"

He stopped laughing.

"I always thought ranching was the most important thing in your life."

He leaned back again. "Well, life doesn't always turn out the way a guy wants."

His words fanned the embers of the guilt she'd carried for ten years. Guilt and regret.

"That's not necessarily bad," he added quickly. "Because what a twenty-year-old kid wants isn't always what he needs. And it isn't always what's best."

Cam's handsome features hardened with resolve. "Some things aren't meant to be, and you've got to adjust your thinking to fit the circumstances. Hell, I adjusted my whole life when Michael came to live with me." A glimmer of affection lit his eyes when he mentioned his son.

Nicole managed a smile. When he talked about things that weren't meant to be, he must have been referring to his broken marriage. Not *their* relationship. No college romance could be as significant as a relationship between husband and wife.

"So just like that, no more ranching for you?"

"Nope," he drawled. "Not what I do anymore. But speaking of the ranch, I'm going up on Sunday to get Michael. Maybe you'd like to come along?"

Her pulse fluttered. "Oh, I—I don't think that's a good idea."

His dark eyebrows snapped together. "Why not? If you're worried about showing up unexpectedly, I'll give Harry a call." He waited a second and then said, "Unless you have other plans?"

She didn't have other plans. Her hesitation had to do with her own emotions, feelings she wasn't sure she could control. Besides, how professional was it to socialize with a parent of one of her students?

On the other hand, why was she reading so much into it? And Michael would only be a student of hers for five more weeks.

"Won't Michael think it's strange?"

"He'll think it's wonderful," he assured her with a smile. "Actually, he suggested it after I told him we were old friends."

Friends. Yes, they'd been that. And if it was his son's idea, not his...

"I promise I won't kidnap you or drag you off to some remote cabin and hold you captive."

That coaxed a smile out of her. And another blush. "I didn't expect you would. You said you've matured. Right?"

He gave her a desultory glance. "Right. I even go golfing once in a while."

Laughter bubbled up inside her. And God, it felt good. "Okay. Maybe I could use a day away from my routine."

"It's settled then." He stood, pulling her up by the hand as he did, then headed for the door.

His touch was warm, his grip confident. With each step, her adrenaline surged—and her apprehension mounted. She shouldn't have said yes, not when he affected her like this.

When they reached the door, he turned to Nicole and gave her hand an affectionate squeeze. A familiar shiver of excitement rippled through her.

"Sunday morning. Eight-thirty. We'll make a day of it. You might even have some fun." He smiled, let go and turned toward the stairs.

Fun with a man she'd once been in love with was just *asking* for trouble. As his foot hit the riser, he hesitated, almost as if he knew she was having second thoughts. He turned, pointed a finger at her and winked. "See you then."

"See you then," she repeated. As she watched him disappear down the stairs, she crossed her arms, her fingertips lingering on the places he'd touched.

She remembered suddenly how his hands used to feel against her bare skin when they made love—hands that were calloused and rough, but like silk when he stroked her.

She felt a surge of panic. It was a mistake to agree to go with him. A colossal mistake. And she had to do something about it.

CAMERON ENTERED THE KITCHEN from the garage and tossed his keys on the center island. The metal clattered against the ceramic tile and echoed off the vaulted ceiling above. He hated that sound. It reminded him how empty the house was.

Another Friday night alone. So what else was new? After making coffee for the morning and setting the automatic timer, he headed down the hall toward the bedroom, stripping off his clothes as he walked. Acutely aware of the silence, he turned the bedroom stereo on, finished undressing and dropped onto the king-size lodgepole bed. Maybe the music would drown out the memories playing over and over in his brain.

Two back-to-back Garth Brooks CDs and an hour with some local talk-show host later, he was still staring at the ceiling, his head filled with thoughts of Nicole.

Always Nicole.

Why had he gone to her place when he could've called? Why had he invited her to come along on Sunday?

He needed her help with his kid, that was why. Michael liked her, she'd been able to communicate with him, and *he'd* been a big whopping failure in that department. Finding out the secret to communicating with his boy was what he needed from her. That was *all* he needed.

Because getting Michael on an even keel was the most important thing in his life. A hell of a lot more important than pining over a relationship gone bad ten years before.

But seeing Nicole, even after all this time, made him realize he hadn't forgotten her at all. He'd only put her out of his mind for a while. He punched his pillow, then thrashed on the bed until, finally, he gave in to a fitful sleep.

In the morning, he woke to the sound of rain pelting against the windows. Damn. Rain meant his crews wouldn't work today, which meant he wouldn't either.

Some of his guys didn't understand why he, as the owner of the business, would sometimes pitch in right alongside them. They didn't believe he actually enjoyed it. But he did. Hard physical work was as much a part of him as riding and ranching had been.

Hard work was gratifying, and it relaxed him—something he particularly needed today.

The aroma of coffee urged a response, so he rolled off the edge of the bed and stood to stretch out the kinks. It was still too early to call Harry. He threw on a pair of jeans and went for the newspaper.

At the front door, he spotted a neighbor sidestepping puddles on his way across the street. The slight man clutched a large clipboard to his chest, his shoulders curled forward as he hid underneath a big black umbrella.

"Mr. Colter," the man called out on his way up Cam's sidewalk. "Jim Bentworth, your neighbor across the street," he introduced himself as he reached the door, then angled his head in the direction of his own nearly identical white stucco, Spanish-style house. He set the open umbrella, tip down, on the Saltillo tile before he extended a hand. "Sorry to bother you so early, but if you have a minute, I'd like to talk with you."

Cam was surprised the man even knew his name, since Bentworth hadn't said two words to either him or Michael since they'd moved in.

"As you probably know, I'm the president of the homeowner's association." Bentworth's gaze darted inside.

Cam opened the door a little farther and motioned his neighbor to come in. "What's on your mind this morning, Jim?"

"What's on my mind is this petition." He held the clipboard up. "There's an issue of great concern to our community, and we're looking for one hundred percent support from association members."

"What's the issue?"

"Recently, we've had several disturbing incidents in the community, including vandalism at the school. None of the incidents occurred prior to the implementation of that after-school program at Barton, and the petitioners believe it's in the community's best interests to have the program discontinued."

Cam scraped a hand over his chin. The program sounded like the one Nicole taught. He wished he'd asked her more about it.

"Don't get me wrong. I believe those boys should get all the help they need, but we don't want our own children to be prey for criminals."

"Criminals?"

"Yes. Some of those students have been in jail. Some are on probation. And the worst part of it is that they don't even live in this neighborhood."

Bentworth's voice rose, and the more he talked, the redder his face got. "As I said, we're counting on the support of every homeowner in the community. We want to keep our children safe. As a father, I'm sure you feel the same."

The only problem Nicole had mentioned was the graffiti incident in her first-grade class, and she hadn't made a big deal of it. "I'd heard about some vandalism, but nothing else. Did the police find out who was responsible?"

"No. But we all know it was one or more of those boys."

Those boys? Cam crossed his arms. As a kid, he and his brothers had heard that term plenty. *Those Colter boys.* When something bad happened, they were always thought of first.

"What boys?"

"The delinquents in that At Risk program. But our *families* are the ones at risk, not them."

"I see. Well, I'd like to learn more about it, but I'm on my way out right now. Maybe I can catch you later?" After he asked Nicole a few more questions.

"Sure. Just so you know, our community's sticking together on this, Colter, and we need your support, too."

If he read the guy right, the underlying message was clear. Not supporting the petition would make him the odd man out. A little like blackmail to Cam's mind.

He'd learned long ago to think first and react later. Hell, he couldn't even form an opinion on this until he knew more about the petition.

"Tell you what, Jim." He placed a firm hand on his neighbor's shoulder. "I'm going to be gone until Monday. Why don't I catch up with you on Tuesday or sometime after that, whenever you're available?"

The man drew himself up, apparently comfortable with Cam's response. "Sure, just remember, the sooner, the better. You can come over and sign any time."

Cam ushered Bentworth toward the door, his hand still on the man's shoulder, subtly directing him out of the house. He let the door slam with a thud.

Damn, he needed a strong cup of coffee.

NICOLE PACED, the phone at her ear.

"I'll ask a few questions, Roy. That's all I can do." It galled her to do even that, since she knew her A.R. students were being unfairly targeted. "But it'll have to wait until the next class on Tuesday." Which he should've known. He could've talked to her on Monday about this.

"I appreciate it, Nicole. Now, on another note, it's come to my attention that one of your first-grade boys has been picking fights on the playground. Are you aware of that?"

Uh-huh. So that was the real reason he'd called her at home on a Saturday afternoon. "Yes, I'm aware there was a scuffle. But we got it straightened out. It's not a problem."

"I suggest you keep a closer eye on your students in the future, Ms. Weston. In a school like this, we depend on the community to keep afloat. Parents choose to send their children here and if we can't handle some of the students, we won't be in business for long. It's critical that we uphold community confidence in our curriculum and in our teachers."

Message received, loud and clear. "I appreciate the heads up, Roy. I'll keep an eye on it."

With that, the principal said goodbye and Nicole hung up. The phone rang again. "Hello."

The voice that greeted her belonged to Letitia Nelson, Dylan McGinnis's aunt, a woman with whom she'd talked several times since the boy had come into the after-school class.

Mrs. Nelson talked about Dylan and her innate belief that he was a good boy. "He's had a rough time of it, and now with all these additional problems—I don't know what's going to happen. I thought maybe you could help."

"I'll be happy to help if I can. What additional problems are we talking about?" Judging by his records Dylan was an extremely bright boy. He was also an angry young man.

What kid wouldn't be angry living the way he had? But other than what she'd read in the files, and the fact that she knew he didn't want to be in the program, she knew little about him.

"Someone—he didn't give his name—called to tell me Dylan was involved in that vandalism at the school. I know it's not true, and I thought you might know why someone would accuse him?"

"Did the caller say why he believed Dylan was involved?"

"No. He just said he was."

"Do you know where he was last Thursday night?"

A long silence ensued, then the woman said softly, "I can see I'm talking to the wrong person. I thought you might help, since Dylan seems to think highly of you. I'm sorry I took up your time."

"No, wait! I only asked the question because it's what others will ask. I don't believe Dylan was involved, and I want to help if I can. What do you think I can do?"

"I wondered if you might know who called and then I was hoping you could talk to him."

"Unfortunately, I don't."

"He knew about Dylan's record. The school and the courts are the only ones with that information. And it's supposed to be confidential, isn't it?"

True, but obviously the caller had found out and was using it against the boy.

"Without knowing the caller's name, Mrs. Nelson, I'm at a loss. It might be a good idea for you to contact the principal and talk to him directly. You can vouch for Dylan from a different perspective than I can."

"I will. I'll call him right away. I'm sorry, I don't want to bother you, but I'm so upset about this, and I didn't know who else to turn to. Dylan said you were different. He said you thought he was smart and even asked me if I thought he was, too. He's never acted as if he cared about anyone's opinion before."

"That's what he *wants* everyone to think—that he doesn't care. It's a defense mechanism."

"Oh." Mrs. Nelson was quiet for a moment. Then she said, "Yes, I can see that. But I know he cares what *you* think and that's a step in the right direction, isn't it?"

"Yes, it sure is. Does Dylan know about the accusation?"

"He overheard the conversation, and then he got angry and left. I didn't have a chance to talk to him about it."

Damn.

"Ms. Weston, if you see him before I do, maybe you could talk to him—before he does something stupid."

"I'd be happy to, but I don't know if he'll listen."

"He'll listen to you. I know it. Even if he doesn't let on. He's a good boy, I know he is. And he respects you."

"I'll do whatever I can. It would be helpful if you and I could meet and talk some more."

"I've been sick and don't get out much. Could you come to my home?"

"Of course. I'll get back to you to work out a date as soon as I can." When she hung up, Nicole was more frustrated than ever. Only cowards made anonymous accusations. Cowards who didn't have the guts or the conviction to say what they wanted to in person.

Listening to garbage like that could permanently damage a kid's psyche. And damn it all! She wasn't going to let that happen to one of her students.

CAMERON ARRIVED on Nicole's doorstep at precisely eight-thirty on Sunday morning. On his way across the street, he breathed in deeply, enjoying the crisp morning air—and strangely excited about the day ahead. The temperature wouldn't stay cool very long, but it didn't matter. They'd be in pine country in an hour and a half and it was always twenty degrees cooler in the mountains than in the valley.

He entered Nicole's building and found the door to her apartment ajar. She knew he was coming and had probably left it open so he wouldn't knock and alert the neighbor—Risa?—that he was there.

The aroma of cinnamon and coffee drew him farther inside. He paused by the archway leading into the kitchen, watching as Nicole stood at the sink pouring coffee into a tall silver thermos—watching and appreciating the sweet curve of her backside in a pair of snug-fitting jeans. It was tough to tell whether his saliva glands were working overtime because of the frosted cinnamon rolls on the counter or the way she looked.

He knocked lightly on the wall. "Something smells mighty good."

She swung around, her eyes lighting up when she saw him. "Cam! I didn't hear you come in."

"I sneaked up so your neighbor wouldn't hear."

She smiled. "I thought we could use some coffee on the road, and I made some cinnamon rolls."

If he wasn't hungry before, he was now. "You got a bib? I think this kid's about to start drooling."

She placed a plate of rolls on the table. "Dig in." She poured two cups of coffee, then sat down.

"Don't mind if I do," he said, joining her. Hungry though he was, he waited, watching her pull off a piece of the bun with two fingers and stuff it into her mouth. He found it more erotic than if she were sitting there naked.

"Mmm." She licked the excess frosting from the tips of her fingers and then, with a swipe of her tongue, from her lips.

"You know what they say about cinnamon, don't you?"

She shook her head, her mouth still full.

"It's an aphrodisiac. Proven to attract men." He picked up a roll and directed it to his mouth.

"Well, then. I guess I'll have to save them until I wish to lure some unsuspecting man into my lair," she said as she snatched the roll from his fingers and returned it to the plate, leaving him with his mouth hanging open.

"Hey." He held up both hands, laughing as he did. "It's a joke, Nicole. Don't go getting all serious on me."

"It's too early for jokes. So behave yourself."

He nodded solemnly, still grinning. "Oh, I will, I will. I promise."

"Well, okay," she said, gesturing him to go ahead. Cam happily ate a roll, polishing it off in two bites. "Mm-mmm. How could I ever forget how much I like your sweet buns?" He gave her a playful wink.

"And how could I ever forget what a smart-ass you are?" She grabbed the thermos and started for the door. "C'mon. Let's get this show on the road." Under her breath, she muttered, "I have a feeling it's going to be a very long day."

CHAPTER FIVE

"OH, YEAH. Smell that air," Cam said, his chest expanding as he took in a deep breath. "Nothing like it." He stood in front of the truck, thumbs in the belt loops of his Wranglers, a melancholy smile on his face.

Nicole knew exactly what he meant. She closed her eyes for a moment, concentrating on the crisp scent of pine in the air. Christmas in April.

They'd stopped midway between Phoenix and Patterson to stretch their legs, and at nearly four thousand feet altitude, the breeze sent Nicole's hair flying. "It's refreshing, isn't it? And gorgeous. Don't you miss it?"

Putting his Stetson back on, Cam walked back to the truck with her. "Sure. Sometimes. That's when I wonder if I made the right decision to move away. But with Michael to care for, it made sense. I can make more money in the construction business in Phoenix than I can in Patterson."

"Is that what it's about? Making money?"

He thought for a second. "Money's nice, but I had other considerations, too. Like I said, people change."

Cam looked at her, his seriousness giving way to a playful gleam in his eyes. "Except for you. I'll bet you're still one of those card-carrying feminists."

"And I'll bet you're still a cowboy—no matter where you live."

He laughed, but didn't disagree. He knew it was true.

She knew it was true. He was and always would be more cowboy than businessman.

Cam held the truck door open and waited for her to climb in. Back on the road, Nicole couldn't stop wondering what Cam's family would think about her showing up again. But then, it was only Harry and his wife she'd be meeting.

Cam still hadn't mentioned his older brothers and she had to wonder why. Maybe he didn't think it was important since they were probably living on their own sections of the ranch as planned. Jackson was the oldest, Ransom next and Cam the youngest of the three with one year separating each of them. Harry, or Harrison as she'd heard his mother call him, had come along five years later and was just young enough not to follow in his brothers' footsteps.

But what made Nicole more nervous than seeing Cam's family again was the fact that being with Cam, even just sitting next to him, felt so damn good. Something inside her came alive when he was around. The very air seemed energized.

It felt as if nothing mattered except what was going on between them—whatever that might be. She was tempted to throw caution to the wind and give their relationship another try. But it was a fleeting thought.

Nicole had learned her lesson. Besides, he didn't seem to be offering anything but friendship.

She noticed that Cam hadn't said much since the rest stop, but the silence suited him. He'd told her when they'd met ten years ago that he didn't engage in idle conversation. When he talked, it was because he had something to say.

"So, what can you tell me about the after-school programs?" he suddenly asked.

The question surprised her. "Well, what would you like to know? Are you considering enrolling Michael in one of them?"

"He's got all he can handle with the regular school day. I was actually wondering about your At Risk class. Are there are other classes like the one you teach?"

"No. There are special interest classes, but my A.R. class is the only one of its kind at Barton. Why?"

He hesitated. "One of my neighbors came by, and apparently, some people in the community think those students might be responsible for the damage at the school."

"My kids?"

He glanced at her and then back to the road. "Yeah. Guess so, if your class is the only one like it."

"Dammit! It ticks me off that everyone jumps to that conclusion. As far as I know, the police haven't arrested anyone, so why do those vigila—"

"Hey..." He reached over and took her hand. "I was just asking a question because I don't know much about this."

"And I'll bet that neighbor of yours doesn't either."

He drew his hand back and grasped the wheel. "I didn't like the guy much, but he said the younger children in the neighborhood could be endangered. So I listened."

"And?"

"And nothing," he said softly. "I told him I wanted to hear more about it, which is why I asked you. I knew you'd give it to me straight." He looked over at her and smiled.

"Sorry. I just get so irritated when people make judgments without knowing anything about it."

"So maybe you can shed some light on the program for me. This neighbor said some of the students are criminals? Is that true?"

"Not only is that *not* true, it's ridiculous."

"I wonder why he'd say it then."

"Perhaps because one of the boys was in a detention center for a while, and they've all been in trouble with the law. *Minor* trouble. But the reason they're in the class is because they have various learning problems, which is why they're at risk for dropping out of school before they finish. It's unfair to label them criminals because they've been in trouble once or twice."

She leaned against the seat and sighed. "Even smart kids from so-called good families get into trouble."

"Well, you're right about that." He grinned engagingly. "I see you still get a little feisty when you're involved in a cause."

"This isn't a cause, Cam," she said fervently. "I'm a teacher. It's my job to help my students in any way I can. I don't pay attention to their parents' credentials, bloodlines or the student's ability to excel. They *need* me and—"

He placed his hand on hers. "I was teasing, Nic." His voice was soft and understanding, and he gave her a look so touched with tenderness that she melted a little inside.

Then he added, "But you're mighty pretty when you get all stormy like that."

Letting a smile emerge, she said, "Okay. I'll behave myself for the rest of the day. I promise."

Cam squeezed her hand as if to assure her everything was fine between them. As she settled back in her seat, she felt a vague sense of familiarity. "Look. There's a sign."

She squinted to make out the faded letters on the weathered board dangling unevenly between two posts. "It's different than I remember. The brand mark looked like a skull and crossbones."

"Yeah. Harry's idea of a joke," Cam said. "Little brother's changed in lots of ways, but his twisted sense of humor hasn't."

They followed the curved road around the base of the mountain and then drove upward through the pines and alligator juniper until they reached a clearing. Several yards ahead, beyond the frontage road, lay a sprawling log house that looked very much like the homestead in the old *Bonanza* television series.

"Are we near your parents' ranch? The terrain is looking familiar."

"Good memory, Nic." He glanced at her and winked.

Her stomach fluttered. He needed to stop that. Right now.

"As a matter of fact, this is, or I should say, *was* part of their property." He pointed to the ranch house. "That's Harry's place." Then he pointed to his right. "And down that road is where we veered off to go to my folks' place."

He stopped the car. "In fact, you might remember that spot over there." He pointed again, this time toward a dilapidated cabin nestled in a grove of fat manzanita trees.

She remembered. They'd spent a couple of unforgettable days in a cabin on the ranch when Cam's parents had gone on a trip and left him in charge. "My memory isn't that good," she lied.

"Need a hint?"

"No, some things are better left to the past," she answered, although she'd called up the memory of that particular weekend more times than she cared to admit—even to herself.

Cam respected her wishes and didn't say another word as he resumed driving. She was still trying to shake off the memory of that erotic weekend as they pulled up to the house. They'd barely stopped when Harry slammed open the screen door and barreled toward them.

"Go ahead," she said to Cam, letting him know it wasn't necessary to get out and open her door. Yet he still reached across and opened it from the inside.

"Where's Michael?" Cam asked as he bounded from the truck.

"Where else?" Harry thrust a thumb toward the back of the house. Next thing she knew, the two men were in a handshaking, backslapping clinch. But when Harry saw her walking toward them, his smile faded as fast as sundown in winter.

Her spirits faded, too, but thankfully, once she got close enough, Cam pulled her against him and wrapped his arm snugly across her back. "You remember Nicole, don't you, Har?"

Cam's brother nodded. "Sure do. How are you?" he asked icily.

"Nice to see you again, Harry," she said and quickly extended her hand.

He nodded a second time and a thick swatch of cocoa-brown hair fell across his forehead. Then he gave her the briefest handshake in history. "Sharon's fixin' some food. We should go in."

The house, built of logs, rock and cedar, had a rustic, lived-in feel. They followed Cam's brother through a huge great room that had a massive floor-to-ceiling natural stone fireplace, then through the dining room and at last, into the kitchen, which was about the size of Nicole's whole apartment.

A tall, large-boned woman stood at the sink, vigorously cleaning vegetables.

"Honey," Harry said over the running water, "look

who's here.'' He reached in front of her to shut off the faucet.

When the woman turned, Nicole was surprised to see how young she was.

''Hey, gorgeous.'' Cam strode over to his sister-in-law, hugged her affectionately, then introduced them. ''Nicole, this is Sharon, my favorite sister-in-law. Sharon, my friend Nicole.''

Sharon came over immediately and hugged Nicole as though she was one of the family. ''Cameron forgot to mention I'm the *only* sister-in-law he's got, and—''

A small angry voice from outside cut off the introductions. ''I did not!''

''You did, too!''

''I did *not* touch your stupid rope!''

''You did. You always take my stuff!''

''Didn't.''

''Did, too.''

Sharon's wide-set eyes filled with concern, but she stayed put, choosing to listen first. When Cameron started forward, Sharon caught his shirtsleeve and tugged him back.

''Give them a minute, Cam. They'll work it out. They always do.'' Her tone was firm, and despite her youth, Sharon seemed the authority here.

Cameron acquiesced, but paced the room, both hands shoved deep into his front pockets.

''He's like a bull bustin' from the chute,'' Sharon said to Nicole. ''Can't wait no how.'' Then to Cameron, ''Michael will be fine. He really will.'' She laid a reassuring hand on his shoulder. ''We'll go out in a minute, *after* they've settled their problems.''

When the high-pitched voices continued, Cam cringed.

''Oh, awright!'' one boy shrieked. ''So what. So maybe I did!''

''Give it!''

''No!'' A taunting giggle filled the air.

''C'mon. *Give it to me!*'' the smaller voice demanded.

''Okay, okay. What's so danged great about that stupid rope anyway?''

''It's a lasso.''

A silence followed and the adults all exchanged relieved looks. Sharon was right. The children had settled it themselves. As Nicole began to offer her help with the meal preparation, a child's bloodcurdling scream split the air.

Cameron flew out the door with the rest of the adults on his heels.

Standing on the deck with the others, Nicole saw Michael in the middle of a small roping arena, his skinny six-year-old legs apart and his arms folded rigidly across his small chest. A satisfied grin lit his face.

Three feet in front of him, another boy, wearing a nasty scowl, was neatly wrapped by a length of rope to a corral post.

''Untie me, Michael, you little puke,'' the boy sputtered and kicked up a cloud of dust as he writhed in the dry earth.

Cam was about to jump in again when Sharon grabbed his pant leg. ''Hold on a minute longer. Let's see what happens.''

Oblivious to the audience, Michael ambled over to stand, arms akimbo, directly in front of the other boy. ''Say you're sorry,'' Michael demanded.

The larger boy squeezed his eyes shut, clamped his mouth into a tight knot and shoved his face forward in defiance.

Michael shrugged as if it made no difference to him and then turned to leave. "Okay. Bye."

All was silent, and Nicole could see the muscles in Cam's cheek twitching as he held himself back. Then the captive boy opened one eye and muttered, "Okay, okay." He lowered his chin to his chest. "I am."

Michael waited. He shook his head. "Uh-uh. You hafta *say it.*"

The larger boy's voice dropped to a repentant whisper. "Awright. I'm sorry I took your stupid rope."

But Michael didn't budge. He stood there with his arms folded across his chest. "What did you say, Devin? I didn't hear you."

Nicole could almost hear the deep breath of resignation coming from the other boy. "I'm sorry I took your rope," he said, this time loudly enough for the neighbors to hear.

Despite appearances, Nicole figured the two boys were just being boys and scenes like this were all part of being buddies. Her thoughts were borne out when Michael untied his cousin and the boys broke into a playful scuffle.

The friendly jostling came to a quick end when Michael spotted Cam.

"Dad! Dad!" Michael made a mad dash toward them, colliding with his father's knees in his excitement.

"Hey, champ. What's up?" Cam balanced himself, then dropped down on one knee. Michael started talking, but stopped abruptly when he noticed his teacher standing there, too. He left his father and walked over to her.

"Are you here with my dad?"

Nicole wasn't sure what to say, but decided a professional response was best. "Yes, Michael. Your father was kind enough to invite me along for the ride."

He gave a huge, if slightly self-conscious, smile. The

other boy ran over to join them and then, just like that, the two went off to play.

Their behavior was so typical she had to laugh. "If only adults could take a cue from kids. The world might be a better place," she said to no one in particular.

"It'll never happen with *some* people," Sharon replied, nudging her brother-in-law in the ribs. "This guy's worse than a stage mother."

Cam scowled. "I can't see letting 'em kill each other when I can stop it." He crossed his arms over his chest and planted his feet apart, exactly the way his son had.

Sharon laughed. "You're going to end up in the nuthouse if you worry so much."

Nicole winced at Sharon's words. They were a sharp reminder that she and Cameron were simply two old friends getting together because she was his son's teacher and he'd asked for her help.

Friends. Teacher. That was all their relationship could be. And that was how it would stay.

"Let the kids work it out, Cameron," Sharon continued. "How else will they learn to deal with conflict when they get older? You won't be there when he goes off to college. When he gets married."

Cam's expression said she'd made her point. He waved to Harry, then to the boys, directing them toward the roping arena. "C'mon guys. Get your ropes."

Sharon smiled, apparently satisfied. "I've got a few more things to do in the kitchen." She turned to go back inside.

"Can I help?" Nicole followed her into the house.

"Sure, sit here." She patted the seat of a wooden stool next to an enormous butcher block in the center of the room. "We're planning a barbecue later. You can clean the strawberries for the fruit salad."

Nicole perched on the stool and Sharon set an amber-colored crockery bowl in front of her, then a box of strawberries. "Grew them in the garden."

"I'm impressed."

"Try one. They're as sweet as honey." She kissed her fingertips.

Nicole pinched the top from the plumpest strawberry, washed it off and popped it into her mouth. She nodded in agreement as the strawberry dissolved in a burst of sweetness.

"I tried growing tomatoes once, but I didn't have much luck." She leaned forward on her elbows. "Of course if I'd had a garden instead of a box on the patio, which I always forgot to water, I might've had better luck." The women laughed together and soon it seemed as if they'd known each other for years.

Nicole liked Sharon's no-nonsense manner, her ingenuous qualities. Sharon, she'd learned, was younger than she by several years and had married Harry when she was only seventeen. Devin, at six, the same age as Michael, was their oldest child, Liza and Rory, short for Aurora, were five and three respectively.

"Coming from a family of eight, I'm used to children and I love it whenever Michael comes to stay. He's like one of my own," she said. "But he's not an easy child. Growing up without a mother...well, I'll just say that's been really hard on Michael. Hard on Cameron, too."

Nicole nodded. She knew exactly how hard it was.

"I wish I had more information about Michael's mom, so I could help, but Cameron's tight-lipped about his personal life," Sharon said as she finished scraping the last of the carrots, then rinsed them and dumped the whole batch in a Tupperware bowl. She went to the double-door refrigerator, pressed the button for crushed ice and spread some on top of the carrots. ''My guess is that Harry knows the whole story, but he's never really talked about it. And I don't pry. A man's business is his own, if you know what I mean.''

Nicole respected Sharon's beliefs, even though they wouldn't be hers. Husbands and wives should be able to talk to each other, confide in each other. Or was that just her fantasy based on limited knowledge?

''Sure, I understand.''

She finished the strawberries and handed the bowl to Sharon, searching her face for the signs of disapproval Harry had shown earlier, but found none. Instead she saw a quick and playful smile that crinkled the corners of Sharon's eyes.

''Weren't you and Cameron almost engaged a while back?'' The smile broadened.

Had Cam said that? Or was it Sharon's interpretation? She and Cam had talked about many things, their hopes and dreams, families and marriage in general, but they'd never planned a future together. They *hadn't* been ''almost engaged.'' Even back then, she wouldn't have let it go that far.

Nicole moved her gaze from Sharon's, got up and went to the screen door. ''I'd call it infatuation at best. It was a college romance, and I was only eighteen when we met.'' She glanced back at Sharon. ''You know how that goes.''

''No, I don't,'' she said frankly. ''I never went to college, and like I told you, I met Harry when I was seventeen. That was it for both of us. Love at first sight.'' Sharon chuckled. ''Most people don't believe in love at first sight, but when it happens to you, you gotta believe it.'' Shrugging, she came over to stand beside Nicole and rested a hand on her shoulder. She looked pointedly at

Cameron, standing outside with Harry and the boys, and then at Nicole. ''Things happen for a reason. You two meeting again—there's a reason for that.''

Just then, two adorable little girls bounded into the room. They had chocolate eyes and hair the color of butterscotch, like their mother's. They could have been twins if not for the difference in size. Sharon introduced the girls, tended to their needs and afterward, they all went out to join the guys.

It wasn't long before both Liza and Rory made a fuss, begging and pleading for roping lessons of their own.

''Boys shouldn't get all the fun,'' Rory pouted.

Cameron tossed Nicole a lariat. ''Remember anything?''

She stared down at the coiled hemp dangling from her hand like a dead rattler. ''Cameron, it's been years. I don't—''

''D'ya know how to rope?'' Michael ran toward her, excitement ringing in his voice.

More than ten years had passed since Cameron had taught her the fundamentals, and even back then, she'd never mastered the skill. She'd only played around with it because it was so much fun to practice with Cameron.

''Do ya?'' The boy peered up at her.

''I used to know a little bit, but it's been so long since I tried, I think I've forgotten everything.''

The boy's face fell, and disappointment filled his eyes. Nicole quickly knelt beside him. ''But maybe you can refresh my memory.''

His eyes brightened again. ''Well, you start like this,'' he said. His small hands crisscrossed over hers to demonstrate the hold. Concentrating heavily, he explained the basic grip and how and when to let the rope slide. Soon they had a wobbly twirl, up and around, both hooting hysterically when the rope dropped onto their heads.

When their laughter subsided, Michael's face grew serious. "I think we need help."

"No, no. I just need a little practice," she said. But it was too late. Michael called, "Da-a-ad!" and before she knew it, Cam had come up behind.

"Show her, Dad. Show her like you did me."

Nicole knew exactly what Michael meant. Cam had taught her all those years ago by placing his arms around her.

When they both just stood there, Michael insisted, "C'mon Dad! I can't do it 'cause I'm too small."

From the glint in Michael's eyes, Nicole suspected the kid knew exactly what he was asking. But thank heaven Cam hesitated, apparently just as reluctant as she was to get that close.

"Like this," Michael said and mimicked the pose Cam had used on Nicole before.

When Michael grabbed Cam's hand and directed it to Nicole's, Cam let out a long breath. He placed stiff arms around her, obviously trying not to touch her with any other part of his body. With his rough hands on hers, Cam guided her into a jerky twirl, finally arcing the rope into a loop above their heads.

With the movement, the tension she'd felt melted away, and in that single moment it was as if she'd been flung ten years into the past. She could almost feel his hard body against hers, moving with her as if they were one. That way, he'd said, she could get the rhythm of the roping motion. And had she ever.

She'd felt his face against her hair, and he'd smelled of fresh air and Irish Spring soap. His breath had warmed her cheek, his lips brushed her ear, and the rest of the world had hummed in a distant haze outside that moment—their moment.

''Remember now?'' Cam's voice pierced her reverie.

''Dad, show her how to pop a loop.''

The past hurtled forward into the here and now, as Michael skipped in a circle around them, twirling his own rope in a tight spiral pattern.

''Sure, kid. Let's do it together.''

That quickly, he was gone, but his touch lingered.

Nicole watched the father-and-son roping routine, and the unadulterated pride that lit Cam's face when he looked at his boy touched her deeply. If life had been different, Michael might have been *their* son.

Should have been, she thought in a crazy burst of longing—longing that quickly shifted to anger at the injustice that had robbed her not only of her childhood, but also her future.

''Okay, guys, time to get the grill fired up,'' Sharon said to the men before sending orders to the kids to wash up. Sharon headed back toward the house, pulling Nicole along with an arm around her shoulders. ''C'mon. We'll get the tables ready.''

Sharon's casual acceptance made Nicole feel as if she was family. A feeling she liked very much. The rest of the afternoon was spent in pleasant conversation, but Nicole made sure the subject never veered toward her former relationship with Cam. Harry had lightened up a bit, and by the time they left, she was no longer sure whether he'd really been distant at first or not.

Maybe she only thought he seemed cool to her because that was the treatment she deserved. Or maybe her imagination was working overtime. That was how it had started with her mother. The doubts. Suspicions.

But all the good feelings inside her chased away her

usual need to examine everything. She wanted to enjoy the time that remained, and on the ride back to Phoenix, Cam seemed as mellow as she felt. Michael, however, still had enough energy to ply her with questions.

"D'ya like macaroni and cheese?" he wanted to know. "Peanut butter sandwiches? GameBoy? Scary movies? How about baseball and soccer?"

Last, but not least, he wanted to know if she had any children for him to play with. "Gena has two kids," he said. "Gena was going to be my mom, but now we don't see them anymore." He gave a big yawn, and a few minutes later, he was sleeping soundly.

Cam didn't say a word.

Nicole leaned over the seat to wipe a smudge of dirt from the boy's cheek and gently pulled his red T-shirt down to cover his bare tummy.

With Michael sleeping, Nicole and Cameron fell into a comfortable silence most of the way back to Phoenix. Comfortable except that she was distracted by Michael's comment about Cameron's relationship with another woman.

Why had she been so surprised? He'd always received more than his share of attention from women, and he *was* single, after all. Did she think he'd been living in a monastery? Just because she'd been practically celibate didn't mean *he* had.

As they were coming down the mountain, the lights in the valley soon appeared as a distant glow on the horizon before them. Cam looked over at her and said, "You did good for someone who never liked playin' with a rope."

She scoffed. "Yeah, right. I can't believe you made me do that. I'm so bad even Michael felt sorry for me."

He laughed, seeming to delight in teasing her. "I know. But it was fun watching."

After that he suggested they drop Michael at home with the housekeeper before driving Nicole to her place. Since Michael had school in the morning, he didn't want to jostle the boy around any more than necessary.

Cam was a good dad. An excellent parent. But then, there'd never been a question in her mind about that. "Sure," she said, even though it meant they'd be alone later.

After arriving at his house, Cam scooped Michael into his arms and carried him inside. Nicole gathered the boy's hat, shoes, blanket, some loose papers he'd been drawing on, and followed.

The housekeeper nodded in greeting. Both she and Nicole trailed Cam into the bedroom where he tucked his son in and planted a kiss on the boy's tousled head before leaving the room.

"Aren't you going to turn off the light?" Nicole asked.

"He likes it on. Makes him feel more secure." Without further explanation, Cam introduced her to Maria, then guided Nicole into the living room with one hand settled on the small of her back.

His easy touch made her feel as if their being together was the most natural thing in the world. A warm sense of belonging coursed through her.

This must be a little like it would feel to be part of a normal family, she decided. She liked the feeling very much. Which was dangerous... And the worst thing about it was that she hadn't expected all those old dreams and fantasies still to be living inside her.

"C'mon, Cam. Time to take me home."

Before she lost it completely.

Fifteen minutes later they were outside her condo. Cam parked, got out and opened her door.

"Thanks," she said. "You don't need to walk me in."

"Yes, I do."

She would've argued with him, but knowing how he'd been brought up, she knew it was useless. His mother had adhered to the old school and drummed the importance of courtesy into her sons. Good manners were as much a part of him as his Stetson.

Now, standing at her door with Cam by her side, Nicole dug in her backpack for her keys, hoping he didn't ask to come in—and wondering where the hell Risa was when she needed her.

"Here, let me help."

He was too close, and he was making her nervous. "Thanks, but I've got it." She held up the key. "Voilà." She aimed it toward the slot in the dead bolt, unsure if she could hit the mark since her fingers had suddenly turned to putty.

"They should put stronger bulbs in these hallways," she muttered, squinting at the lock. "Or maybe I'm just too tired to see straight." She hoped he'd take the hint and go home. Because she doubted she could handle any more closeness tonight.

Cameron reached out, enclosed her hand in his and firmly directed the key into place. With another deliberate movement, he turned the lock and pushed open the door.

He made no move to leave, so she said, "I enjoyed the day, and I hope Michael did, too."

A funny, almost relieved smile formed on Cam's face before he said, "He did. A lot. I could tell. His old man did, too. Thanks for coming along."

And then he was gone.

CHAPTER SIX

THE NEXT DAY AT SCHOOL, Michael was the perfect student. It was almost unnatural, and Nicole wondered what he was up to.

At the end of the school day, when all the other kids had filed out, Michael approached her desk.

"Hey, you're going to miss the bus if you hang around here too long." It was only 2:45 and he still had ten minutes, but she had to leave to visit her mom and after that, Mrs. Nelson.

"My dad likes you," he said matter-of-factly. "Are you going to marry him?"

Whoa. Where did *that* come from? "No-o-o. We're just friends, Michael. Didn't your dad tell you that?"

The boy shook his head. "He said he'd get me a mom."

"Well..." Nicole cleared her throat. "That's good, Michael. But people usually marry someone they've been seeing for a long time, so your dad must've been talking about someone else."

"You mean like Gena?"

Hmm. "Yes, I suppose...if he's been seeing her for a while."

"She moved away. But my dad told me he'd find someone else. I want him to marry a lady like Aunt Sharon. She's pretty and she's nice to me."

Something sharp lodged in Nicole's chest. Which was

a ridiculous reaction. So why did she feel as if she'd just found out her lover was cheating on her?

"But I think you're even prettier. And I like you better."

Oh, the honesty of children. She smiled. "And I like you, too, Michael. But I'm your teacher, and that's different. While your dad and I are old friends, it's good for him to have lots of other friends, too. Now you'd better get going before you miss your bus."

Nicole was still thinking about their conversation when the guard nodded her through the electronic gates at the hospital. She removed her visitor's card from the slot and drove into the compound. The card was a courtesy extended to family members of long-term patients so they could enter the grounds without signing in each time.

She parked in her usual spot, then walked through the parking lot to the plain brick building, paying little notice to the high fencing that surrounded the building. Or the razor wire in some areas.

Unit A. She hit the buzzer next to the steel door and waited for one of the staff to open it from inside. In silence, the two of them walked down another empty corridor and through more locked doors. Once in, Nicole approached the station and Mary Beth, the on-duty attendant, flashed a welcoming smile.

"She's had a good day today, Miss Weston. Very quiet, no problems whatsoever."

Nicole bit back the urge to remind the attendant that in her mother's case, "quiet" wasn't necessarily good. In fact, it often meant just the opposite. She and Mary Beth reached the gray double doors and again waited to be buzzed in.

Passing through the common area, Nicole steeled herself against the malodorous smell, a combination of ammonia, disinfectants, cigarettes and the heavy air that accompanied a roomful of people. She'd never get used to it. She wondered if anyone ever did.

A rumpled young man, not more than twenty-five, shoved his unshaven face under her nose. Blinking heavy-lidded eyes, he mumbled something unintelligible.

Nicole knew his sluggishness and slurred words were caused by medications. Haldol, once known in the facility as vitamin H, Clozapine, Thorazine, Risperidone and a host of others were familiar names to her—and like old friends to her mom. Lord knows, her mom's doctors had tried them all.

More doors into the women's unit where an overweight woman sidled up next to Nicole. "Got a cigarette? Gimme a cigarette."

Nicole smiled pleasantly and shook her head. "I'm sorry. I don't smoke."

Blank faced, the woman shuffled off, the back of her dress gaping open. Nicole stopped Mary Beth with a hand on her arm. "Wait. She needs her dress zipped."

Mary Beth motioned for her to stay put while she took care of it. Then they walked shoulder to shoulder through the gray-walled corridor to her mother's gray room.

Everything in the place, except Jenny's white, gauze-thin bedspread, looked gray. Even Jenny, who blended into her surroundings like a chameleon, seemed tinged with a gray pallor.

Nicole nodded to the nurse, who quickly left, and then approached her mother. Jenny sat rigidly in a straight-backed chair facing the window.

"Hi, Mom." She bent down, gently pressed her cheek against Jenny's and gave her a light squeeze. Turning, she crossed the narrow space and dropped onto the foot of the twin-size metal bed.

Looking at her mother, Nicole felt her sense of loss rise anew. She'd never get used to seeing her like this, though sometimes it was hard to remember when it *hadn't* been this way.

Schizophrenia was insidious and, in its early stages, easily masked by drugs or alcohol and worsened by both when left untreated.

"I spent Sunday with an old friend." She talked with her mother as she always had, convinced that somewhere in that frail shell of a body, Jenny would somehow know she was loved.

"You met him once. His name's Cameron Colter. The guy I dated early on in college. Remember?" She recalled how years ago she'd told Cameron her mother was never home because she traveled so much with her job.

It was a lie, of course. She'd lied because she couldn't bring herself to tell him the truth.

The one time he'd met her mom, Cameron had stopped over unexpectedly and Jenny was on a home visit. Nicole had quickly explained her mother's behavior as jet lag. Fortunately, it was one of Jenny's better days and Cameron had never questioned her explanation.

"But that was a long time ago. It's no wonder you don't remember him." She sighed wistfully. *A very long time ago.* "You'd like him, though. I know you would."

Attuned to her mother's tiniest movements, Nicole thought she saw Jenny turn a little toward her, so she went to the window and sat on the ledge facing her. But her mother continued to stare beyond her with blank gray eyes.

Nicole twisted around, searching the landscape, trying to see what Jenny did, wanting desperately to know what was going on inside her mother's head, wanting desperately to help her.

Oh, she'd learned a long time ago that when Jenny was in this state, no one could help. She was actively listening. Listening for the voices inside her head telling her to do things. Voices as real to Jenny as if someone were talking to her.

Over the years, Nicole had learned that for people with her mother's illness, external stimuli were amplified. All sounds, background noises, car traffic, phones ringing, machines humming, people talking, even the rustling wind, became louder and louder, increasing in intensity until the noise filled their heads and there wasn't room for anything else. So, between the delusions, hallucinations and the noise, her mom simply sat there and listened, transfixed, immobilized by the chaos in her head.

Catatonic sometimes. Over the years, Nicole had also learned that her mother's illness had different degrees of severity. There were remissions. And there were even times when Jenny remembered things that happened during her "quiet time," as Nicole had come to call it.

So, Nicole carried on as always, as if everything was normal. And for her mother, it was. This was her life. It would always be her life.

"We dated in college. But we were too young and finally went our separate ways."

She bit her lip at the memory of her teenaged attitude about her mother's unpredictable behavior. Denial, embarrassment, resentment, guilt for feeling resentment, sadness for her mom and the life she'd never have, sadness for herself and the life *she* would never have—all were emotions she'd experienced.

Typical emotions, she knew, common in family members of the mentally ill. And she'd hated herself for having every one of them. Even now, regret ambushed her when she thought about those days.

"Anyway..." She rose from the ledge and pulled a tortoiseshell hairbrush from her pack and smiled at her mom. "It's ancient history." She moved behind Jenny and began to stroke her waist-length hair with the brush.

A lighter auburn than Nicole's, her mother's hair was streaked with strands of silver, but still gleamed like shiny copper. Nicole washed and brushed her mother's hair for her as often as she could, using her own herbal shampoo.

With each rhythmic stroke, she watched her mother's reflection in the window, waiting for a sign of recognition. But the eyes were vacant, like silver-gray coins with no depth.

Yet Jenny wasn't always like this and sometimes, on her better days, she managed quite well.

Nicole was certain that communication would come again once Jenny left the hospital and went to the smaller residential facility. At the very least, it would be a more natural environment. A home rather than an institution.

But housing with appropriate care for her mom wasn't easy to find. She'd tried several already, yet Jenny always ended up back at the hospital. If her mother wasn't approved for the new home Nicole had applied for, she didn't know what she'd do.

State laws required that institutionalized persons who weren't a danger to themselves or others be "transitioned" into alternative living situations rather than remaining in state hospitals. Her mother's physicians believed Jenny was ready and Nicole wanted it for her more than anything.

Nicole leaned forward and looked directly into her eyes. "How about a French braid today?"

Jenny nodded almost imperceptibly.

Nicole smiled. Any kind of response was good. "Great. I always liked that look on you. Simple but elegant."

At forty-six, despite her problems, Jenny was still pretty, and she *was* elegant. If she'd had flowers in her silky hair, the picture would be complete. Her mom, a flower child of the early seventies, had left home at fifteen. How she ended up on a commune in Northern California, Nicole never knew.

But living on a commune wasn't conducive to lasting relationships, either. Her father had left when she was an infant, and Nicole had never wanted to know anything more about him. Because any man who could walk out on a sick wife and his own child wasn't worth knowing.

She brushed Jenny's hair until it was smooth, then parted the top evenly into thirds. Pulling the right section over the middle and the left over that, she continued plaiting, happy when she felt her mother relax.

When she'd finished the braid, she took a mirror from her bag, placed it in Jenny's hand and raised it to her face.

"See how beautiful you are, Mother?"

IT WAS STILL EARLY when Nicole left the hospital, so she drove into south Phoenix to keep her appointment with Mrs. Nelson. Risa's warning that the neighborhood wasn't the safest meant little to Nicole. She and Jenny had lived in some of the worst areas. And when you're homeless, any house in any neighborhood looks good.

As she cruised the streets, scanning the addresses, heat rose in waves from the asphalt. Yards were filled with debris, old bicycles and rusted-out cars. Shirtless teens loitered in hot alleys and music blared from low-riding cars that bounced up and down—"juicing" it was called—their stereo bass volumes cranked so high the vehicles vibrated with the rhythms.

Some whitewashed older homes boasted front yards with miniature shrines of the Madonna, many adorned with small bouquets of red and purple flowers. With her car window down so she could better see the addresses, Nicole heard laughter and saw several children darting through a spray of water from a propped-up hose. She was tempted to join them.

Finally locating the house, she parked in the driveway and got out, then went to the door and knocked.

There was no answer. As she turned to leave, a woman appeared behind the screen door.

"Mrs. Nelson?"

The older woman nodded.

"I'm Nicole Weston. We spoke on the phone earlier today—about my visit."

"Yes, I remember."

"I'm not interrupting your dinner, am I?"

"No, no." Mrs. Nelson opened the sagging screen door for Nicole to come in.

As she followed her through the austere living room and into the kitchen, shades of the past flashed through Nicole's mind. The spare apartments. The cold. The hunger. But the most vivid memory of all was one of incredible loneliness. She felt it here, too.

In Mrs. Nelson's kitchen, a chrome-and-gray Formica table, flanked by two chrome chairs with red plastic seats, was centered on a large square of tan linoleum. The refrigerator, a round-cornered relic, yellowed with age, stood against the wall on her right.

Next to the fridge was a rectangular cast-iron sink with a skirt of faded blue gingham gathered around the base. Somehow, that one addition transformed the dilapidated house into a home.

Mrs. Nelson pointed to a teakettle sitting on a hot plate. After a nod from Nicole, she filled the kettle with water from the tap and placed it on a burner.

"Where's Dylan?" Nicole asked.

"He's out getting some medication for Roland. It'll be a while before he gets back, since he's got to take the bus." The woman, a great deal older than Nicole had thought she'd be, shuffled across the room to get cups from an open shelf. She inspected each one closely, and her hands trembled a little when she set the cups on the table. She didn't look well at all.

Mrs. Nelson filled the cups with hot water, and added a tea bag to each, then handed one to Nicole.

"Who's Roland?" Nicole asked as the older woman eased slowly back into her chair.

"My son. He's in the bedroom. He's sick, but you don't have to worry, it's not catching." She pointed to a photo on a shelf. "That's Roland there with Dylan."

"I'm sorry he's not well. Is there something I can do?" Nicole got up to look at the photo. Dylan stood with his cousin, a smiling cherub-faced older boy who dwarfed Dylan in size.

Mrs. Nelson shook her head. "No, he's comfortable," she said. "I called you because Dylan is the one I'm worried about. I was hoping you could help. Dylan likes you. If you talk to him, he'll listen."

Nicole went back to the table and sat down. That was the second time Mrs. Nelson had said something about Dylan putting stock in what she said. But Nicole had had no indication from Dylan that it was how he really felt.

"Yes, of course. If I can help, I will. What can I do?"

"Will you talk to those people? Tell them Dylan's helping me with Roland, and he's not out doing all the things they say he is."

Nicole took a deep breath. "What people? What things?"

"I don't know who the man was, but he said Dylan

wrecked that classroom. Maybe the school principal would know. He called here about Dylan before. He said he knew there were better places for Dylan, that he could get better help at another school.''

Mrs. Nelson looked down, as if realizing what she'd just said. ''I'm sorry. That didn't come out right. I'm sure you're a good teacher.''

Nicole smiled. ''I'm not offended. Do you mean Mr. Bergman, the charter school principal?'' Odd. Why hadn't he discussed this change with her?

''No. Mr. Sipowitz.''

That was even more bizarre. Roy had nothing to do with the A.R. program. And as far as she knew, there weren't any other programs that could give Dylan the individualized attention he needed to graduate in a condensed period of time. ''Did Mr. Sipowitz mention what school or program he thought would work better?''

''No.'' She shook her head. ''He said he'd call me back when he had more information. I said fine, because I wanted to make sure I've done everything I can. You see, I'm very sick—kidney disease—and the doctors don't give me much time. I worry about what'll happen to Roland when I'm gone.'' She hesitated a moment, then said, ''Roland is slow.''

Mrs. Nelson touched her temple. ''Up here. He needs someone to take care of him. I know Dylan will watch out for him, but if Dylan gets into more trouble...well, then he can't.''

''Yes,'' Nicole murmured sympathetically.

Despair shone in Mrs. Nelson's eyes. ''I thought I was doing the right thing by talking to Mr. Sipowitz, but when I told Dylan, he got mad and said if he's going anywhere, it wouldn't be to another school.''

Nicole didn't like the sound of that.

"I'm worried he'll leave. Could you talk to Dylan? And maybe someone at the school, so they don't make him change?"

She couldn't blame Dylan for being upset. In his situation, she would've felt the same. "I'll be happy to talk with both of them." She patted Mrs. Nelson's hand.

Nicole wasn't sure how to approach Sipowitz, though. She certainly didn't want to jeopardize her chances for a full-time contract next year; from what she'd heard, the chances of getting the job were good. Mrs. Jessup wasn't planning to return. But if Roy wanted changes that involved one of her students, he should have consulted with her and the charter school first. She had to do something about that.

CAMERON DROPPED THE RECEIVER into the cradle without making the call. It was the third time in the past week he'd started to call and then changed his mind. He wanted to see Nicole again, but he knew it wasn't wise. He wanted to talk with her, but he didn't have any real reason to.

According to the progress note she'd sent home, Michael had had a great week at school. And his son's behavior at home had been exemplary. He sighed. There was no reason to call. No reason whatsoever.

He was a fool to have invited her out to the ranch. Being with Nicole had made him *want* her, just like he had ten years ago. Worse yet, when he realized he'd brought her home that night with every intent of seducing her, he knew his thinking was fatally flawed.

It would have been a way to get her out of his system once and for all—was that what he'd hoped? Worse, had he seen it as a way to get even? He winced at the thought.

Yeah. He was a fool. And it was a good thing he'd gotten the hell out of there when he had.

Because in the one lucid moment he'd had that day, he knew any such plan wouldn't work. Not with Nicole. She was in his blood. Had been from the moment he first laid eyes on her.

Ten years ago she'd come to a frat party with a girlfriend who'd introduced them and then disappeared for the rest of the evening. Nicole had seemed a little shy, so he'd asked her to dance. She held out a hand and he pulled her close—so close he could smell her freshly shampooed hair.

"When a Man Loves a Woman." He could still hear that song, still practically feel her body against him, her heartbeat keeping time with his own as they moved slowly to the music.

Most of the girls he'd dated back then had been easy to get to know. But Nicole was different. She'd always held something back—a part of herself she wasn't willing to share. He'd wondered at first if she even liked him.

Then he'd made her laugh, and she'd opened up a bit more and he'd felt ecstatic, felt as if he was the one person she'd been waiting for, the one person who could do what no one else could. He'd felt almost drunk on the power of it.

It'd been a defining moment for him, and he'd never forgotten it. He'd never felt that way about another woman.

No, with Nicole it would be all too easy to let himself go—and where would that leave him except involved with a woman he couldn't trust?

That was scarier than breaking a bronc without a grip.

Besides, she'd only agreed to go to the ranch with him because of Michael.

He had no reason to call her and he should be damn well satisfied with that. It might keep him from making a fool of himself.

But he *wasn't* satisfied. He knew he wouldn't be satisfied until he found out what had gone wrong ten years before.

Cam picked up the phone again and dialed her number. The hell with pussyfooting around. *He* needed to talk and he was going to do just that. Maybe then he'd be able to put the past to rest. And get a good night's sleep.

"Nicole. It's Cameron," he said when she answered.

Silence. Then she asked sleepily, "Do you know what time it is?"

He looked at the clock radio next to the bed. 4:00 a.m. "Sorry," he said, a little embarrassed. "I guess I forget the world doesn't get up when I do."

"What's going on? Is this about Michael?"

"Yeah. He's got a dad who's an idiot. Sorry I woke you. Go back to sleep."

He was about to hang up when he heard, "Don't you *dare* hang up, Cameron Colter! You can't wake me in the middle of the night and then just tell me to go back to sleep—not without explaining what you called about. I'll lie here awake for the rest of the night trying to figure it out."

"You were always too curious for your own good."

"Right now I'm anything *but* curious. I'd just like to know I wasn't awakened for no good reason."

"I'd like to talk. Is that a good enough reason?"

"Is it about Michael?" she asked again.

"No, he's fine. He's perfect. At least for the moment. No, I wanted to talk about us, about what happened."

More silence. Then she said, "I'm afraid to ask. What do you mean? What happened?"

"What happened with you and me..."

"That was a very long time ago."

"I know. But I need to talk, Nic." His voice softened. "I need to talk and not on the phone."

She let out a long breath. "Okay. When?"

"How about now?"

HAD IT ALL BEEN A DREAM? For twenty minutes she'd paced the floor in her living room, waiting for him to arrive. What was keeping him? She glanced at the door and back at the clock again. It shouldn't take this long to get from his place to hers, not at this hour.

The whole thing was bizarre. Why did he want to talk about the past? It was done. Finished.

Her only tie to him now was Michael; she was his son's teacher and Cam had asked for her help. Their former relationship had nothing to do with it. But he wanted to know what had happened. Perhaps he needed to clear the air so the past wouldn't interfere with their parent-teacher relationship.

That she could understand. In fact, she'd thought about it more than once herself. But every time she'd considered telling him, she couldn't bring herself to do it.

Maybe it was selfishness that kept her from it. Maybe she wanted to preserve the memory of what they'd had.

And once he knew about her mother, he would never look at her the same way again. Not only that, it could affect his perception of her as a teacher, destroy his confidence in her abilities to help his son.

Michael was the important issue here, she reminded herself. He was the sole reason they'd met again. If clearing the air would allow them to work together to help Michael, then that was what they had to do.

She needed to be honest with him, and then let him decide if he wanted her assistance.

Finally—a knock. Okay. She whirled around, went to the door. Her hands were clammy. Okay. She'd tell him and then he'd leave.

She jerked open the door. Dread lodged deep in her chest as they stood face-to-face.

"Sorry to bother you—"

"It's okay." She gestured to the couch. "Make yourself comfortable. Please."

She didn't offer coffee or drinks, but immediately sat down in the chair opposite the couch where he hovered, apparently too agitated to sit.

"What do you want to know?"

He ran a hand across the back of his neck and glanced around, as if trying to decide whether to sit or stand. "Yeah... Well, after we spent the day together at the ranch, I realized that, well...there's this...thing hanging between us and I need to deal with it."

"So where do you want to start?"

"All I need to know is...why we didn't work. I don't care what the reason was, I just need to *know* it. Because every time I see you, I think about it, and I don't want anything to interfere with helping Michael."

Nicole clenched her hands in her lap. "I handled things badly back then."

His eyes widened in surprise, and he sat on the edge of the couch, elbow on one knee. Waiting.

Nicole had to tell him. She had to tell him what she should've told him ten years ago.

"I wasn't straightforward with you when we were going together. My whole life was a lie then. I left because I couldn't face telling you the truth. Because I was... ashamed."

Cam's back was rigid. "So I was right." He drove a fist into the palm of his other hand and stood abruptly. "You don't need to drag it out. I don't need a name or any details."

"Name?"

"The other guy."

Oh, dear God. "That's what you thought?"

He gave a mocking laugh. "I was young and arrogant, Nicole, but I wasn't stupid. Did you think I wouldn't notice the private phone calls, broken dates, running late all the time, leaving early whenever you had the chance..."

He turned away in obvious disgust. A second later he faced her again, his expression hard and angry. "Dammit, Nicole. You should've been honest with me."

Stunned by his revelation, Nicole pressed her fingers to her lips. "You thought I was *cheating* on you? I would never have done that," she said in a whisper. "Never."

He stood in front of her, his body taut, demanding answers that his words didn't. "Well, I must be dumber than a post. You said you were living a lie. What else could you be talking about?"

She stiffened. "I—I'm talking about the truth," she sputtered, totally taken aback. "I wasn't cheating on you. I was ashamed to tell you about my mother. Back then, I never told anyone about her."

His hands tightened into fists at his sides. "Your mother? What's she got to do with anything?"

This was so hard. She knew exactly what he'd think when she finished, exactly how he'd look at her, how he'd see her from now on.

"She's got everything to do with it, Cam. She's mentally ill. Paranoid schizophrenia with psychotic episodes. She's been that way since I was a kid."

CHAPTER SEVEN

CAM'S ANGRY EXPRESSION slowly shifted to one of confusion. "I don't understand."

She shored up her reserves and forced herself to go on. She said quietly, "I didn't think you would, which is why I couldn't tell you ten years ago."

He paced, then came toward her again. "You left because you didn't think I'd understand?" His expression and the tone of his voice were incredulous. "If you fell in love with someone else, at least *that's* a reason. This...this is no reason at all. You didn't think I'd understand about your mother's illness, so you left instead? That doesn't make sense."

He stopped in front of her. "Why? Why couldn't you tell me? And why would that be a reason to end our relationship? I *loved* you, Nicole."

A squeezing pain centered in her chest. His eyes filled with hurt, and unable to bear it, she looked away. "I couldn't because I was too immature to handle it myself, much less believe that someone else could. But there's so much more to it, I can't..." Her throat closed and she couldn't speak for a moment.

Pulling herself together, she did the only thing she could—what she'd always done. She dissociated her feelings from her words and went on. "From the time I was about five, I knew my mom was different from other kids' mothers. I was too young to know what was really wrong.

I don't think she knew, either, because...well, because there were other things that masked the illness. In California, we lived in a commune and there were lots of drugs...

"Anyway, when I was nine, the commune disbanded and we—my mom, her boyfriend and I—moved to a tiny apartment in Phoenix. My mom got worse. She was hospitalized and the boyfriend left. But the good part was that she was diagnosed and given medication. Life got better for a while. But the meds had side effects and she hated taking them. So she didn't. She had a lot of episodes and was in and out of the hospital dozens of times—I was in and out of foster care just as many times because of it. We moved around a lot," she said, skimming over most of the experiences. "Finally, when I was sixteen, we rented a room in an old house and, with money from my mom's disability checks, I paid the owner to tell Child Services she'd take care of me whenever my mom was hospitalized. I soon got the system figured out, and even though we moved a few more times, I managed to stay by myself. I got a part-time job cleaning offices at night and saved as much money as I could for when I'd need it. But my life was a nightmare. School wasn't even an escape. The kids—"

She swallowed the pain and anger that surfaced whenever she thought about the past. Habit told her to downplay it, but she couldn't. She had to tell him all of it, and then he'd know her actions had nothing to do with him. "All the kids knew about my mom and treated me like an outcast. I hated school. When we moved again in my junior year and I changed schools, I did everything I could to keep my secret. Finally I had a few friends, started dating and even had a boyfriend."

She stopped for breath. "Then somehow, somebody found out and again, everyone knew. My friends got real busy. They suddenly had other things to do, and my boyfriend—'' she let out a cynical burst of laughter ''—my boyfriend split faster than an atom. All the boys I met bolted when they learned about my mom. I guess they thought I'd turn into a raving lunatic or Lizzie Borden or something. After that, I kept to myself.''

She stared down at her hands. ''I decided that if I wanted a normal life, I couldn't tell anyone about my mom, ever. It was stupid, I know, but I wanted so much to have what the other kids had. In the end, though, it was just easier not to get close to anyone.''

Twisting a corner of her T-shirt, she looked up at him. After graduation I managed to get some student loans, started college—and then I met you.'' She took a shaky breath before she continued.

''I fell in love. At first I didn't tell you because, like I said, I wanted a normal life. I wanted to have fun. I'd never experienced a relationship like ours, and I wanted it to keep going. But that was a mistake, because it just got harder and harder to tell you the truth. So I didn't, not even when I knew I had to end it.''

He ground his teeth, and the cords in his neck tightened noticeably. ''Why did you have to end it?''

''I'd thought we could enjoy what we had together and leave it at that. When you started getting serious, I panicked. You wanted children. Lots of them. By that time, I'd learned enough to know my mother's illness is often hereditary, and any child of mine could be afflicted. And the more children I had, the greater the likelihood. I'm not immune, either. So, I had a decision to make and I made it.''

''You didn't think you should ask me how *I* felt about it?''

''Actually, I did. I asked how you'd feel if the person

you married didn't want children. Your response was that you could never fall in love with someone who didn't want the same things you did."

He frowned. "That's it? What about adoption? Did you think about that?"

She shook her head. "I couldn't ask that of you, Cam. You were adamant about having a large family, living on the ranch, carrying on tradition. If I'd asked and you'd gone along with it, I knew that sooner or later you'd realize what you'd missed and hate me for it."

"So, you made the decision for me."

"It was the only decision I *could* make."

With that said, it seemed there was nothing left to say. They sat in heavy silence for what felt like a long, long time.

Finally, he spoke. "Well, none of that applies now. Does it?"

She took another shaky breath. What was he suggesting?

"I'm not living on the ranch. And Michael's such a handful, it's not likely I'll have any more kids. You ever give any thought to trying again? You and me?"

Had she ever given it any thought? Only every minute of every day and every night since he'd appeared outside her classroom door. Could they? Was there any chance whatsoever?

She knew the answer as well as she knew her name. "My mother has spent most of her adult life in and out of hospitals, Cam. That's where she is now. I'm her guardian. She's my responsibility, and if the group home I've applied for doesn't come through, she'll be staying with me. And if it *does* come through, I'll still have her at home sometimes. That responsibility and my job are all I can handle. And I can't ask you or anyone to assume my burdens."

His eyes were cold, his words precise and measured. "It's not for you to decide what I can handle and what I should assume."

"I *know* what happens, Cam. It's not easy living with someone who has a mental illness. I've been there. My mom's been abandoned by everyone who ever meant anything to her. My father, her supposedly good friends—even her own parents. They kicked her out when she was only fifteen, the time she needed them the most. If they'd caught it then—" She couldn't get the words out. She shook her head. "It happens all the time."

"And you thought I'd do the same? That's how much faith you had in me?"

Oh, God. "It wasn't about you, Cam. It was *never* about you."

He exhaled, long and hard. "Well, I asked for the truth and I got it. Considering how little trust you placed in me, I guess it wouldn't have worked, anyway." He slapped his hands on his knees and stood up.

She ached for him. She'd only done what she thought was right. And still, she'd hurt him terribly. More than she'd ever known. Then and now.

But there'd been no other choice.

There still wasn't. She could easily end up exactly like her mother. She got up, walked to the door and opened it. Despite the dull throb of grief in her chest, she said evenly, "I'm sorry. I'm truly sorry and I hope you can forgive me."

For a long painful moment, he just stared at her. Then he strode to the door. "There's nothing to forgive. I'm glad I know." He stuck out his hand. "Friends?"

It took every ounce of inner strength she had to put her hand in his, smile and say, "Friends."

With a nod, he turned and walked away.

Nicole closed the door and leaned against it, sapped of energy and filled with despair. Tears welled in her eyes. Because no matter what lie she told herself, she was still in love with him.

A few minutes later, she was startled by a knock on the door. Had he forgotten something? God, she hoped not, but who else could it be at this hour? She peered out the peephole, relieved when she saw Risa's blond head. She opened the door.

"Hi, I couldn't sleep."

"Me, either." She drew Risa inside and onto the couch and blurted out the whole story: how she'd visited her mom and then gone to Mrs. Nelson's, the call from Cam and his request to talk. She left out nothing. And somehow, saying it all strengthened her sense of resolve.

"So, what're you going to do now?"

She got up and moved toward the kitchen. "I'm going to make coffee, get dressed and go to school. I'm going to talk with Sipowitz and find out why he's making plans for my students without talking to me about it."

Risa walked with her. "That's not what I meant, and you know it. What're you going to do about the hunk who just left looking like he'd lost his dog?"

Nicole switched on the coffeepot. "There's nothing to do. I told him I have all I can handle and that's the truth."

"All you can handle and yet you're ready to jump in and help this delinquent kid and his guardian?" Risa sat at the table.

"He's not a delinquent, and it's my job."

"It's your job to help *all* your students. Including your ex-boyfriend's son. Right?"

"Right. That's why I saw Cameron in the first place. He asked for my help, and as a teacher I have an obligation to do whatever I can. Professionally."

"Uh-huh. And you went to your old boyfriend's ranch so you could give his son some English lessons? Or was it math?"

Nicole let out an exasperated breath. "There's more to teaching than reading, writing and arithmetic."

Risa grinned sardonically. "Yeah. And I bet you even believe all that."

Risa's bluntness might have offended her if it wasn't so damn close to the truth. "Of course I do. I wish I'd had a teacher to turn to, someone who could've given me guidance when I needed it. Kids can be very cruel."

"Yeah, and the older those kids get, the more skilled they are at going for the jugular. I know about that, too."

The intensity in Risa's voice surprised Nicole.

"We've all been there, one way or another. You think you're the only one who ever got a raw deal?"

Nicole poured the coffee. "No. But that's beside the point. Cameron knows where I stand. He knows that as his son's teacher, I'll do whatever I can." She sat down and slumped in the chair. "But he may not want my help after this."

"'Course he will. You said he came over to clear the air. Right?"

She nodded. "Yeah. I just don't think he had any idea it would turn out the way it did. He was truly shocked. Angry, too. But I couldn't whitewash it. He asked for the truth and I told him. The strange part is, he's angrier now than when he thought I'd been cheating on him."

"My guess is that he's angry because you weren't truthful with him when you broke up."

Nicole rested her chin in one hand. "I know that. I

screwed up back then, but I can't change it. Besides, it's ancient history. There hasn't been anything between us for ten years."

"I'm not so sure that's true. It hasn't been ten years since he found out why you split. Give him time. He'll come around."

Nicole shot to her feet. "That's exactly what I *don't* want."

"And what *do* you want?"

She thought for a moment. "I want him to be happy and remember the good things about our relationship. I want him to forget about me. And *I* want my life to go back to the way it was before he showed up in my classroom. I don't want to see him or think about him and be reminded of what we could've had if..."

Tears welled up again. She waved a hand. "It's pointless to dwell on it."

Her friend's eyes softened. Her voice, too. "How can you say that when you're still in love with him? It's so obvious."

Nicole didn't have a response.

Love had nothing to do with it.

"Some of us have never had that experience," Risa said wistfully, lifting her cup. "You're lucky to have someone who feels that way about you. If it were me, I'd fight like hell to make it work." Before taking a sip, she said, "But then, that's me. I'm not noble, and I don't get off on self-sacrifice."

Yeah, as if *she* did. She had a responsibility, one that wasn't going to disappear. That was all there was to it. A far cry from *noble* or *self-sacrificing.*

"Of course, it's not like any of that matters in my case," Risa added. "I'm not exactly fighting off suitors declaring undying love, and it looks like I never will."

"That's ridiculous!"

Risa gave her the *puh-leeze* look. "No, it's not. I rub most people the wrong way and I know it. I wish things were different, but they aren't."

"Jeez, Risa." She'd never heard her friend talk this way before. She'd thought Risa was the most grounded person she knew; she'd always seemed happy with her life. "If you want something to be different, then you have to make some changes to make that happen."

"Precisely."

THE MORNING DRAGGED. She'd gone to see Sipowitz, only to find he had a meeting off campus and wouldn't return until after lunch. She was about to check again when Michael came to her desk.

"Hey, how come you're not out on the playground with the other kids?" she asked.

"I think there was a bug or something in my lunch 'cause I don't feel so good."

He looked fine. She touched his forehead—neither hot nor cold. "Where don't you feel so good?"

He placed a hand on his tummy. "Here."

"Well, maybe I'd better take you to the nurse's office. If she thinks you're sick enough, she may have to call your dad."

"Can you stay with me till he comes?"

Looking at him, she doubted the glint in his eyes had anything to do with a tummy ache. "First things first, buddy. And that's getting you to the nurse's office so she can check you out."

As they walked down the hall, Nicole saw Roy entering his office. "While you're seeing Mrs. Ferguson, I'm going to talk with Mr. Sipowitz about something. When I'm done, I'll come back and see how you're doing,'' she said, leading the boy by the hand into the nurse's room.

Michael looked puzzled. ''Did I do something bad again? Is that why you're talking to Mr. Sipowitz?''

''No. I'm not talking to him about you, Michael. It's a business matter.'' Her answer seemed to satisfy him, but on her way out, she heard him call her. ''Make sure you come back. Okay?''

''Absolutely.'' What was going on with him today? Well, whatever it was, it would have to wait. She needed to impress upon Roy that she wanted to be consulted regarding her students. If changes were to be made with Dylan or any other student, she should be part of that decision.

Reaching his office, she said from the doorway. ''Roy. I'm glad you're back.'' She smiled. ''I'd like to talk with you about a student.''

He glanced up at her, his face a mask of indifference. Portly, balding and looking older than his forty-five years, the man had never mastered the art of diplomacy. But he'd hired her and she desperately wanted a full-time contract in the fall.

''Okay. But I only have a few minutes. I have a parent coming in at one.''

Roy was always meeting with parents—far more than she ever remembered seeing when she was a kid, or at the school where she'd done her student teaching. ''I'll make it quick,'' she said and slipped inside his office. ''Shall I close the door?''

He seemed surprised, frowning slightly. ''If you think it's necessary.''

She pulled it shut behind her, then sat in the chair.

Ensconced behind the desk, Roy folded his hands over his round stomach. ''What can I do for you, Nicole?''

Might as well plunge in. ''I was curious about whether

you've heard anything more from the police. Have they uncovered any leads on the graffiti artists who decided to use my classroom to exhibit their work?"

The eyebrows rose. "No, can't say that I have." He pulled a card from a stack of papers and handed it to her. "This is the officer in charge. You can call him. Arnette's his name."

When he didn't offer anything else, she took the card and reminded herself to be tactful. With her contract status, she could be fired without cause.

"I learned recently from Mrs. Nelson, Dylan McGinnis's aunt and guardian, that there's been some discussion about Dylan attending a different program. I figured you'd need my input, since he's one of my students."

She squared her shoulders. "You see, he's just now started to make some progress and I'd hate to see—"

He interrupted her sharply. "There's nothing to discuss, Ms. Weston. Barton has a contract with the charter school for space. We're not involved with the program. I suggest you talk to Mr. Bergman about your student's progress." He gave her a conciliatory smile, then looked conspicuously at his watch. "I'm sorry but I really don't have any more time."

She felt her cheeks grow warm. Dismissed like a recalcitrant student. And there was nothing she could do about it. She couldn't challenge his truthfulness, not if she wanted to keep the job. Rising to her feet, she gave her own conciliatory smile. "Thanks Roy. I really appreciate the time. As an educator, you know the importance of communication."

He grinned weakly, as if unsure whether he'd been complimented or insulted. It was definitely time for her to leave—before she made the point perfectly clear.

On her way back to the classroom, she swung by the

nurse's office to check on Michael. He was still in the waiting room. ''What's going on? Did Mrs. Ferguson get the bugs out?'' She tousled his hair.

''I called his father to take him home,'' the nurse said as she came in. ''I'm not sure what the problem is, but an afternoon of rest won't hurt. We don't want a little boy with a bellyache hanging around when he could be home resting up for tomorrow. Right, Michael?''

Michael smiled up at them. Guiltily, it seemed to Nicole. The little scamp was faking. She was sure of it.

''Well, I'll go back to the room and get your stuff. And I'll pack up your homework assignment so you can bring it in tomorrow.'' Widening her eyes, she added, ''If you're feeling better, that is.''

He frowned. ''Okay. But you'll be here when my dad comes, won't you?''

''Maybe.'' What was Michael up to? She *didn't* want to be there when Cam arrived, so she hustled back to her room. She was surprised to find Dylan inside waiting for her. He never showed up during the day.

''Dylan. Is something wrong?''

''No, but I wanted to give these to you before class tonight, in case you had time to look at them.'' He held out a folder. ''It's makeup work.''

He seemed embarrassed and didn't meet her eyes.

''Great. I'll take a look the first chance I get.'' She was elated, but didn't want to make him more self-conscious by reacting too much. This was progress. And for him it was huge.

Not long after Dylan left, the bell rang and the kids poured into the room from lunch break. At almost the same time, Cam appeared at her classroom door. She grabbed Michael's backpack and jammed his homework pages inside.

"I'm sorry, but I tried to get Michael's things back to the nurse's office before lunch was over, but as you can see..."

He smiled. "I can see you're busy. I just wanted to ask if there was anything I should know before I go get the kid."

"No, it's just a tummy ache. I'm sure he'll be fine in the morning." She whirled around to go back in.

"Oh, I also wanted to ask if you'd like to spend a day at the rodeo with a couple of guys on Saturday?"

She stopped midstride. She stared at Cam, who was smiling slyly. "The rodeo," she repeated. "With two guys."

"Yeah. Michael and me. It'll be fun."

Her mouth fell open.

"We're friends, right? And friends hang out together. So why don't you see if you're available, and I'll call tonight to firm up the details."

"HEY, CHAMP, you'll have to move to the back once we pick up Nicole," Cam said, reaching over to double-check Michael's seat belt while they were still in the driveway.

"Dad!" Michael pushed Cameron's hand away. "I did it myself, like I always do."

"Just making sure. Saturday traffic going to the mountains can get kind of heavy."

Pouting, Michael folded his arms across his chest and stared straight ahead.

"Hey. What's wrong?"

Silence.

"C'mon, talk to me. I'm not leaving until you do. Don't you want to go to the rodeo with your cousins?"

Michael wrinkled up his face as he said, "I wanna go. But I don't want you to treat me like a baby so much."

"What are you talking about?" Cam turned to look at Michael, surprised at his son's declaration of independence, behavior the boy usually displayed only when he was mad.

"Well, maybe...maybe you could *not* make sure so much?" Michael's blond hair fell like a mushroom cap across his forehead, his blue gaze searching for his dad's reaction. "You know how you're always fixing my seat belt when I already did and making sure I'm safe all the time and all that stuff."

Draping one arm across the back of the seat, Cam turned to face the boy. "And you don't think I should, huh?" While he wasn't sure he agreed, he was glad his son was talking about it.

Michael pursed his lips, arms still crossed tightly over his chest. "Well," he said, lowering his voice as far as he could. "I'm six now. I'm big enough to take care of lotsa stuff myself."

Cam suppressed a chuckle. Michael was serious, and he needed to respect that. If he didn't, he'd be doing the same thing his own father had done. "Okay. Yep." He nodded. "You're probably right." He nodded again and playfully squeezed Michael's knee. "I'll try to remember, and if I don't, you be sure to remind me."

He reached for the ignition, started the truck and headed for Nicole's school. To save time, he'd said he'd pick her up after her Saturday class, since it was on the way.

Michael seemed to accept his peace offering and settled in for the ride. *The kid has a point.*

He *was* overprotective. God knows he'd heard that often enough from Sharon. Sure, Michael would have his own battles to fight, and there was nothing Cam could do about those. But he *could* support Michael's desire to feel some sense of control over his life. God knows, he'd never felt in control of his own until he left the ranch for California. He didn't want Michael to grow up feeling the way he had.

Which meant *he* had to restrain his vigilance.

His thoughts shifted to Nicole. Just thinking of her as an unhappy child made him want to protect her, too. He suspected he felt that way because of his own experiences as a kid. The hell of it was, she didn't need anyone's protection.

"Excited about the rodeo?" he asked, not sure that asking Nicole to come along had been the best idea in the world. It'd been Sharon's doing. She'd purchased the tickets and then convinced him it would be good for Michael to go. Michael in turn had begged him to bring Nicole. Had they conspired in this plan? Probably not, but…

"Uh-huh." Michael's eyes brightened. "And I'm excited to see my teacher." He grinned at Cam. "She's nice, Dad. You like her, too, don't you?"

How much could he tell a six-year-old? Not much, he concluded. Michael was too young to understand his history with Nicole. Hell, he didn't understand it himself. And with all that had gone on between him and Nicole, he sure didn't know why he felt so hopeful today, almost like a kid on a first date.

"Sure, Michael. I like her, too. Remember I told you we've known each other for a long, long time? Before you were born."

"Were you friends in the olden days?"

He smiled. His son's shining innocence lit all the dark places in Cam's heart. "Yep. We were very good friends."

"Were you married?"

"Married?" Cam couldn't help laughing.

"Yeah. Jeff's dad was married to another lady before

he married his mom. So, that means you and my teacher coulda been married before you married my mom."

"Hmm." Michael's question raised a more significant one. He hadn't told Michael that he was never married to his mother. No six-year-old kid needed that kind of information.

But he wouldn't keep it from him forever, either. He didn't believe lying was best under any circumstances. But he *would* wait to tell Michael about his mom until he was old enough to really grasp what it meant.

"Nope. Nicole and I were never married. We were almost engaged, though."

"Is that like getting married?"

Cam shook his head. "No. It's when two people love each other and plan to get married. The man buys an engagement ring for the woman, and then they're engaged. It's a promise between them. The wedding comes later."

"And after the wedding, then they're married?"

Cam nodded.

"Jeff's older sister got a ring. She says it's bigger than a Cadillac and costs even more money. Did ya buy Nicole a big 'gagement ring?"

Regret caught him by surprise. He'd bought a ring but had never given it to her. Never even asked because she'd left before he had the chance. "It was a long time ago and I was a college kid who didn't have much money. If I bought anyone a ring, it would've been more like a Volkswagen than a Cadillac."

"Then you didn't have no wedding?"

"Nope. No engagement. No wedding." He rumpled Michael's hair.

The boy frowned, then he squinted, as if he was thinking really hard. "If you and my teacher *had* a wedding before you met my mom,'' he said slowly, ''then my teacher would be my mom.'' His face relaxed, he was obviously satisfied with his conclusion.

Considering the serious thought his son had put into the question, Cam refrained from chuckling. ''Not exactly,'' he said as he pulled into the parking area at Barton Elementary.

Before Cam got out, Michael frowned again. ''And if you *didn't* get engaged and *didn't* get married, then you still gotta do it, 'cause you said you'd get me a mom.''

''Someday, champ. When we find the right person.''

''But I already did find the right person. I want my teacher to be my mom.''

Cam rolled his eyes upward. Hoo, boy! He had about thirty seconds to get himself out of this one.

CHAPTER EIGHT

WITH HER SATURDAY CLASS over, Nicole shoved the day's paperwork into her briefcase. Dylan was in the lavatory, the last one to leave, and she wanted him gone before Cameron and Michael arrived to pick her up. Why had she even agreed to go? A rodeo, for God's sake!

It'd been years since she'd gone to a rodeo and the last time had, of course, been with Cam. She'd loved every minute.

So what was she doing now? Was she hoping to recapture the past?

When Cam had asked her to come along, and then when he'd called later to firm things up, he'd phrased the invitation in such a way that she couldn't refuse.

"I'm taking you at your word about remaining friends," he'd said. "I know you meant it. Right?"

Truth be told, if they *could* be friends, she'd like it very much. So, why did she have to keep making more of it? Why couldn't she take his offer of friendship at face value, do what she could to help Michael and be happy about it? She vowed right then to do just that. She'd be a good friend—period.

"So is there any chance at all?"

"What?... Oh." Dylan was standing in front of her, and she'd been so preoccupied, she hadn't even heard him come back in. "I'm sorry. What was the question?"

"Is there a chance I can catch up?"

"That depends on you. If you continue to do what you've done here—" she patted the folder "—then yes, I think so."

A tiny smile broke out. She could tell he felt self-conscious and a little proud all at once. He was a great-looking kid when he smiled, and he'd be a real heart-breaker in a few years.

"You've missed so much, but if you do the makeup work for the last two weeks and all the assignments from here on in, you just might pass."

He shifted his weight, his pose reminding her of the rebellious teen in an old James Dean movie she'd seen once. *Rebel Without a Cause.* All he needed was the cigarette dangling from his mouth. She wondered if he smoked outside of class.

"And if I could do more?"

"Well, there isn't a whole lot of time left before graduation. Only so many assignments."

"How about if I made up some of the past stuff I missed?"

"You know the rules. Two weeks' makeup work is all that's allowed. Besides, you wouldn't learn anything from doing the early work. It's too easy. What you did in this folder is far beyond those assignments."

He was quiet, and for a second she worried that she'd doused his spark of interest. "But I might be able to find some extra work. If you can do it, you won't be the class valedictorian or anything, but you'll certainly graduate."

His dark eyes grew so hopeful, she added, "In fact, I'll put together something over the weekend. If you can pick it up on Monday before I go home, you'll have an extra day to work on it. But I can't get it organized before then."

She heard a cough, glanced up and saw Cam standing

in the doorway. ''Hi. C'mon in. I'd like you to meet one of my students.''

Cameron walked over and she introduced them.

''Nice to meet you, Dylan.'' Cam extended a hand.

Dylan eyed him suspiciously, almost as if the older man was horning in on his time—or his territory. The teen lifted his chin, then took Cam's hand. ''Hey.''

Their handshake looked more like a power struggle, in Nicole's opinion. When they finally ended it, Cam said, ''Michael's waiting in the truck.''

Dylan turned and started for the door.

''See you next week, Dylan,'' Nicole called after him. As the boy sauntered off, Cam's face went tight.

His parents had taught their sons respect with a capital *R,* and she knew he expected the same from others. He would see Dylan's attitude as disrespectful.

Hoping to ease the moment, she placed a hand on his arm and smiled. ''I'm all set, and I'm really looking forward to it. I'll just pack up the rest of my things and we'll be off.''

HARRY STOOD at the entrance to the rodeo grounds when they arrived, one foot on the weathered wooden gate, and waved them over. Nicole was struck by how little the two brothers resembled each other. And how opposite their personalities were.

Cam with his raven hair and electric blue eyes was tall, over six feet, and muscular. He carried himself with confidence and pride. Harry was shorter, five ten at best. He was stockier, and his walk had attitude written all over it. His cocoa-brown hair almost matched the color of his eyes. Eyes rimmed with the same dark lashes as Cam's.

Quite the pair they were. Double trouble. Teeming masculinity—enough to jump-start any woman's latent desires. Yet they were so different, it was like comparing Antonio Banderas with Russell Crowe.

Though Harry was younger, all his hard living showed, and he appeared the older of the two. Where Cam was forthright, Harry had a cautious air about him, as if some anger festered inside, something that kept him aloof and closed off.

Ten years ago, Harry was Cam's rowdy teenage brother, and everyone excused his behavior, saying he'd grow up soon enough. She'd suspected then that Harry couldn't live up to his older brothers' image in their parents' eyes and early on, he'd decided to travel a very different route.

Ironic the way it had turned out. Harry now had everything Cam had once professed he wanted, the ranch Cameron had always dreamed of, the wife and flock of children. A major role reversal there.

Harry pushed off the gate and pumped hands with Cam. "Sharon and the kids are holdin' a spot for us inside." Squinting into the sun, he nodded to acknowledge Nicole, and nearly lost his balance when Michael tackled his legs. "Hey, Mikey. How are ya, guy?" Harry's voice crackled with delight.

The earthy scents of animals, dirt, sweat and leather permeated the air as they followed Harry single file across the bleachers to where Sharon sat. An element of excitement hummed through the crowd.

The sights and scents catapulted Nicole back to the days when Cam had lived for the rodeo. She'd spent her fair share of time watching him, admiring him. He was expert enough to participate in almost all the events, but his specialty was bareback broncs.

Lord, she remembered the myriad emotions that had coursed through her as he'd gone through the paces. Anxiety because she didn't want him to get hurt, outright adoration as she listened to the crowd scream and cheer, happiness that *she* was there with *him*.

"Nicole. Over here," Sharon called out from a seat down in front. Flanked by her children, Sharon stood to wave them over. "Well, aren't you cute," she said as Nicole neared.

Nicole never gave much thought to what she wore, but today, she'd gone rodeo with worn faded jeans, a white T-shirt, suede vest and her old boots. "I thought I'd play the part."

"Here, I brought this for you," Sharon said, handing her a tan and very broken-in hat. "It's one of mine and doesn't look so good anymore, but you'll be a crispy critter if you don't wear something."

Nicole put the hat on, adjusting the long French braid she'd worn to stay cool.

"She looks perfect, doesn't she, Cam?"

Cam smiled, then brought his gaze to linger on Nicole's backside. "Absolutely perfect."

"Cameron doesn't look too bad, either," Sharon said softly to Nicole, pointedly eliciting a response.

"He looks like the guy I used to know," Nicole answered as casually as possible although she thought he'd never looked better.

But she had no intention of letting him know that.

They had excellent seats, right next to the starting chute. Sitting so close, she could smell the bulls and hear them snort.

"Colter, you son of a buck. Where ya been?" A barrel-chested older man with a leathery face waved at them from below.

"Hey, Bolo. How are ya?" Cam waved back, a broad smile on his face.

"When are we gonna see the Colter brothers ride again?"

Cam stiffened visibly. "Not likely that'll happen. I'm retired. Harry, too. You know that."

The man made a dismissive gesture in response. "That's hogwash, Colter. Once a rider, always a rider."

Cam laughed and turned to Nicole. "Bolo was the best bull rassler in these parts till he got stomped. Since then, he hangs around doing odd jobs. Guess the rodeo's in his blood."

Et tu, Cameron Colter. Close observation told her this was the first event her onetime lover had attended in years, but he was definitely happy to be there. The pure joy in his eyes was infectious, especially when he greeted people he'd probably known all his life. Especially when he looked at her.

This was the man she'd known before, the man who delighted in the closeness of family and friends, a man who loved the small-town way of life. His heart was here.

And Michael seemed to blossom in this setting, too. He literally bounced in his seat with excitement.

A hush spread through the crowd. Tension mounted as they waited for the first competitor. Watching the riders mentally prepare, Nicole remembered when she'd watched Cam do the same. It took more guts than she could imagine to do what these guys did on a regular basis. It was a true test of courage.

The announcement came. The first rider hit the saddle, set his hold and nodded. The gate shot open and the horse burst out the side delivery chute, bucking high. The powerful horse did a spin, bucked, jumped and kicked with a vengeance. The rider, holding a thick rein attached to the horse's halter in one hand, raised his free hand in the air. He was required to keep it there without touching the animal, himself or his equipment; Nicole recalled that much. He stayed on less than four seconds.

"Is he hurt, Dad?" Michael's eyes widened with concern.

"Nope. Although a rider can get badly hurt if he's not careful. That's why these guys really need to know what they're doing."

Cam explained to Michael that the rider was disqualified because he'd failed to *mark out.* He hadn't placed his feet above the horse's shoulders in that split second before the horse's front hooves first hit the ground. For that, he'd received a "no time" disqualification.

It hardly seemed fair to Nicole. All that preparation, all that work for four seconds and a disqualification. Broken bones, dislocated joints, neck and back problems—all were common ailments with riders, and she never really understood why they did it. The money didn't even compare to that in other sports.

After the saddle bronc riders came the bareback riders, the steer wrestlers, team roping and calf ropers, followed by barrel racers, all of whom were women, and then the grand finale, the bull riders.

Dust and dirt churned in air now laced with the scent of manure. When a rider was thrown, clown-painted matadors played with the bull, distracting the animal until the rider escaped to the nearest railing or open gate. Cam told Michael that a clown's job was dangerous, because he had to divert the bull from its rider and at the same time, entertain the audience.

Watching them, Nicole laughed. She was still laughing when Cam abruptly stood up.

"I need to see someone," he said. "Can you keep an eye on Michael for a few?"

Almost before she said yes, he was gone. When she

turned back to Michael, she saw one of Cam's older brothers heading their way. Jackson Colter resembled Cam, but with his dark eyes and chiseled features, their father's heritage was more evident in him. He was a quiet, stoic man, but could hold his own on a horse or in a fight.

Jackson and Harry shook hands, then Harry gestured toward the chute. She peered around them. The next rider was Ransom, apparently the only brother still on the circuit. He was the practical joker in the family, she remembered, and he'd loved the girls. Still did, it seemed, as he threw a kiss to his squealing female fans in the front row.

Cameron didn't return until Jackson had left, but she'd seen him standing to the side as Ransom took his ride. She was so absorbed in watching Cam, she didn't hear the announcement on his brother's time, but figured from the applause that he'd probably won.

Once, years ago, the brothers all would've been there, each cheering the others on. Cam hadn't even clapped. She took a cue from Sharon about a man's business being his own and decided Cam's was none of hers. If he wanted to tell her what had gone wrong between them, he would.

By the time they started the return trip to Harry and Sharon's place, Michael was so wound up Cam practically had to wrestle him into the truck to settle him down. On the way there, Michael asked, "How come you don't do the rodeo anymore, Dad?"

Cameron whistled through his teeth. "Your old man is too old, that's why."

"Nuh-uh. I saw guys lots older. Uncle Rans is older than you, ain't he?"

"Isn't he," Cam corrected, his knuckles tightening on the wheel. "Yep, he's older, but not as smart. If he was, he'd have given it up by now."

''I think it's cool. Can you teach me to ride? Huh, Dad? Please, please, please? Then I could do something better'n all those bigger kids.''

Cam looked at Nicole. She shrugged.

''We'll see. Maybe when you're a little older.''

Later, after they'd filled up on hamburgers and hot dogs, the adults sipped iced tea and frosty mugs of beer on the wide redwood veranda while the children romped on the dry grass in front of them.

Cam, sitting across from Nicole on a redwood chair, kept watching her. Every time she looked up, he was watching her, and when he wasn't, she found herself looking at him. Then his eyes met hers and in that single moment, she could actually feel the current of desire that passed between them. She broke her gaze.

Being with him again was like...well, she didn't know what it was like. Christmas, maybe, back when she was a little girl and all the feelings were good ones. This was the most wonderful day she'd spent in as long as she could remember, and she didn't want it to end.

Ever.

''I suppose purple people-eaters or puce-colored elephants might work. What do you think, Nicole?''

Sharon was talking and she hadn't heard a thing. Except for something about elephants. ''Purple elephants?''

Michael and Dev giggled in the background, then ran off to tackle each other on the grass.

Sharon laughed and so did Harry. ''Just checking to see what zone you two were in,'' Sharon added.

Nicole took a quick sip of her beer, sure her face was as red as it felt.

Embarrassed, she focused on the children playing in the yard and changed the subject. ''This is a wonderful place to raise a family.''

"No better place on earth, in my opinion. We were hoping Cam would build on his piece someday."

They all turned to Cam, who cleared his throat. Scowling, he got up to join the kids wrestling in the grass.

"And maybe he will, when he comes to his senses," Sharon called after him, laughing as she did.

Cam had a great rapport with Harry's family. They all shared the same spontaneous joking, teasing camaraderie that Cam used to have with his older brothers. She so envied that and reveled in her small part.

When they finally began the drive home, everyone was relaxed. Even Harry's earlier reticence had disappeared.

On the way home, Michael snored in the back seat while Chris LeDoux's country voice lulled them from the speakers. Outside, a fat yellow moon, cradled in an ethereal swirl of silvery clouds, lit their way home.

Nicole felt truly contented. Almost...happy.

Cam drove with his left hand on the wheel and his right on the seat next to hers. She thought, even hoped, that he might place his hand over hers. She wanted him to touch her, she realized, wanted to feel his skin against hers and feel that close to someone again. But not just *someone*.

She wanted to feel close to *him*.

Despite that, she was glad when he didn't make any move to touch her. Because then she'd have to think about the future, about consequences, and she wanted to bask in the moment.

Cam dropped Michael off with Maria as he had before, and then drove Nicole to the school, where she'd left her car. "Just wait in front," she said. "I'll walk around."

"I'll go with you." He pulled into the drive.

"You don't need to do that. I'll be fine. And you probably want to get home. It's been a long day."

He'd already opened the door to get out, but stopped

to look at her. ''It's been a *great* day.'' He exited, locked the car, then circled around it to walk with her. ''Michael was really glad that you came along. His old man was, too.''

Her stomach fluttered.

''And you?'' He brought his gaze to hers.

The air was balmy and a wisp of breeze touched her face. For just a second, she caught her breath. How could she answer that? She felt wonderful and alive. More so than she had in a very long time.

She kept her voice even, because that was more than she could tell him. ''I had a good time, too.''

He took her hand and as they reached her car, he pulled her around to face him. Before she knew it, he'd stepped closer, his body a fraction of an inch from touching hers, his lips a breath away.

He placed a finger under her chin. ''It was more than fun, Nicole. I know it and you know it.''

Her pulse raced. She nodded. ''More than fun.'' And if he thought she was going to push him away, he wasn't thinking clearly. Right now, she couldn't have done that if her life depended on it.

She wanted him to kiss her. She wanted to kiss him. She wanted to taste his mouth and feel his body against hers.

And she needed to stop all this before it went too far. But somehow, what she wanted and what she needed were getting all confused. She *needed* not to get involved.

But she *wanted* to kiss him.

His lips brushed hers, featherlight, testing, teasing.

Delicious.

All good sense vanished, and she slipped her arms around his neck.

He pressed against her, his body hard, molding perfectly with hers, and she kissed him more deeply. And still, she wanted more. She savored the tang of beer on his tongue, the scent of soap on his skin. She kissed him again and again. And he kissed her back. Passionately. As if there were no tomorrow. As if there were only this one last time and they had to make it go on forever.

He leaned heavily against her. His hand rose up under her shirt and she felt the warmth of his skin on hers. Desire grew hot and low in her stomach.

A distant thud made her jump. A door closing or… She drew back, her breath short, her chest heaving. "What was that?"

"What?"

"I heard a noise. Over there near the portable. Like a door or something."

Cam's breathing was as labored as hers. "Janitor?"

She shook her head and whispered, "He doesn't work on Saturdays."

"Maybe one of the teachers forgot something?"

"Maybe." She glanced around his shoulder. "Maybe we should call someone."

Cam eased his hold on her. "I'm not going to call anyone unless I need to. I don't see a thing. Maybe you imagined it."

She stiffened. "I didn't *imagine* anything. I heard a noise." She raised her voice slightly.

"Okay. Why don't you get in your car, and I'll take a look."

"What if someone's there?"

He laughed, no longer trying to keep his voice down. "Well, if anyone was, I'll bet we scared them away."

"I'd better go," she said, glad the mood had been broken. "This isn't a wise idea, anyway."

He rubbed a hand over his chin. "Yeah? It seemed like a good idea a few seconds ago."

She pushed away from the car and stepped out of his reach.

"That doesn't make it a *wise* idea. Thanks for a nice day, Cam. I really did enjoy it."

He gave a patently false smile. "Me, too. Especially the last part."

He was still standing there when she pulled out and drove away.

ALL THE WAY HOME, Nicole applauded her sense of caution, then alternately cursed it for not allowing her a few moments of pleasure. So what if they didn't have a future together? He wasn't even offering that. It was a kiss, that was all. Though he might've offered more if she hadn't run scared....

And what would be the harm in that? What was wrong with sharing some time, having fun, enjoying each other's company?

Making love.

But that was exactly what she'd thought ten years ago. She'd wanted to have fun, to have a taste of what others had. In the end, it had been a selfish thing to do, and Cameron had been deeply hurt because of it. They'd *both* been hurt, but her pain was of her own making.

She deserved the results of her selfishness. He didn't. And there was no way she could ever make it up to him.

But now, he knew where she stood. Still, even if *he* could be "just friends," she wasn't sure *she* could. It was pointless to even consider the possibility. Besides, her social life was hardly a top priority.

She needed a permanent job, and getting a contract for next year was a major concern. She had four teens who needed her help to graduate. Three of them were doing well, and Dylan had recently made progress. If he could keep the momentum going, he would pass.

In addition, her mother's move was looming. Once a facility was approved, the physicians and clinical staff would meet to write up both a transition plan and a service plan. She'd have to be involved.

She knew from past experience with her mom that it was important to visit regularly and take her out as much as possible. She'd seen too many people whose families had abandoned them. She wasn't going to let that happen to her mom.

So…with all that to worry about, she had no business even entertaining the idea of being anything more than friends with Cameron Colter.

As she drove into her parking space and then entered the building, she thought about what she had to do. She would explain to Cam that as a teacher, she would do everything she could to help his son, but that was it as far as a relationship was concerned.

She unlocked the door and flicked on the light. If Risa didn't drop by, she'd put together the work she'd promised Dylan, and then get some much-needed sleep—if she could stop thinking about Cam….

Closing the door, she noticed a plain white envelope on the floor. Odd. She bent down to pick it up. No identification.

She tore open the envelope, pulled out a sheet of white paper and unfolded it. She gasped.

Another cut-and-paste message.

A chill crawled up her spine and, without reading the message, she jerked back and flung the paper away.

Staring at it, she reached out for the arm of the couch and eased herself onto it. She should call the police.

But maybe this wasn't a threat? Maybe it was a prank? A joke? From someone with a sick sense of humor.

Hands shaking, she plucked up the paper. It was a picture message. A crudely cut-out magazine photo of a lady with long auburn hair, wearing a business suit, was pasted on the left. Next to that was a red danger sign with a large X across the front. The ragged letters in random sizes and colors spelled out, *Warning number 3! You're out!*

For the longest time, she just sat there feeling oddly detached, as if this couldn't be happening to her. She'd notified the police about the other messages, the one written on her desk and the one in her drawer. Detective Arnette, the officer assigned to the case, had pointed out, however, that none were actual threats, and they had no way of knowing whether the note was directed to her or the school or someone else.

But this…this was hand delivered to her home.

Which meant the other warnings *had* been meant for her, too.

She shivered at the thought. Was she being stalked? Who would do that? What was the warning about? What was she supposed to do—or not do?

The idea of some creep lurking around her apartment, watching and waiting, made her shudder. Well, she wasn't going to sit back and do nothing.

She pulled the detective's card from her wallet, picked up the phone and called.

CHAPTER NINE

"DAMN!" Cameron caught the sleeve of his shirt on a nail jutting out from the door frame in the entry between the garage and the kitchen. He gave one swift yank, heard a rip and cursed again.

"Who's there?" Maria called out.

"It's just me, Maria." He flung the car keys onto the countertop and slammed his briefcase down beside them. His shirt was ruined, so he took it off and threw it into the garbage can under the sink.

"Is something wrong, Mr. Colter?" Maria entered the kitchen. Seeing him standing there, half-naked, she halted, averting her gaze.

"No, nothing's wrong. I just ruined a shirt, that's all." *Yeah, that's all. Nothing's wrong. Everything is just* perfect.

Except that his good sense had gone missing right about the time he'd run into Nicole again.

After spending yesterday together, he realized he was just as confused as he'd been before. Learning what had happened ten years ago hadn't cleared things up at all. In fact, it blurred the lines even more.

All these years, he'd blamed her for something that wasn't true and although he hadn't enjoyed hearing that she hadn't trusted him enough to confide in him, he could no longer blame her for the failure of their relationship.

Which put things in a different light altogether. He didn't like that—he liked things clean and simple.

"Where's Michael?"

"He's playing with the boy across the street, Jimmy Bentworth."

"Yeah? How did that come about?"

"Jimmy came over and asked if Michael wanted to play ball with him and some other boys. His father took them to the park a block away. I thought it would be okay since an adult was with them."

Bentworth. The man hadn't won any points with him. But Michael needed friends and Cam was glad to see it happening. It was a step toward a normal childhood for the boy.

"I hope that was okay, Mr. Colter. I can go to the park and get him if—"

"It's fine. Did he say when they'd return?"

"Mr. Bentworth said in an hour or two. So, if you don't need me anymore—"

"No. Go on home, Maria. I'll be here for the rest of the day. Thanks for staying."

After Maria had left, he changed into his sweats, took the briefcase into his office and sat down to do the estimate on the McClellan Mall. It was a major contract, one that could put his company over the top. Even so, he wouldn't come in as the lowest bid on the job.

He didn't believe in low-balling just to get a contract. In the short time he'd been in business, his company had established a reputation for honest, reliable, high-quality work. He prided himself on conducting his business in the same way he conducted his life.

He sat back and let out a long breath. If he was going to be honest with himself, he needed to admit that he still cared about Nicole. He cared too damn much.

He'd thought more than once about pursuing a new relationship with her, but every time he did, he got nervous. If she'd lied to him then, wouldn't she lie again? How could he ever be sure? He hadn't talked to his older brothers in two years for that very reason. They hadn't told him how sick his mother was, and although technically it wasn't a lie, the result was the same. It had kept him from seeing her before she died. His brothers had made the decision for him, just as Nicole had in not telling him about her mother.

A man's character hung on his word, and it was no different with a woman. Especially a woman he cared about. If there was no trust between two people, what the hell was there?

Shoot. He was sitting on the fence again. Either he was going to pursue a deeper relationship with Nicole or he wasn't. And if he *wasn't,* then he had to stop thinking about it all the time. He made a mental list of pros and cons and finally realized that none of them really mattered.

He decided to go with his gut, as he always did.

The only thing that would tip the scales one way or the other was how Michael felt about Nicole.

And he already knew that.

NICOLE'S MOTHER WAS WAITING in the straight-backed chair by the window, her thin hands resting lightly on her thighs. ''She's having a good day,'' the aide said, and looking at her mother, Nicole had to agree. Jenny had actually glanced up at Nicole when she entered the room.

She gently hugged her mom around the shoulders and placed a soft kiss on the top of her head. ''Someone did your hair, huh?'' She gazed directly into Jenny's deep-set eyes, searching for some sign that she knew what was going on.

Jenny wore navy knit pants and a pink blouse Nicole had bought as a birthday present. ''You look extra pretty today, Mom. Pink becomes you.'' After a moment, she added, ''I thought we'd go for a Sunday drive and then we'll have lunch at my place. It'll be fun.''

Once they arrived at the condo, Nicole led Jenny to the couch and turned on the television. Then she set about making lunch. She desperately wanted today to go smoothly because it was a test of sorts.

The last few times Nicole had brought her mother home, it hadn't gone well. Because of that, her mother's caseworker had volunteered to come along. But Nicole wanted to spend the day alone with Jenny to see how she'd react without staff around in case the new facility didn't work out and she had to bring her mother home to stay. If this went badly, well...

She shouldn't think about that. Still, she couldn't help feeling anxious, and to cover her apprehensions, Nicole talked nonstop while preparing the food. She kept up the patter as they settled at the small table in the kitchen, where Jenny placed her napkin in her lap and picked up one half of the sandwich.

''Let me know how you like it, Mom,'' Nicole said, although she didn't expect a response. Sitting there, she was struck by the thought that no matter how poor they'd been, how little food they'd had or how bleak the surroundings, her mom had loved and cared for her daughter as best she could. Sometimes Jenny's best wasn't very good, but it wasn't because she hadn't tried.

She could do no less for her mother. No matter how it affected her own life...

If the new facility worked out, Nicole would be truly

thankful. Jenny would be able to live away from the hospital and still have the clinical care and medication monitoring that she required.

Watching her fold her napkin into a neat triangle, Nicole said, "Keep the napkin, Mom. When we're done, there's dessert. I made brownies, your favorite."

Jenny nodded. No expression of interest, just a nod. They'd been so close when Nicole was small, but the illness had snatched it all away, robbing them of the mother-daughter relationship they could've had.

If only she could have hidden the good memories somewhere to keep them being tainted by all the bad ones…

As a teenager, she'd kept a journal, and at one point when things were at their worst, she'd actually made a list of her good childhood memories so she wouldn't forget them. The time they'd planted a garden in California and watched the vegetables grow. The time they'd taken the bus to Fisherman's Wharf and watched the seals playing near the pier, and once when her mom, after receiving a tiny bit of money from her parents' estate, had taken seven-year-old Nicole on a shopping spree and spent every last cent on school clothes so her daughter could look as pretty as the other little girls.

Since then, she'd recited that list more times than she wanted to think about.

Sadly, those memories were so distant, they sometimes seemed more like long-ago dreams. She longed for that closeness again. She wanted to tell her mom about Cameron and her feelings for him, the concerns she had. She wanted her mom to know the achievements she'd made, that she'd finally received her degree, and that she was a teacher now.

Oh, she'd *told* Jenny about all those things, but what

she really wanted was for her to understand, and to be proud of the person her daughter had become.

She longed for motherly advice, to know how her mom had felt when her dad had left them. She wanted to ask whether having love for a little while was worth the pain later, when love died. Those were questions Nicole had no answers to, no experience with. And sometimes, in the middle of the night, it seemed the loneliness inside her just grew larger and larger.

''Remember the man I told you about last week, Mom? The old friend I saw?'' Nicole prodded, looking for some way to nudge Jenny into the world again.

''Remember I told you we were going to a rodeo? Well, we did, and then...''

MICHAEL HIGHTAILED IT into the school building while the rest of the class was still out at recess. He was headed for Nicole's desk again, and she could only wonder what had happened this time.

Since the rodeo last weekend, he'd been staying close to her. She was glad the school year was almost over; it wouldn't be good for the rest of the class to know she'd shown more than a professional interest in Michael's father. That could cause all manner of repercussions, and possibly affect the way Michael's classmates viewed him.

She wasn't sure how it would sit with the school board, either. But there was no reason to think about it anymore, since she'd made the decision to keep her distance.

''Hi, Michael,'' she said as he bolted through the door. ''Too hot out there for you?''

He approached the desk. ''Nuh-uh. I just don't feel like playing anymore.''

Something was wrong. ''Are you feeling sick?''

He shook his head.

"Did someone say mean things or pick a fight?"

He shook his head again.

"Oh, I know. You've come in for some extra homework?"

"No way!" he insisted. "Ackshully, I wanted to ask a question."

"Sure."

He looked down, then tapped the leg of her desk with the toe of his sneaker. "Well, uh, I was wondering how come you have to teach those big boys after school."

Nicole sat back in her chair and folded her hands. What a strange question—and from out of the blue. "Well, there are lots of reasons. But the main one is that I'm a teacher and it's my job to help students learn."

He thought for a moment, then said, "But can't somebody else teach them someplace else? I mean, not here at this school."

"Sure. Someone else could, but this program is working well for these boys. Do you think someone else *should* teach them in a different place instead of here?"

He frowned, as if he was trying to decide. Nicole wondered whether Michael was getting possessive. Some children had a tendency to do that when they were receiving undivided attention and that attention was diverted elsewhere. But it wasn't the most likely answer because she hadn't stinted her efforts in this class in order to teach the At Risk students.

She said, "You know, everyone needs help once in a while."

"But some of the kids said those big boys were bad and they said their moms and dads don't want them at our school."

Well, that cleared up a few things. "Michael, sometimes we have to ignore what other people think and do what we believe is the right thing. Some of those boys made bad decisions and got in trouble for it. But if they're sorry and are trying to be better, we can't hold that against them, can we? We all make a bad decision now and then, and it's only fair to get a second chance, don't you think?" She took a breath, then added, "I help them when they need it. Just like I help you sometimes."

He puzzled on that for a bit, then his eyes lit up. "Can you help me be good so I don't do bad things?"

She smiled. "If I could, I would. But usually, if we want to improve at something, we have to do it alone. It's like playing the piano." Not the best analogy, she knew, but the first one that came to mind. "If we want to get better at playing the piano, we have to practice. It's okay if we make some mistakes and don't get it right the first time, because if we keep practicing, we'll learn."

He gave a huge sigh, and tears welled in his eyes.

"Why are you so worried, Michael?"

His bottom lip quivered. "'Cause if I can't be good, my dad will give me away."

Shocked, she held him at arm's length. "Michael, whatever made you think that? Your father loves you more than anything."

He rubbed his eyes with both fists, trying hard, she thought, to be brave. "Nuh-uh. My mom said she'd give me away if I was bad, and she did. Lots of times. I tried and tried to be good but I wasn't good enough 'cause I always got sent away again. Then one time I must've been extra-bad 'cause she gave me away, and she never came back. My dad said she died."

Oh, dear God. She enclosed him in her arms and pulled him close. "Michael," she said softly. "Things happen—bad things—no matter what we do. They happen for many reasons that we don't even know about. Your mommy didn't go away because you were bad. There was a different reason."

She didn't know what that reason was, although she had her suspicions, but she sure wasn't going to let him think such a hurtful thing. "And I know your daddy loves you very, very much. He'd *never* do that." She gave him a squeeze. "No matter how ornery you might be."

"But what if I *can't* be good?"

"Hey, all you have to do is try. That's what counts. Your dad thinks you're a pretty darn good kid already. So do I."

His behavior problems, she realized now, might be related to this fear of abandonment, and he was unconsciously testing his dad.

Her heart ached for the little boy. And she definitely needed to talk with Cameron.

AFTER SCHOOL that same day, Nicole waited for Dylan to show up for their Tuesday class. She crossed her fingers, hoping he'd come through with the extra assignments she'd given him.

Apparently he hadn't said anything about it to the other boys in the class. Probably figured it would mar his tough-guy image.

As the minutes passed and there was still no Dylan, a small twinge of disappointment grew inside her.

Loud music caught her attention—a car stereo cranked up—and then the screech of tires and gravel. Thirty seconds later, Dylan sauntered in and laid a large manila envelope on her desk. "That's it."

"The assignment, I presume?" She picked up the envelope. "Great. When you finish the rest of it—"

"That's all of it."

It took her a second to realize he was talking about *all*

the work she'd assigned him. "That's wonderful, but it's a lot to do in such a short time."

"Did you bring something else for me?"

"Ah…no, I didn't. Actually, I didn't expect you to finish everything."

"You're sure I'll be able to graduate if I finish the work?"

"Absolutely."

"Can you give me more work on Thursday?"

Nicole nodded. She'd do it, even if she had to stay up all night. Which would probably be the case, since she couldn't cancel tonight's movie with Risa again, tomorrow night was booked solid, and she had to grade his current papers first.

He hesitated, then looked away and said, "Thanks." She got the impression that he wasn't used to thanking people—or having anything to thank them for.

"Dylan," she began, wondering how to phrase the question she'd had for days. "The other day you asked if I knew who vandalized my room. And I got to wondering if maybe you had some idea who it was."

He stared down at the floor.

"So you know who did it?"

"I didn't say that." He lifted his chin.

Right. And even if he did know, he *wouldn't* say. Questioning him about it now might prove counterproductive. "I was only concerned about the children. I'd hate to see their work destroyed again."

She glanced up and saw Mitchell come in. As he cruised by Dylan, he said, "Caruso wants to see you outside, man."

Nicole didn't like the sound of that. Dylan left immediately, which worried her, because Dennis Caruso was the kid who'd dropped out of her class. She hoped his attitude didn't rub off on Dylan. He had enough trouble with his own.

"So," she said, once Dylan had come back and all the boys were assembled. "Tonight we're going to do something a little different. Essays. You know how to write essays, correct?"

Silence and blank stares. "One of you want to explain what an essay is?"

More silence.

Then, a moment later, "It's a paper that tells what someone thinks about something."

All heads turned. It was the first time Dylan had volunteered an answer on anything. "That's exactly right, Dylan. An essay is an interpretive, often reflective, composition that usually expresses the author's outlook. But that's a formal definition. Dylan's explanation is better. Why? Because it's more concise and easier to understand than mine."

Glancing at each boy, she saw a hint of interest in some of their expressions. She grinned as she leaned against her desk.

"Tonight, we're going to read a few short essays and then discuss them, just to give you a feel for how they can be written. After that, you'll get a chance to write your own essay, which you'll turn in on Saturday."

A low moan reverberated through the room. So much for interest. She ignored the protests and went on. "There are only two requirements. One is that you pick a topic from my list, which I'll give you later, and two is that your essay is, if typed, double-spaced and two to five pages long. If you write it in longhand, that means eight to ten double-spaced pages."

"Oh, man." Justin slumped in his chair. "Ih ate writing."

"And when you write your essays, keep Dylan's definition in mind. Make it easy to understand. Don't worry about fancy words or descriptive passages, just make it clear. Proper sentence structure and punctuation would be nice, but for the first go-round, don't let that hold you back. Just write it as you feel it."

"What if I don't feel nothin'?" Mitchell said.

"Then you pick a topic from the list and explain why you feel nothing about it."

A few laughs erupted. "Yeah," Aaron said, "Just do it, man, and quit complaining."

As she handed out copies of the reading material, she said, "One of my favorite quotations is written at the top of the page. 'I think somehow, we learn who we really are and live with that decision.' That says so much in a few simple words. It's something to remember when you're writing your essay."

"So who's this Eleanor Roosevelt babe?"

She laughed. "I don't know if you'd think she's much of a babe, but she was an insightful woman who never quite fit in with the world around her. She decided to make her own mark—which we all have the ability to do. Now let's start with the first essay."

AFTER CLASS, Nicole took a different street to the freeway, since her usual route was undergoing construction. She cursed the never-ending widening of the highways needed to accommodate the rapidly growing population in the Valley of the Sun, but even bumper-to-bumper traffic couldn't quell her excitement.

Tonight had gone superbly and, for the first time since she'd begun teaching the A.R. class, she felt completely positive about it. Her boys had actually engaged in a discussion and enjoyed doing it. They might even have learned something.

Michael might've been headed on the same course as her older students if Cam hadn't entered the picture. Initially she'd had no idea the boy had had such a traumatic childhood. How terrible for a child to believe his mother would give him away if he was bad!

Cam had said Michael's mother had problems, but he hadn't elaborated. Well, he was going to have to tell her a little more. She couldn't work in a vacuum.

She'd call him the minute she got home. Or would it be better to talk in person? If Michael really needed professional help, Cam shouldn't wait too long, or the small problems would become larger ones. Maybe if she found a counselor to come to the school, or went with him to—

No. She was doing it again. Getting too involved. She needed to step back, stay within her defined role. She would phone Cam and talk to him about Michael's revelation, and he'd have to take it from there.

Hitting the entrance ramp to the freeway, she looked over her shoulder, then merged into traffic, paying particular attention to her surroundings and the cars nearby. She'd been watchful since receiving that last note, but she also guarded against becoming *too* watchful. Excessive caution could lead to paranoia and constant fear.

She was glad to be going to the movies with Risa tonight. Arriving at her building, she took a quick glance around the parking lot, got out of her car and raced up the stairs.

Seeing Risa's door open, Nicole called out, "Will you be ready by eight, Risa?"

"I'll be ready. Don't sweat it."

She looked down the hallway and went inside. The first thing she did was call Cam. He was out on a job bid, so she left a message telling him she'd be back from the movies around ten-thirty and that he should call her no matter what time he returned.

She hung up and pressed the button to listen to her messages. She had only one. Mrs. Nelson wanted Nicole to call her back, which she did. There was no answer. Thinking about Dylan, she suddenly realized she'd left his completed assignments at the school. Damn! Well, there was no alternative; they'd have to stop by the classroom to pick up the envelope.

A half hour later, they were off. "So, what's the reason we're making ourselves late for the movies?" Risa asked.

"I told you, I forgot the work Dylan left for me, and if I don't have his papers to grade later tonight, I can't give him any more assignments on Thursday. Tomorrow night I have two parent-teacher meetings, my mom to visit and my reglar class work to do. It's now or never. Anyway, we're not going to be late."

"Dylan—isn't he the kid who'd rather scrub toilets than do schoolwork?"

Nicole smiled to herself, pleased at Dylan's newfound interest in graduating. "One and the same, but if he keeps up this level of work, he'll graduate with the rest of his class."

"And to what do you attribute this miracle?"

"I don't have a clue, but I'm grateful for whatever it was."

"Don't be disappointed if it doesn't work out."

"Risa! Don't even talk like that."

"Hey, I'm being realistic. I think you should, too."

"I am. Anything he does is more than he did before, and it's a step in the right direction. That's progress."

Nicole pulled into the school parking lot, got out, then

peered through the open window. Risa was busy filing a snag on a fingernail.

"You sure you don't want to come in? It might take me a few minutes because I'm going to try returning Mrs. Nelson's call. She sounded a little distraught in the message she left on my machine. If I do it now, I won't be thinking about it all through the movie."

"Nah, you go on. I need to fix this." Risa waved her off and Nicole smiled to herself. Her friend's fingernails were her trademark, and she wasn't about to let a snag go untended. How she managed to give a massage without stabbing her clients was a mystery.

Nicole walked around the side of the school to the portable. The area was dark, except for the illumination provided by two streetlights, one at the opposite end of the playground, and the other near her. She could feel the afternoon's intense heat radiating up from the concrete through the soles of her shoes.

At the door, she searched in her backpack for the key. She couldn't find it. As she stood there rummaging through the pack, perspiration trickled down the side of her face. Served her right for carrying so much junk. But if the lights had been a little brighter, she might've been able to see something.

Was it darker than usual? She glanced around. No, not really. But something didn't seem right. Her nerves tensed, and she glanced around again. Nothing unusual. She didn't notice anything different.

Nicole forcefully dismissed the thought, refusing to entertain paranoid fears. Refusing to act like Jenny…

When her fingers touched the cold metal of the key at the bottom of her pack, she realized it had come off the ring. She shoved open the door and reached inside to flip on the light.

Nothing happened. She flipped the switch again. What the— Flick, flick. Nothing. Maybe a blown fuse? That had to be it, since the air conditioning had gone off and it was stifling hot inside.

In a moment, her eyes adjusted to the darkness, and with the door open and the streetlight shining through the blinds, she could see well enough to do what she needed to do.

She made her way to the desk, found the folder Dylan had left, then groped for the phone to call Mrs. Nelson. She moved to the right and hit the phone cord with her leg. Before she could catch it, the phone crashed to the floor. She jumped, dropping the folder and scattering Dylan's papers. Dammit. She'd thought the phone was on the other side.

A slight draft blew in, and the door shut with a bang. Her nerves leaped. Quickly, she ducked down to replace the receiver in the cradle and pick up the papers.

Then…she heard a rustling sound. A shuffling movement not her own. Or was her mind playing tricks?

Still, terror ran through her and in a second, she'd scooped up as many of the papers she could, held them against her chest, and scrambled for the door. The call to Mrs. Nelson would have to wait.

She scraped a knuckle reaching for the knob, jerked her hand back and brought it to her mouth. She heard another noise—like someone breathing. Heavy, labored breathing.

Sheer fright shot up her spine. She seized the knob and pulled. The door didn't budge.

Oh, God! She pulled harder. *Locked.* Her hands shook and sweat rolled down her face as she strained to get the door open.

Whomp! An arm suddenly grabbed her from behind. She screamed. A hand clamped over her mouth, and the arm tightened around her neck, crushing her throat, cutting off her air.

She clawed at the thick fingers. They were squeezing harder and harder, silencing her desperate screams.

She was hoisted off her feet and dragged upward…and then they were moving.

She flailed her arms and kicked her feet, struggling helplessly against the choking grip. The more she struggled, the tighter he squeezed. No air. Oh, God. Oh, God. She couldn't breathe. She would die. Suffocate. She had to go limp. Yes, she vaguely remembered. *Go limp.* But too late.

Stars burst in her eyes. Her senses dimmed. She was sinking. Falling. Fading.

CHAPTER TEN

SIRENS WAILED. Distant, then louder, coming closer and closer.

All black. Everything was black. She was slipping away. Going down. *Get up.* She had to get up. Pull herself from the blackness.

A blur. Movement around her. Bright lights flashed and voices echoed in her head. *Wake up.* Got to wake up. Everything a blur. Blinding light.

The white jackets! The faces, always the faces. Like her dreams? No. Not a dream. Oh, God! What was happening? Was she going crazy? Was she trapped like her mother? No, no, no! She had to get out of there.

Scream. She had to scream and fight back. But the sounds went mute in her throat. All she felt was a burning, scalding pain—it hurt too much to scream. Or talk.

And she was cold. So cold. A hand under her head. Something soft. Wetness against her face, over her eyes. The hand. She remembered the big hand, crushing, hard over her mouth, her screams cut off, stifled, like her breath.

Someone had tried to kill her.

Nicole ripped the wet thing from her eyes, forcing herself to focus on the form hovering over her.

"Nicci? It's me. It's okay, Nic."

Risa's voice. Her face was blurry, but there.

"You're okay. You're okay."

She tried to speak, but all that came out was a croak. "Wh-what's going on?" She managed a whisper. She raised a hand to her neck where it hurt and tried to raise herself to a sitting position, only to be pushed back down by someone on the opposite side. She turned her head, annoyed at the resistance.

"You'll have to stay where you are for a bit." The white-coated man smiled at her. "I'm a paramedic and we need to make sure you're okay."

"I'm fine," she mouthed.

"Shhh." Risa pressed a finger to Nicole's lips. "Don't try to talk now. You can talk later. First we're going to get you to the hospital with these guys to make sure you're—"

Risa was interrupted by two burly paramedics who slid Nicole onto a gurney. A police officer appeared from somewhere and announced that he and his partner would follow to get her statement.

Nicole closed her eyes. A statement? What would she say? That when she thought she heard something, she'd dismissed it because she'd been having too many feelings like that lately? Could she tell them she was afraid that when she heard things she wasn't sure she really did? That she saw shadows everywhere? That she was afraid she was imagining things and would eventually be like her mother?

She tried to swallow, but a needle-sharp stab of pain made it impossible. She touched her throat again.

No, she hadn't imagined this at all. This was real. Very real. And although it was frightening, she felt an overwhelming sense of relief.

This is real. You didn't imagine it.

"They won't let me ride with you, so I'll follow in the car." Risa's voice trailed off as the paramedics lifted the gurney into the ambulance. One by one, the vehicle's doors slammed shut and in seconds, they were rocketing through the streets, sirens shrieking.

By the time they reached the hospital, Nicole's head had cleared a little. Moments later, Risa appeared. Her friend assured her that she'd been unconscious for only a few seconds.

"I don't know what woulda happened if I hadn't been there," Risa rattled on. "The man was big." Risa's hands flew into the air. "I didn't get a good look, though, because the minute he sees me, I'm screaming like a banshee and he was outta there."

Nicole thought back to the body behind her, the thick arm closing around her neck. She shuddered at what might have happened if she'd been alone.

"The minute I heard you scream, I came running. And when I saw him dragging you from that building, I started screaming. Then, bam!" She smacked her hands together. "He split. It took forever for the security guard to come. He must've been napping because he shows up rubbing his eyes like he just got out of bed. Some security!"

"Thanks, Risa." Nicole massaged her temples with two fingers. Her head throbbed.

"Anything could've happened before that guard got there." Risa muttered. "You could've been *murdered.*"

"But I wasn't," Nicole whispered. "So let's forget about it. Okay?"

"Forget about it?" Risa swung around. "He might be a serial killer or rapist. Who knows what was on that creep's mind!"

Nicole wondered, too, thinking back to the massive form behind her.

A policeman, who identified himself as Detective Arnette, entered the room. He looked familiar, but her thought processes weren't exactly functioning at their best. He had a notebook in hand and was obviously intent on questioning her.

Her throat hurt and she could barely talk. In addition, she hadn't even seen the man who attacked her.

"No," she whispered, shaking her head in answer to his question. She didn't know anyone who might want to hurt her.

"He was big," Risa chimed in. "I saw him put Nicole down, but when he saw me, he took off."

"Put her down?" The police officer pushed the brim of his hat upward so it sat on the back of his head.

Nicole recognized him now. He was the officer who'd been sent to the school when her room was trashed—the same officer she'd called about the messages. He'd come to her apartment to talk with her and pick up the second one.

"Yeah." Risa said. "It was kinda strange now that I think about it. He didn't just drop her and run." Risa turned to face Nicole instead of Detective Arnette and acted out the movements. "He gently put her down, because she'd passed out, I guess."

"Would you be able to identify him?"

Risa shrugged. "It was dark."

Officer Arnette's blond brows drew together as he glanced from Risa to Nicole. "I've already taken Ms. Beaumont's statement, Ms. Weston. I'd like to get your version."

She shook her head and pointed at her throat.

He smiled. "I'll speak with your doctor then, to find out when might be a good time."

After he left, Risa whirled on Nicole. "Darn! I still had stuff to tell him."

"It's okay, Risa," Nicole whispered. "He'll be back."

Risa sank down on the chair next to the bed, and a few minutes later, Cameron appeared in the doorway.

"Oh, yeah. I forgot to tell you, I called Tex when we got to the hospital. I thought you'd want him to know."

Cam's tie hung loosely around a crisp, white collar. His double-breasted, navy suit jacket flapped to the sides as he barreled in and stood next to her opposite Risa.

"You all right?" He reached out to touch her cheek, his eyes full of concern.

"I'm fine," she mouthed, trying to coax her voice into more than a whisper. She forced a tiny smile to let him know everything really was all right. "Not hurt."

His eyes narrowed as he stared at her throat. "Yeah. Right. And I'm the Lone Ranger."

NICOLE AGREED to let Cameron drive her home from the hospital. He'd insisted.

"I think you should stay at my place for a while, at least until you recover."

"Thanks, I really appreciate the offer, but it's best if I don't. I'll be fine." Staying with him was definitely not a good idea. Because right now, she wanted nothing more than to be held by him.

Anyway, she wasn't sure she was in any real danger. No one except Risa had even known she'd be at the school. And Risa hadn't known until the last minute. The attack couldn't have been planned.

After arriving at her condo, Cam said, "You're too damned independent for your own good. You know that, don't you."

She nodded and smiled.

"I really wish you'd reconsider."

Inside, she tossed her backpack onto the side table in

the living room. "Thanks. Like I said, I appreciate the offer. Truly. But I…can't."

"Can't or won't?"

"Both."

"Okay. Then I'll stay here."

She did a double take. "Cam, I'm fine—"

"You're not fine. You can barely talk." He stood there like a sentry, legs apart, body taut, arms crossed over his wide chest.

"Sorry, you're stuck with me."

She pursed her lips, ready to speak again.

"You," he said, making a zipping motion across his mouth, "save your voice. I'm staying, and that's that." His expression grew stern.

"Suit yourself," she whispered, then stomped off to the bathroom. When she emerged, he was pacing her small living room.

"I called Maria, and she's staying with Michael tonight. C'mon. Let's get you comfortable and I'll make some dinner." He gestured for her to sit on the couch.

"I don't think I can eat."

"Right. I wasn't thinking." He spent a couple of seconds in thought, then said, "Okay. I'll be right back. I'm going to talk to Risa."

Nicole watched him leave, her emotions warring with her good sense. She shouldn't let him stay. But she wanted him to. She wasn't afraid—but she didn't want to be alone, either.

He returned a few minutes later and stood in front of her with a silly smile on his face. "There. That's done. Dinner will be here shortly."

She opened her mouth to speak, but before the words got out, he held up a hand. "Don't say a thing. You'll eat if you can, and I'll eat what you can't." His smile widened. Then as if remembering something, he frowned. "C'mon. You were supposed to get comfortable."

He led her to the couch and when he said, "Sit," she did. She didn't even complain when he went into the bedroom and brought her a pillow and her favorite down comforter. She'd never seen him so attentive.

It felt good to have someone look after her for a change. Of course, she'd seen him taking care of Michael, but that was different and it reminded her… "What will you tell Michael?" Her voice was half whisper, half croak. "He can't be told what happ—"

"Will you stop." He rolled his eyes. "You're going to make yourself worse. Michael's fine. I'll go home early tomorrow to get him off to school and I'll explain then."

"But—"

"No buts! And you might as well stop talking, because I'm not going to listen." He walked to her desk, grabbed a notebook and pen and slapped them on the table in front of her. "If you need to say something, use that."

She smirked, picked up paper and pen and scribbled, *Bite me!* Then she tossed it back across the table.

He snatched it up to read. "Hmm. Y'know, tempting as that is, I think we ought to wait till you're feeling a little better."

There was a knock at the door, and he went to answer it.

"That would be dinner." He took a bag from Risa. Nicole waved her in, but Risa shook her head. "Sorry. Got to run. But I'll check back tomorrow."

Cameron closed the door, locked it and headed for the kitchen without another word.

Great. A prisoner in her own home. She grabbed the remote and turned on the television. After a few minutes of news, Cam was back, balancing a tray with two giant ice cream sundaes. A tower of vanilla, layered with chocolate, whipped cream, nuts on one and cherries on top of both.

"Hot fudge," he said. "Soothing for the throat. I get the one with the nuts."

She picked up the notebook and pen. *My favorite.*

He took the pen and wrote something. As she read his response, she felt his eyes on her, watching, assessing. *I know. I remember all your favorites.*

Looking into her eyes, he said, "Would you like me to list them or show you?"

Her cheeks warmed. She snatched back the pen and paper and scribbled, *I'd like you to take a cold shower, cowboy.*

He read it and laughed out loud, eyes glinting. "Sweetheart, if there's one thing I've learned in life—" he paused to lick chocolate from the tip of his spoon before he pointed it at her "—it's that most times what we profess to want isn't even close to what we *really* want."

She grabbed the remote again and changed the channel, turning up the volume. She should have thrown it at him.

When they finished the sundaes, she wrote, *Thanks for dinner. There's a blanket in the linen closet. I hope the couch is comfy.* She smiled, then sashayed into the bedroom and closed the door. Maybe she should have locked it.

Because he was right. What she professed to want wasn't even close to what she really wanted.

And it was going to be one helluva long night.

CAMERON WATCHED TELEVISION for a long time, but even then, sleep wouldn't come. His stomach churned. Every protective instinct within him seemed to be on high alert.

The woman *was* too damned independent for her own

good. Well, whether she liked it or not, he wasn't about to leave her by herself. Not with some stalker out there.

The attack had shaken him badly. He could've lost her. Again. And he couldn't stop thinking about it.

Sometime in the wee hours of the morning, he got up and went to the kitchen for a glass of milk.

This whole thing bothered the hell out of him, and the more he thought about it, the angrier he got. Every nerve in his body rebelled at the thought that some creep had put his hands on her, had hurt her. He felt like punching something.

Hell, if he had half a chance, he'd kill the bastard.

He grabbed a beer instead of milk, stalked back to the living room and lay on the couch again. At the hospital, after he'd visited Nicole, Risa had told him about the cut-and-paste messages Nicole had received.

He'd been livid. Why the police hadn't done something prior to the attack was beyond comprehension.

Dammit, he was still furious. He spent the next two hours pacing. He wanted to wake Nicole to ask her more questions, but he didn't. She'd had enough trauma for one night, and he refused to upset her even more.

The police had those notes, so they should've done some kind of testing for fingerprints, talked to the neighbors, checked their files for similar cases. If they'd done any of that, they might even have a lead.

But if they had evidence, why had they done nothing to prevent the attack? And why hadn't she mentioned any of this to him? He and Nicole had certainly reached the point where they could confide in each other. At least *he'd* thought so.

He leaned against the pillow and rubbed the back of his neck. The knowledge that she might still be in danger fanned the embers of rage within him, and his inability to do anything to protect her made it worse.

So, maybe he'd just call the station and find out if they had any more information or new leads. He picked up the phone, got the number and called. No one was willing to give him information, so remembering the name of the cop at the hospital, he asked for Officer Arnette.

Arnette wasn't in, so Cam left a message. After hanging up, he called Risa and asked if she could come over for an hour or so until he returned. It was almost 6:00 a.m. and he had to drive home to get Michael ready for school.

A few minutes later, Risa appeared at the door in a fuzzy pink robe and glasses with large red frames. He must've looked surprised because she said, "You sounded in a hurry so I didn't bother with the contacts." She came in and settled on the couch.

"Do you know any reason someone might want to attack Nicole?" He didn't want to think it, but had to ask. "One of her problem students, maybe? Has she said anything to you?"

"No. Nothing." She paused. "Except she did talk about one kid. Dylan somebody. I only remember the first name because I've been practicing that memory association thing and I thought of Bob Dylan when I heard it."

He remembered, too. He'd met the kid, the one hauling a chip the size of the Titanic. "You think he might've had something to do with it?"

"All I know is that Nicole said the police were asking about him and some of her other students as possible suspects in the vandalism. Him because he has a record. Of course, Nicole's positive it wasn't any of her students."

If the police thought the culprit was one of the students, how could she be so sure it wasn't? Remembering that his neighbor, Bentworth, had said he had hard facts to back up his claim that Nicole's students had been involved, he decided maybe it was time he took a look at it.

"Okay, thanks. Listen, I'll be back in an hour or so. Don't leave before that and don't let anyone in."

Risa saluted. "Yessir, Cap'n sir."

"Sorry. I'm just worried. If she gets up, please don't let her out of your sight. Okay?"

"I'll try. But school starts in a few hours. I don't think I can stop her from going."

"Don't worry. I'll be back before then. I'm sure the school was notified about last night, since it happened on their premises, and I'm sure they won't expect her to come in today." When he got to the door, he turned to Risa again. "Thanks for helping out."

She waved him off. "What're friends for?"

Cam left the condo feeling more unsettled than when he'd arrived. He had to confront Nicole with what Risa had told him about the note, and knowing the police suspected one or more of her students didn't make him feel any better.

The kid he'd met had been openly hostile.

On his way home, he glanced at the time. Michael would be getting up for school in less than an hour, so if he got him ready and then begged Maria to take his son to the bus, he'd be back before Nicole even woke up.

Then he could get some straight answers. If the police weren't going to protect her, he would.

When he returned to Nicole's, Risa was sprawled on the couch fast asleep. He had to nudge her twice before she stirred. Great help she would've been. "Risa, wake up." He shook her gently.

"What?" She groped for her eyeglasses on the table.

Cam picked them up and slid them on for her, whispering his thanks for staying with Nicole.

"No problem. You want I should do anything else?" Risa stumbled to her feet.

"Not now, but if I think of anything later, I'll let you know." He followed her to the door, locking it after she was gone.

"What's going on?" Nicole's scratchy voice sounded behind him.

Cameron turned around. Nicole was standing in the bedroom doorway rubbing her eyes, her curls even more tousled from sleeping. She wore a short blue nightshirt with a teddy bear on the front. The shirt barely skimmed the tops of her thighs, and if he wasn't so worried about her, she'd be in deep trouble.

Noticing that her slippers were shaped like teddy bears, too, he smiled. A powerful surge of protectiveness coursed through him. "Nothing. It was just Risa."

"What time is it?" She yawned and stretched, her voice a little less raspy, but not yet normal.

"It must be late. Risa never gets up early." Then her eyes widened. "Oh, no. *I'm* going to be late."

He walked over to where she stood, draped an arm around her shoulders and led her gently toward the couch.

She looked at his clothes, then at the two-day growth of beard. He'd taken a quick shower and changed into a clean T-shirt and jeans before returning, but he hadn't bothered to shave. "You might want to rest for a few days."

Nicole realized she was still groggy from the sedatives she'd been given for pain, but that didn't mean she was going to miss class. "The kids'll be there. I've got to get dressed." She started to stand, but he stopped her, pulling her back to sit beside him.

He said softly, "I'm worried about you, Nic. And listen to you. What will the kids think? How will you explain the bruises on your neck?" He studied her closely, as if he'd just noticed something, then reached up to gently touch her cheek near her mouth. "And the ones on your face." He clenched his fists. "If I ever get my hands on that bastard, I'll—"

"I'm fine, Cam," Nicole cut in. "I don't want you to do anything to anyone." But he was right about going to school. Her voice was still little more than a whisper. It would be hard to teach anything if she couldn't talk. And it would upset the children if they knew what had happened. She picked a puffy throw pillow and held it against her chest.

He glowered at her. "You're not fine."

"Okay. Maybe my voice could use a rest. I'll call the office so they can get a sub." She placed the call and was told they'd already arranged for a sub for the rest of the week.

When she hung up, Cam said, "Good. And now I want you to reconsider staying at my place, at least until the police find out who assaulted you."

She chewed on her bottom lip, mentally listing all the reasons she shouldn't, then countering those with the reasons she should: her safety and the fact that she didn't really want to be alone.

"Cam, they may never find the person who did it." She brought a hand to her neck and suddenly noticed the silver chain was gone. She glanced to the floor but didn't see it anywhere. Tears welled up in her eyes because the chain was a gift from her mother, one of the few she had. Good Lord, she was more emotional about all of this than she'd thought.

Maybe she ought to stay with Cam. Just then the phone

rang, and she snatched the receiver from the cradle, happy to have a moment to think about what to do.

The voice on the other end belonged to Dylan's aunt.

"No, it's okay. You didn't wake me." Nicole got up and went to sit in the chair next to the window. "No, I'm not sick. My throat's...a little scratchy this morning."

"Dylan's gone."

"Gone? What do you mean?" She leaned forward and opened the blinds to a bright sun breaking over the distant horizon.

"He didn't come home last night and I'm really worried."

"Maybe he stayed with a friend and forgot to call?"

"I don't think so. He's never done that before, not since he's been here with me. He knows I need his help with Roland."

"Did you call any of his friends?"

"No. I don't know his friends. I don't even know if he has any. And I didn't want to call the police or anything. They already think he was involved in that school incident, and if I report this, it wouldn't look good."

Jeez.

"I thought you might know where he went—or maybe he said something to you."

"No, he didn't. But I'll see what I can find out and call you back." She hung up and remained curled in the chair, thinking. Now what? Why had she said she'd find out anything? She didn't even know where to start. And she was in no condition to go searching for anyone.

"What's going on?"

She wasn't sure Cam would understand, but he'd find out sooner or later, anyway. And maybe he could help. "Dylan's missing." Another thought hit her. "I guess that's what Mrs. Nelson called about last night. Damn. I wish I'd known."

"So do I. Pack your stuff," Cam ordered. "You're coming with me." She couldn't deny it felt good to have someone worry about *her* for a change. But was moving in with him really the answer?

CHAPTER ELEVEN

"CAM—" She rose from her chair and walked over to where he stood. "I know you're concerned about what happened last night, but maybe it had nothing to do with me. Maybe I just surprised whoever was there."

The lines around his mouth deepened. "Your classroom was trashed, you were assaulted and, at the same time, one of your problem students disappears. I can't believe you don't see a connection."

He paced a few steps, then swung around to look at her. "You're kidding yourself, Nicole. Big time."

"He's not a problem student!"

"And what about those notes? That's not random. Whether it's your student or not doesn't really matter."

Risa must've told him about the notes, she realized. She shifted her gaze to the table. Taken together, all those facts *did* look suspicious. While her gut told her Dylan had nothing to do with this, Cam was right. Right now, it didn't matter.

"I hope you're keeping the police informed. After last night, it's pretty obvious you need protection of some kind."

"They know everything, but they're not doing a thing that I know of. The last I heard, they said the vandalism at the school could've been perpetrated by kids playing a prank."

His face went stony. "Last night was no prank."

She touched her neck, her voice a little stronger now. 'Believe me, I know. But I also know Dylan wasn't in-volved. He wants to graduate. He's been trying really hard and doing extra work. What would be the point? There has to be another explanation."

"Such as?"

"I might've been mistaken for someone else," she said stubbornly. "There are a number of teachers at the school. The teacher who taught my class before wasn't anyone's favorite, either. It's just as reasonable to think someone was out to trash *her* room. It's also reasonable to think I might've interrupted a burglar or vandal, and he got scared. It could've been the same guy who trashed the classroom. Maybe he came back to do more damage and I got in the way."

Cam dropped down onto the couch and took her hand in his. "Those are all possibilities. But the person who left a message under your door wasn't soliciting for charity. He knows where you live."

Right. And whether she wanted to admit it or not, that worried her. Hell, she was *scared.* She wouldn't be able to sleep at night if she stayed here alone, and she couldn't help Dylan or anyone else if she got hurt again.

A knock on the door startled her and she realized just how jumpy she was. She hurried over to answer, but checked the peephole first. It was the same detective she'd talked to before. The one she'd talked to about the messages.

"Hello, Ms. Weston," he said when she opened the door. "I'm Detective Arnette. We spoke before."

"I remember. C'mon in." She stepped inside.

"I've been trying to convince her it's not safe to stay here alone," Cam said. "At least not until you guys catch whoever attacked her."

The two men eyed each other, as if communicating in some silent male language. Arnette said, "We have reason to believe the incidents are connected."

"So the police think someone's stalking me?" Nicole whispered.

"Stalkers usually make themselves known in some way or other. This case is a little different, but as I said, there's evidence suggesting the incidents are related."

"What kind of evidence?"

"I can't comment on that. But we have a couple of suspects."

She hoped Dylan wasn't one of them.

"It wouldn't hurt to stay with someone or have someone stay with you for a little while."

"What about police protection?" Cam asked.

"The department can set up a watch, but unless there's a direct threat, we can't do much more than an intermittent drive-by."

"Okay," Nicole said to Cam after the detective had asked his questions and then left to talk with Risa again. "I'll stay with you, but on two conditions. One—that we don't tell Michael why I'm there. It might scare him."

"Makes sense. What do you think we should tell him?"

"I don't know. Maybe that my condo needs some work. That's true. It's not a lie."

"Okay. What's the other thing?"

"That we set a time limit. If the police have no results or nothing happens within a specific period, I'll come back home and you won't give me an argument about it. I'm not going to let some vandal coward who creeps around in the dark keep me from living my life."

Cam arched a brow, and she realized how silly that was, considering what had actually happened last night. "Well, you know what I mean."

He smiled. "Yes. Now get ready."

She started for the bedroom, then turned. "We may be giving whoever did this exactly what he wants."

"And what would that be?"

"He has me running scared."

"Running scared isn't a bad thing," Cameron said. "Especially when you could get hurt if you don't. But have it your way. The reason you come doesn't matter, as long as you leave here with me now."

She went into the bedroom, showered, tossed a nightshirt, some casual outfits and enough work clothes for a few days—since she wouldn't be teaching for the rest of the week—into her suitcase. If she stayed any longer than that, she could come back for more or wash clothes at his place.

She wouldn't be there most of the time, anyway, she reasoned. Between his being at work and her visiting Jenny, they wouldn't be together much at all.

And she wasn't sure if she liked that or not.

SHE THOUGHT THAT STAYING at Cam's would be awkward, but she was wrong. She felt at home almost immediately.

When they'd arrived, Maria had lunch waiting for them and Cam spent the afternoon with her, helping her get established in the guest room. Then he went to pick up Michael at school rather than let him take the bus. She'd wondered why he didn't walk since they lived only four blocks from the school and discovered it was Michael's choice because he'd recently had a run-in with a couple of bigger boys.

When they returned, Michael was more excited than she'd ever seen him. Cam had explained that she was staying with them and the child had accepted it without question. Then he launched into a series of tales about the substitute and how she was horrible and mean and all the kids had started throwing things.

"Good Lord! You weren't one of them, I hope," she said.

He shook his head. "Nuh-uh. I was good. I'm trying to practice like you said."

Cam sent her a questioning look.

She shrugged, palms up. "That's good, Michael. But remember I said you don't have to worry about that other part?"

"I'm still gonna practice," he said. "A little bit."

"Can't hurt." She smiled and ruffled his hair, and he ran off to play—but not before taking her aside and swearing her to secrecy about what he'd told her.

"What was that all about?" Cam asked after the boy had gone.

She'd intended to tell Cam about her last talk with Michael, but now she felt uncomfortable betraying the child's confidence. Even the reason for telling Cam no longer seemed valid. "Just a little student-teacher stuff."

To her relief, Cam accepted her explanation without question, and she felt he understood that the relationship she had with Michael as his teacher was different from the relationship the three of them had.

With the rest of the week off from work, she had more time to spend with her mother, but Cam initially refused to let her go alone. If she didn't agree to let him come, he said he'd follow her, which was laughable but gave her a sense of comfort as well.

She'd never had anyone care that much, at least not that she could remember. So, he came along and waited for her in the car, and after a couple of times, she convinced him that no one could possibly know where she was going because she hadn't been to school or her condo.

After talking with Arnette, who set up a limited watch on her, Cam agreed, and she started moving about more freely.

The next Monday she went back to school, and for a couple of days, life seemed wonderfully normal, except that she was going home to a different place. Or maybe because of that... Some nights were later than others, since she had her A.R. class and also her mother to visit. The school had even stationed an extra security guard on the premises during the nights she was there late.

Despite their busy schedules, she and Cam fit seamlessly into each other's lives. It felt like the most natural thing in the world to be together. *This,* she finally decided, was what it was like to be a part of a real family, and she wished it could go on forever.

But there was no point in fantasizing. She vowed to take it one day at a time and simply enjoy each one. In any event, she'd be going home soon because they'd tentatively set a two-week deadline, and it was getting close. But she didn't want to think about that.

Adopting a laissez-faire attitude allowed her to derive pleasure from their closeness. Some evenings, as they sat together in the family room, Nicole was filled with a contentment she'd rarely experienced before.

On Tuesday, when Nicole returned from visiting her mom, Cam called her into the kitchen where he was opening a beer. "How'd it go?"

"Great. Well, as great as can be, I guess."

He looked straight at her. "I was thinking maybe you'd like to bring your mom here some night." He handed her an open bottle of beer.

A sharp pain in her chest took her by surprise. As she

reached for the beer, she shook her head. ‘‘Not a good idea.’’

His left eyebrow rose a fraction. ‘‘Why not? She might enjoy meeting Michael.’’

‘‘I don’t think this is a good time for that.’’ She hadn’t known what to say to the boy when he’d asked why her mom was in the hospital. She’d said her mother was sick and let it go at that.

It wasn’t her place to explain, it was Cam’s and he hadn’t done so. She hoped it wasn’t because— She cut off the thought. She had to stop attributing motives.

‘‘She might get confused. I’ve been preparing her for a move to a smaller facility, a group home, and if she came here first, she might think this was it.’’

Cam knocked back a swig of beer. ‘‘When’s that supposed to happen?’’

‘‘It’s been put off twice, but next week, I hope. I’m waiting to get the final word.’’

‘‘Okay. Maybe before that I can go with you to visit?’’

‘‘Maybe.’’ The idea made her uneasy. Why was he pushing to meet her mom? To bring her to the house?

‘‘And you know if there’s anything I can do, you just need to holler.’’

‘‘I know.’’ She’d always known that about him. He was being supportive in wanting to go with her, wanting to meet her mom. That was all it was. Still, she couldn’t help feeling that doubt. What would he think? How would he feel about her afterward?

She suddenly realized that he hadn’t changed at all since she’d told him the truth. In fact, their relationship was better than ever. They were closer and more relaxed around each other. Did that mean she’d been wrong about him, about his ability to accept her background? But, he hadn’t told Michael. What was holding him back?

"Nic? You okay?"

Cam stepped closer and rested a gentle hand on her shoulder. His sensitivity spurred a rush of need and she wanted more than anything to lean against him, to absorb some of his strength.

"I'm fine. Why?"

"You look sad, like something's really bothering you."

"Nope." She shrugged. "I'm fine. Really. Just a little tired. And after a warm bath, I'll be as good as new."

"Then get to it." He gave her a little nudge.

She went to her room, two doors away from Cam's and set her beer on the side table. Then she drew the bath and slipped into the warm silky bubbles. The best place in the world to sort out her thoughts—when she wasn't imagining what it would be like if Cam were in the tub with her, his big rough hands sliding over her slippery body, touching all the places he'd once known so well.

She wondered if he remembered. Because she did...

But she had too many worries to waste time fantasizing. Besides her mom's move, there was her concern about Dylan. She didn't know where he was or what he was doing.

Even though he hadn't shown up at home, she'd held out hope that, somehow, he'd make it to class tonight. He hadn't. And she couldn't shake the conviction that she'd failed him somehow.

Still, the fact that he'd done some assignments *had* to mean he was interested in graduating. There'd be no reason to do the work otherwise, and she couldn't believe he'd show that much commitment and then just abandon all his efforts.

She talked to Mrs. Nelson regularly, and with each passing day that the woman hadn't heard from her nephew, Nicole's spirits flagged a little more. Mrs. Nelson's biggest fear was that she'd die and Roland would have no one to take care of him. She'd been counting on Dylan for his help and he'd willingly given it.

Now he was gone.

All Nicole could do was offer her support. But it didn't seem enough. She couldn't forget the hopelessness in Mrs. Nelson's voice. So far, the police hadn't taken anyone into custody for the assault or the vandalism. She knew they still suspected Dylan, and her anger surged each time she thought about it. How could the boy get his life turned around if no one gave him a chance?

Cam had once said she got too emotionally involved when she believed in a cause. But she just didn't know any other way to be. If she was involved, she couldn't do it halfway. She wasn't going to forsake her principles, even if the only help she could give Dylan and his aunt was encouragement.

"How's your appetite?" Cam asked when she returned to the kitchen after her bath. "Michael and I made dinner."

She looked around. "Really?" There was no Michael and no dinner that she could see.

"Michael's finishing his homework, but he'll be done soon. The food's warming in the microwave and I'm going to start getting things ready. Okay? Or do you need more time?"

She beamed. "I'm good to go."

"I see that," he said, giving her cutoff shorts and tank top an approving glance.

"This dinner thing ought to be interesting. I wasn't aware that six-year-old boys could cook anything, but hey, I'm all for men learning how to take care of themselves at an early age."

"Hmm. I suppose that comment was directed at me."

She laughed. ''If the boot fits.''

''Remember, I said I've matured. Guess I forgot to mention that also means I'm a little more self-sufficient than before.''

Now it was her turn to arch an eyebrow. ''I'll check with Maria on that before I believe it.'' They laughed together and for the first time today, she felt relaxed.

Cam directed her to one of the bar stools at the island, then filled two chilled long-stemmed, salt-rimmed Mexican glasses with frozen margaritas.

At that moment, Michael bounced into the room and his dad put him to work. It was a pleasure watching the two of them—until she noticed Michael wielding a butcher knife almost as big as he was to shred some lettuce. She held her breath and let it out only when he'd finished.

''That's for the garrishments,'' he said proudly.

''Garnishments,'' Cam corrected.

''Yeah. The stuff that goes on top.''

''And there's more.'' Cam pulled out a couple of bowls from the fridge, filled with diced tomatoes and onions and shredded cheese.

''And what, pray tell, does it go on top *of?*''

''Enchiladas. And to go *with* it—'' He whirled around and produced a bowl of tortilla chips and another filled with salsa.

''Ta da!'' Michael said, grinning from ear to ear.

''Michael made the salsa.''

''Really? I'm impressed. Where'd you learn how to do that, Michael?''

''Maria helped me,'' the boy said. ''She helps me lots.''

''Oh, and do we have a budding chef in our midst?''

She tousled his hair, then took a tortilla chip and dipped it into the salsa.

"Nuh-uh. She tells me lots of things like when I need to wash up and brush my teeth and stuff like that."

Nicole felt a twinge of sadness. Maria, the housekeeper, was the boy's only motherly influence. Maria and the child's aunt Sharon, who saw him only on occasional weekends.

Michael was growing up without a mother to nurture him and give him the love every child needed. He had surrogates, but it wasn't the same. She knew there'd always be an empty place in the little boy's heart because of it.

However, Michael had a devoted father; she just hoped for Michael's sake that it was enough.

"Maria taught you well. Your salsa is absolutely magnifico!" Nicole kissed her fingertips.

Michael beamed at the compliment.

When they'd finished dinner, they all cleaned up the kitchen and then headed for the family room, where father challenged son to a game of checkers. Nicole curled her bare feet under her in the easy chair and resumed the novel she was reading. As she read, she stole intermittent glances at the two of them.

Cameron and Michael seemed to have developed a closer relationship in the short time she'd been there. Cam was still overprotective, but she couldn't deny she'd be the same way if she had children of her own. She smiled to herself. She might even be worse.

As a girl, she'd dreamed of what it would be like when she had a real family, a husband and children.... Unable to stop the flood of thought, she remembered the exact moment she'd known she would never realize that dream.

In one single second, her future had been snatched away from her.

Now, looking at the two of them, she felt as if she'd been given something precious. A gift, a gift of knowledge. She finally knew what it was like to be part of a real family. It didn't matter that it was temporary.

She looked at Cam, a proud and principled man. She'd fallen in love with him all over again.

"Yowee," Michael sang out. He jumped up, so excited he could hardly contain himself. "I won! I won!"

A second later, his face grew serious and he frowned at his father. "You didn't *let* me win, did you?"

Cam gave a whoop of laughter. "No, dang it all. I didn't *let* you win. You beat the pants off me!"

Nicole laughed right along with them and almost didn't hear the doorbell when it chimed.

"I won!" he repeated gleefully.

"Okay, okay. Don't rub it in."

"Does that mean I get to stay up late?"

"It means you get to go to bed smiling. Now hop to it." Still grinning, Michael went happily off to his room and Cam answered the door.

She shifted position in the overstuffed chair, a warm glow settling within her. She heard a male voice, quiet at first, then slightly raised. She couldn't make out the conversation, though. Soon she heard the door shut and a moment later, Cam came back.

"Nothing urgent, I hope," she murmured.

His gaze didn't meet hers, and when he didn't respond, she asked, "Cam? Everything okay?"

He glanced up. "Oh, sure. It was just a neighbor about a community association meeting. It's a once-a-month thing. No big deal." He started for the hallway. "I'm going to tuck Michael in."

Nicole relaxed again. Then Cam called her to come into Michael's room. She got up and hurried down the hall.

As she reached the doorway, Cam said, "We've got a kid here who wants to say good-night to you, Nicole."

Michael looked up at her. "Can you read me a story?"

"If it's okay with your dad." She knew Cam always read to him at night and figured it was a special time for the two of them.

Cam checked his watch. "Okay. But pick a short one."

Nicole searched the stack of books Michael had by the bed and together they chose *The Boy With Green Hair.*

"You hafta sit with us, too, Dad," Michael said. Cam sat directly behind Nicole on the bed, facing his son. He leaned to the side and forward, almost curled around her, his elbow bent, head resting on his hand.

She read a couple of pages. With Cam so close she broke out into a sweat—even though the air conditioner was going full blast. Fortunately, Michael dropped off to sleep halfway through the book.

Together, she and Cam tiptoed out of the room. As he closed the door, she whispered, "I hope that was okay."

"Okay? Of course it was. You were great."

She moved away from the door and walked down the hall toward the family room, with Cam at her side. "Well, I didn't want you to think I'm...horning in on your relationship with Michael."

He stopped her with a hand on her arm and turned her so they faced each other. "Now, that's about the most ridiculous thing I've ever heard anyone say. He *asked* for you to come in."

"I know. But I didn't want to intrude. I thought you might think I was overstep—"

He let out an exasperated breath and held her at arm's length.

"Jeez, Nicole," he said in exasperation. "Don't keep putting *your* thoughts in *my* head. If I didn't want you there, I wouldn't have asked. If I didn't want you to get close to Michael, I wouldn't have brought you here in the first place."

"Sorry. I didn't mean to—"

"No!" He broke in midsentence. "Don't say you're sorry about anything. Y'know, sometimes you just have to stop thinking so much and do what you feel in here." He tapped her lightly on the chest, his fingers lingering just long enough for her to enjoy the contact. "Don't keep examining things all the time."

"That's easy for you to—"

"Shhh. Stop. Or I'll do it for you."

"But—"

In one swift movement his mouth landed on hers. He stopped her, all right, and his lips were warm and sexy and full of passion and need, and he didn't let up for a second. He pressed against her, his body hot and hard. Just the way she'd imagined it... Just the way she remembered...

She parted her lips, kissing him back without a thought. She wanted him to possess her, wanted to possess him. In the short time she'd been there, her need for him had become almost more than she could bear.

After what seemed the longest kiss in history, he came up for air, his chest heaving, his brooding eyes seeking hers—eyes as blue as a mountain lake. Eyes she could drown in. And right now, that was what she wanted to do.

Because with him, she felt desired and loved and all she could think of was that she wanted him. More than anything.

"I've been hankering to do that forever," he said.

"Me, too," she breathed.

And when he slid his fingers under her chin and raised her lips to his, she let the rhythm of need and want and desire flow through her. She parted her lips again, inviting him back for more.

His mouth descended on hers, this time with a slow intensity that made her knees tremble and her pulse slow.

He backed her against the wall. His hands dropped from her chin to her breasts, softly touching, caressing, tracing a path to her nipples. He kissed her eyes, her cheeks, her neck, her earlobes and she returned each kiss—making up for lost time.

Kissing him was more than pleasure. For so long she'd been starved for a simple loving touch, for *his* touch. She'd longed for him to hold her, caress her, make her feel wanted, needed. Loved.

"Nicole," he murmured. "Nicole."

His husky voice urged her on and she obliged, her hands all over him, exploring every muscle, every contour. She wanted to breathe him in, taste him, touch him. She wanted to crawl into his mind and into his skin, to know what he was thinking and feeling. She wanted it all.

"Remember how we used to shower and then make love right after I finished a competition?" He leaned one arm against the wall, his body pressing into hers, his face nestled in her hair.

"And sometimes we didn't even make it to the shower," she added.

"I thought about that the whole time we were at Harry's." He nibbled her ear and trailed moist kisses down her neck.

All she managed in response was a low moan. *Remember?* How could she not remember? She'd never forget that sweet culmination of lust and love, the sweaty tangle of their bodies, the heightened awareness that made her every cell ultrasensitive to his touch.

Remember? Yes, she remembered. Every kiss, every caress, every mind-exploding orgasm.

And if she didn't stop him, this very second, they'd be doing it on the floor in the hallway. She brought both hands up between them, placing them flat against his chest.

"Cam," she whispered, her breath coming in gasps. "What about Michael?"

CHAPTER TWELVE

"I'LL LOCK MY BEDROOM DOOR," he whispered back, his breath hot on her cheek as he reached for the doorknob behind her.

"What if he wakes up?" She didn't know what the protocol was with a child in the house, but knew it was something they had to figure out right this minute. And there was that other worry still hanging over her, telling her she shouldn't be doing this at all.

"We should stop." Her words were hardly more than a whisper.

"You sure about that?"

Yeah. Like she was sure she hated chocolate. With his body flush against hers, she wasn't sure about anything. His nearness was dizzying and threatened to snap her control. Breathing heavily, she nodded. "Yes. I'm sure."

"Okay, I'll stop." He nuzzled her neck. "In a thousand years." She heard a click behind her. Cam's bedroom door swung open and they tumbled inside. Still holding her in his arms, he maneuvered them both around and shut the door.

"Cam. I can't be here in your room. What will Michael think?"

"He'll think you spent the night in his dad's bed because you were scared of the dark." He laced his fingers through hers, then brought both her arms up and pressed er against the door with his body, his desire ragingly pparent. "Besides, it's too late for thinking."

Her stomach contracted. Her blood rushed. "Are you *ure* he won't wake up?"

"Hey, the kid sleeps like the dead." He nuzzled her eck again. "And if you're worried about protection, I an take care of that."

He ran his tongue along the soft skin at the curve beveen her neck and collarbone and raised his head to kiss er again.

Yes, he could protect her. Physically. But what about er heart? What about his?

T WAS A WONDER Cam could think at all. They'd been eaded here from the get-go. He knew that now. And he'd nown the second she tilted her head against the wall and arted her lips that they were destined to be together.

Every movement, every touch, was an erotic exploraon, igniting in him a deep, deep need that had nothing—nd everything—to do with sex and love and all those varring passions that filled him so completely there was o room for anything else.

Her breathing matched his own shallow rumble and hen she wrapped a leg around his, he knew this night vas not over. Not by a long shot. He reached down, ocked the door, and in one quick movement he'd placed er on the bed. A flash of uncertainty crossed her beautiful eatures.

Though engulfed by passion, he reached up to frame er face in his hands, and restraining his physical desires, e traced a thumb across her cheekbone, where only last veek he'd wanted to kiss away her tears. If he'd thought e could remain detached, he'd never been more wrong.

"Nic," he began, but the words lodged in his throat.

An enormous ache of longing welled within him, catchi
him off guard.

If he let himself get caught up in her again, he mig
never be able to recover. Yet he wanted her. Hell, he
never *stopped* wanting her, in every possible way.

Slowly he drew his hands down her arms, fingerti
caressing smooth skin, remembering every texture, eve
curve, until finally he pulled her into his embrace. "I wa
to make love to you, Nicole," he whispered. "But i
more than that. It's been so long since I've felt anythin
much less what I'm feeling now, I don't know how
explain it." He drew away from her and shoved his han
through his hair. He almost laughed out loud at his ov
erratic behavior.

Finally, he just said, "It's always been you, Nicole.
still care about you. I don't think I ever stopped."

If Nicole had any reserve at all, it melted right then a
there. Tears burned in her eyes and she wanted to t
Cam she'd never stopped loving him, either.

But she hadn't truly known how much she'd hurt hi
until now. He seemed so vulnerable it scared her.

She had to be very careful—and very sure of what s
was doing. She couldn't hurt him again. She just couldn

She reached out, enclosing his hands in hers. "I nev
meant to hurt you, Cam." She wanted to tell him th
she'd hurt, too, that she'd carried the pain of regret f
ten years—but she couldn't.

Moments ago, her passion had been fueled by wi
physical urges that hurtled through her. Passions that r
fused to die. Emotions that wouldn't be denied.

But she couldn't lie to him. She couldn't keep siler
"This…this can't be anything more than it is right no
I want you more than anything, but I need you to unde
stand that."

Slowly, but without hesitation, Cam pulled her to him. liding his fingers through her hair, he inhaled, as if filling imself with her scent. "It's okay," he whispered. "I un-erstand."

In that moment, with those simple words, he freed her. 'reed her to love and make love and live as she'd never eally lived before. She sought his mouth, and as if he new the significance of the moment, he kissed her leeply, seductively, tenderly. Somehow in the middle of t all, she found the buttons on his shirt, unfastened them nd placed one hand on his chest.

Skin against skin, she felt a connection that hadn't been here before. With fingertips following the well-defined ontours of his chest, downward over his hard stomach, he kept going until she touched his belt buckle.

He stood up, allowing her to release the desire that grew t her touch and in a moment he was naked before her. ust looking at him produced a longing so intense she ouldn't wait another second.

She didn't need to, because he brought her to him, slip-ing her shorts and panties down around the curve of her ips while she shrugged off her shirt. His mouth covered ers, his tongue seeking, probing, intimate in its knowl-dge of her. She returned his passion with equal force, heir kisses insistent and demanding.

Instinctively, they rolled onto the bed together. He uickly put on a condom, as he'd promised. She slid un-lerneath as he braced himself on his arms above her. She aised herself to him, and watched the hard muscles of his tomach flex as he slowly entered her. With each rhythmic hrust he entered a little farther, repeating her name, urg-ng her on until she moaned in pleasure and tremors of cstasy shot through her again and again until they found heir release together.

Afterward, Cam lowered his forehead to hers. He shi
ered and finally, ever so slowly, lay next to her, as clo
as he could get, allowing them both to come down gentl
Sweetly.

NICOLE AWAKENED wrapped in Cam's arms, entwined t
same way they used to be years before. But that was t
only similarity with the past. Everything else had been
very different, the experience deeper, more meaningf
than any other time they'd been together.

She'd been honest with him, and he'd accepted it. He
accepted that this was all she could share with him, a
he'd let her know it was enough.

What freedom that had given her. The freedom to
herself, and to let him know how much she cared. Nico
snuggled against him, feeling safe in his arms. She w
determined to enjoy their closeness for as long as s
could.

Because she loved him—even if love didn't mean fo
ever the way she'd once thought it would.

He stirred a little, and she felt his fingers tangling
her hair. He took a deep breath. "I love your hair,"
murmured in a sleepy voice, then pulled her around
face him. His lips brushed hers. "Good morning, su
shine."

She smiled. "Is it morning already?"

He glanced at the clock on the stand behind her hea
brought his mouth to hers again. "Four a.m. I guess it
true."

"What's true?"

"Time flies when you're having fun."

"I should go to my room before Michael wakes up."

"Not a chance."

“Cam,” she whispered. “I don’t want him to find me here. I really don’t.”

“Okay, but he doesn’t usually wake up until 6:30. Until then, I’m going to hold you hostage.”

“Oh, yeah?” she said. “Well, maybe I’ll hold you hostage instead.”

“Hmm.” His voice was still husky. “I might like that even better. Do you treat your hostages well? Or do you make them sex slaves and—”

She disappeared under the sheets and he stopped talking altogether. The next thing she heard was a low and very satisfied moan.

“SO WHEN ARE YOU COMING BACK?” Risa asked. “Or is this a permanent move.”

School had let out early today, and Nicole was so filled with happiness, she’d gone to Risa’s shop for a manicure—and a visit, complete with a little girl talk.

“Soon. We set a limit of two weeks. Nothing’s happened since then, so I think I’ll be safe going home.” She felt a twinge of regret at the idea of leaving Cam’s. Well…more than a twinge.

“Are you sure you don’t want some color? Green, maybe?” Risa placed Nicole’s right hand into a small bowl of moisturizing liquid and started work on the left.

“That would generate a lot of teacher confidence with the parents, wouldn’t it? Maybe I should get a tattoo, as well.”

“Yeah. I like that idea.” Risa looked up at Nicole from under arched brows. “Okay, maybe green’s a bit extreme for a teacher. How about a French manicure?”

“French.”

“Yes. Natural on the bottom and white on the top. *Très élégant.*”

Nicole narrowed her gaze.

"All right, already. Don't give me that look. Plain an natural it is." She frowned in concentration. "So tell m what's going on. Why are you *really* here?"

Last night had been…thrilling. But she couldn't te Risa that. Instead, she talked about other things, mostl her classes and Mrs. Nelson.

"Maria told me that a neighbor of Cam's is spearhea ing efforts to get the At Risk program removed from th school. That, plus the fact that Dylan's still missing, up sets me. I just wish there was more I could do."

"Sounds like you've done everything you can, as fa as your students are concerned. Maybe you need to lear not to get so involved."

Where had she heard that before? "I don't think I ca do my job *without* being involved." And if that was wha being a teacher required, she'd be enormously disap pointed. "I wouldn't have become a teacher if I wasn willing to get involved with my students' problems."

"I didn't say you shouldn't get involved at all, I sai not so much. A little versus a lot."

"In a way, that's what bothers me. I only did a littl for Dylan. I should've done more."

"Uh-oh. Sounds like a guilt job to me."

"No, it's true. I was too worried about rocking the boa I was concerned about my job."

"Makes sense to me. Think of all the time and effo you put into getting where you are. You don't want it a to go down the tubes because of one kid. If you did, th other kids would lose a great teacher."

"Sacrifice one for the good of the whole." Intellectu ally it made sense. Professionally. But emotionally, sh just couldn't do it.

"Sometimes you can't make all the pieces fit, Nic. Shoot, the way I see it, most of life is a compromise."

Unfortunately, Risa was probably right about that. Some things *couldn't* be fixed. Still, she was convinced Dylan genuinely wanted to change the direction his life was headed. He'd already shown her that.

She had faith in him, and if she didn't show *him* she believed he was capable of improvement, regardless of what other people thought, she was a hypocrite.

"Are you saying *you* make compromises?" Nicole teased. "Somehow I doubt that."

"I do it all the time." Risa's expression turned serious. "It wasn't my lifetime dream to become a masseuse and a manicurist, you know."

Nicole was surprised. Risa didn't seem to be a dreams-and-goals kind of person, at least not that she'd ever let on. She'd always struck Nicole as eminently practical, someone who accepted whatever life threw her way. In fact, this was the most revealing thing Risa had said about herself since Nicole had known her. "And what was your dream?"

"That's irrelevant. I was making a point."

"No, I asked if you compromised and you said all the time."

"That *is* the point."

So, it made Risa uncomfortable to talk about herself. Nicole had assumed she knew her friend, but maybe she didn't. "Okay, give me another example and I might consider the point, whatever it is."

Risa thought for a minute. "Okay. I wouldn't have picked a younger guy to go out with, but I think I'm going to do it, anyway—particularly since the only guy who's asked me out is younger. That's a compromise."

"You're kidding! When did this happen? You never

said a thing.'' Nicole got so excited she clapped her hand and spattered water all over the two of them.

Risa jerked back.

''Sorry.''

''Yeah, well, it's not a done deal, so there's no reaso to make more of it than there is.''

Nicole felt another tingle of excitement for her frien ''I think it's great. Who cares how old he is? Who is it?''

Risa concentrated on Nicole's nails again, jabbing little harder than Nicole thought necessary.

''So—'' Risa continued as if Nicole hadn't asked th question. ''The *point* is that we all compromise in on way or another. You don't always get exactly what yo want, and if you don't compromise you end up with noth ing. That's just how life is.''

''And you're compromising so you don't end up wit nothing?''

''Hey, love when it comes is better than no love at all.''

Risa, she knew, didn't want to get her hopes up in cas this relationship didn't work out. ''Okay, but don't thin I'll let you off the hook so easily. I want details, and whe I get back home, you're going to tell all.''

Risa smiled wryly. ''Yeah, but it may be all over b then and there'll be nothing to tell.''

''Well, that's a winning attitude if I ever heard one.'' Nicole sat back, letting all this new information sink in ''Just do it, Risa, and don't worry about what is going t happen. Sometimes you've just got to stop thinking s much.'' Oh, jeez. Cam's words were now coming out o *her* mouth.

Risa smirked. ''Exactly.''

So, okay...that was the real point and she'd bee tricked into admitting it. Risa knew her too well.

"I've changed my mind. Give me the French manicure."

WHEN MICHAEL SHOT IN THE DOOR, home from school on Friday, Cam said, "Hey, I've got a surprise for you. Devin wants you to go with him on his Cub Scout camp-out this weekend. Tents and all."

Michael frowned, then crossed his arms. "I don't wanna go."

Cam's antennae went up. "You're usually champing at the bit to go see your cousins. You love being at the ranch and you love camping. What's up?"

"I do like them things. But I like being here, too. Do I *hafta* go?"

Well, that was a switch. "No. You don't *have* to go. I only agreed because you love camping, and you always want to go the ranch rather than stay here."

Michael shoved his fists in the front pockets of his faded Levi's and with eyes cast down, rubbed a spot on the ceramic tile floor with the toe of one sneaker. "But it's different now."

Cam leaned against the counter, giving Michael his full attention. "What d'you mean? What's different now?"

The boy hedged, then muttered, "It's different *here* now. It's like the other kids. Y'know, kids who have a mom and a dad."

With a sudden wrenching insight, Cam crouched to his son's height and wrapped an arm around him. Up until now, Michael hadn't said a word on the subject. When he'd first come to live with Cam, he'd asked about his mom, but seemed satisfied with the answer his dad had given him. Cam had no idea that Nicole's presence held such significance for the boy.

How could he tell him he didn't know if anything

would ever come of his relationship with Nicole? It wouldn't if she had her way, and he had to respect her feelings, even though he didn't fully understand them.

He'd figured a little time might be all she needed, and he was planning to give it to her. Now he had something else to think about. Should he continue this relationship when it could end in hurt for Michael? He hadn't realized how intense Michael's need for her had become.

As Cam pondered a response, Michael's mood changed abruptly. He scooted onto a kitchen stool at the island, his short legs dangling. He picked up a napkin from the basket, rolled it into a cylinder and peeked through the hole as though it were a telescope. Then he sent Cam a glance from the corner of his eye and said, ''But it's okay with just us two guys, too.''

Cam's heart cramped. His six-year-old son was trying not to hurt his feelings. The kid was more mature than his father was sometimes.

If he and Nicole continued this relationship and if he knew it wasn't going to end in permanence, wasn't he shirking his duties as a father? All because he wanted a little fulfillment of his own. The thought had been nagging him lately, and sooner or later, he'd have to make a decision.

''Well, I'm glad to hear that, champ. Us guys got to stick together. If you don't want to go, that's okay. It'll be a pretty boring weekend here, though. I've got a meeting tonight, and tomorrow I need to work at one of my sites. Nicole's visiting her mom tonight and tomorrow she has to teach her other class.''

Michael's face crumpled.

''And Harry said he's got a new pony for you to ride.''

In an instant, the boy's eyes brightened again. ''Awright! Okay. I'll go,'' he said excitedly.

Just like that, Cam thought. He wished he could bounce back that fast.

NICOLE SAT AT HER DESK, absorbed in good feelings. The rest of the week had been blessedly normal. Wonderfully normal. Between their jobs, homework, and her visits to her mom, they went to the park and played ball, watched *Shrek* on a DVD, and even stopped in at a video arcade where children of all sizes engaged in battle with assorted electronic enemies. She'd had to drag both Michael and Cam away from that one.

But the best times of all were when they spent the evening quietly together, with Michael doing homework or working on puzzles while the adults read. Feeling renewed confidence in Cam's acceptance of their relationship—and the limitations she'd placed on it—she'd finally agreed to take him with her one evening to meet her mother.

Cameron was pleased, and when Michael had asked why her mom was in the hospital, he'd explained in simple terms the child could understand. They'd left Michael with Maria, and Nicole made arrangements to see her mother and one of the nurses in what the hospital called the garden room.

Nicole had been more nervous than anyone. When they arrived, Jenny was sitting in a chair, her pretty hair loose but caught up in a barrette at the back. Nicole introduced Cam; he said, "Ms. Jenny Weston, it's my pleasure," and bending at the waist, he took her hand in his and kissed it.

Her mother actually smiled at the courtly gesture. The nurse stayed with them for their short visit, and Cam charmed her, too. When they were ready to leave, he held both of Jenny's hands and said he'd like to come back with Nicole to see her again, if she didn't mind.

Not an earth-shattering meeting, she'd thought later, lying in bed next to him, but one that had given her hope. And it seemed as though all the good feelings of the past week had culminated in this Friday afternoon.

Nicole had just cleared her desk and was getting up to go when the phone rang. She answered and couldn't hold back her surprise or her excitement at hearing Dylan's voice.

"Dylan! Where are you?"

"I can't say."

Nicole glanced around to make sure no one was within earshot. Most of the teachers and staff had gone home for the weekend, but she shut her classroom door, anyway.

"Are you okay?"

"Yeah. I just wanted to make sure *you* were okay 'cause I heard about what happened. I tried to call before, but some sub answered the phone."

She smiled. "I'm fine. I appreciate your concern and—"

"I...I wanted you to know it wasn't me. I know it looks bad but—"

"Dylan, I *know* it wasn't you. I couldn't see who it was, but I didn't suspect you for even a second."

"How come?"

Good question. One she didn't have a ready answer for. It would sound stupid to say she had a gut feeling. That she understood what it was like to have people believe things about you that weren't true. "I think you're too smart to do something that stupid," she finally replied.

A silence ensued before Dylan said, "I finished that essay you gave me."

"Wonderful! Are you planning on bringing it to class?

You've missed a lot, and you can't graduate if you..." She stopped. "But you know that, don't you."

"I can do the work. I just can't come back right now."

"Why not? No one can prove you did something if you didn't."

"Yeah, sure."

Okay, he probably knew more about that than she did, but she had to try. "Staying away makes you look guilty. You can see that, can't you?"

"They thought I was guilty before without any proof. So I'm not taking any chances. Not yet. But I'll do the work if I can get it."

She didn't know what his situation was, but he had a point. He'd already been accused and found guilty without doing a thing. The story of his life. And it did sound as if he was coming back, but not immediately. He needed to know someone believed in him.

"Your aunt's very worried about you."

"I'm going to call her soon. I have to go now."

Lord, she couldn't let him just disappear. Not when he was reaching out for help. "We can work something out about the lessons."

"Like what?"

"I don't know. Maybe I can leave the homework for you to pick up somehow and return to me. Is there a way to do that? Or someone who can do it for you?"

"Yeah. There's a guy I can ask. But how do I know you won't tell someone?"

"You don't. You just have to trust me, Dylan."

"HOW LONG WILL the meeting take?" Nicole asked later that night as she searched for a cool drink in the fridge. Talking with Dylan and then visiting her mother had drained her emotionally.

"An hour or two. Depends on the discussion," Cam said. "We don't need to stay for the whole meeting. I just thought you might be interested in going, since it's your class they're discussing."

"I appreciate that. But really, any decision regarding the program is up to the school board."

"Some of these people *are* on the board," Cam said.

Maybe he was right, and she should go. Lord knows, Sipowitz wasn't confiding in her. It might even help if she got to say a few words on her students' behalf. "How much time do I have? I'd like to wash up first, and change clothes."

"Fifteen minutes."

It was so hot out, she did a quick change into tan cotton shorts, a white, spaghetti strap T-shirt and sandals. She'd have to prepare the lessons for Dylan later.

They'd figured out a plan for exchanging the work Dylan would need to complete in the time they had left. She'd leave the work at school under the steps of the portable, and the rest was up to Dylan. She didn't question him about the details because it was best not to know. She assumed he'd have help from a friend.

What she was doing felt vaguely illegal, but it really wasn't. There was no warrant out for his arrest or anything like that. She just hoped he'd call his aunt.

The visit with her mom after school had not gone well. The residential facility had made a final decision and turned down the application. Once they'd studied Jenny's treatment plan, they'd decided she didn't fit their criteria. They weren't staffed for such a complicated case, they couldn't provide the clinical care she needed, they couldn't effect the crisis plan as it was written.

The news had all but overwhelmed Nicole, but with a

little pressure from her mom's physician, the facility had agreed to reconsider.

As if that would do any good.

Going to the homeowners' association meeting with Cam would only add to her agitation. But, given the agenda, she had to do it.

CHAPTER THIRTEEN

THEY WALKED to the community building, since it was only three blocks from the house, and made it just before the meeting started. Most seats were filled, so they took two empty chairs in the back row. A skinny man with glasses sat at a table in front.

Cam told her the man was Jim Bentworth, his neighbor across the street and the association president.

The first part of the meeting was taken up with association business. Nicole's eyes were heavy. It'd been a long, tiring day and all she wanted was to go to bed and sleep. Ten minutes later, she perked up when she heard the next topic for discussion was the At Risk program at Barton Elementary.

Bentworth launched into a lengthy explanation of the petition they planned to present to get the program out of Barton. Apparently, though, they hadn't obtained the required number of signatures yet.

Another man sitting next to Bentworth added, "The bottom line is that when this program went into effect, we, the community, weren't notified that we'd have criminals in our midst. As parents, we have a right to know that. We want to keep our children safe and give them the opportunity to excel. That's why we chose to make our homes in this outstanding community, and we want the neighborhood to stay that way."

Bentworth said, "Here's the petition. Those of you who

haven't signed can do so when we're finished. We need all of you to make this work.'' He glanced around, then smiled at certain people. Cam was one. ''The topic is now open for discussion from the floor.''

She looked about the room. No one raised a hand in protest. Which meant that her program could be canceled, just like that. What would happen to her students then?

She nudged Cam and whispered, ''Those kids aren't criminals. And there isn't that much time left. Surely they can wait till the end of the school year.''

Cam raised his hand and when acknowledged, he stood. ''There's only a short time left in the school year. Wouldn't it make sense to let the program finish?''

Another hand rose, and a thirty-something woman got to her feet. ''I think the vandalism at the school and the assault on that poor woman is more than enough reason to do it now. Why wait until someone else gets hurt? The sooner that program and those students are gone, the better.''

Nicole saw another hand go up. This time a man, but she could only see the back of his balding head. ''We never had problems like this before the program came into the school.''

Nicole listened as the next two people said basically the same thing. Cam looked at her quickly, then placed a hand on her arm. He raised his hand again and got up, his expression now dark. ''How do we know these students are criminals? Do we know that for a fact?''

This time, Bentworth glared at Cam.

A chubby middle-aged woman sitting beside the balding man rose from her seat, and without being called on, turned and said, ''Of course we do! That's why they're there in the first place. That poor woman was beaten and left for dead, and I for one don't want to fear for my lif when I go out at night."

Cam's expression shifted to an angry scowl, which h directed at the woman talking. Nicole knew he wouldn' like being reminded of the assault; he'd made his feeling about that abundantly clear.

"As far as I know," he said, "the police haven't ar rested anyone. Do you know something they don't?"

The woman's face turned the same color as her pin floral dress and Nicole saw the balding man's arm reac up to pull her to her seat. She opened her mouth to re spond, but Bentworth interrupted. "Mr. Colter had th floor, Mrs. Sipowitz." The woman sputtered, then glow ered at Cam as she was yanked down again.

Nicole flinched when she heard the woman's name *Mrs. Sipowitz?* Roy's wife? She studied the man's head Her stomach knotted. Was that why he was trying to ge Dylan moved to another school? Was his wife pushin him to do it?

Cam went on, "I want my son and those I care abou to be safe, too. But I believe it's important to get the fact first, and that's what I intend to do." Cam finished an then took his place next to Nicole.

Her love for him swelled. He knew how much the pro- gram meant to her and was willing to support it, eve though he was still worried that the culprit might be on of her students. She placed her hand over his in gratitude

She wondered if she should get up and say something tc the group herself. But knowing that Roy was there with his wife, and that some members of the school board also sa in the audience, worried her. If she was perceived as a trou- blemaker, she might not get hired permanently in the fall She might even get herself fired right now—from both jobs What good would she be to any of her students then?

What good were her principles if she didn't stand behind them?

If she kept quiet, people in the community would go on believing that what they'd heard was true. Her A.R. students, Dylan in particular, would be blamed. It wasn't fair.

She raised her hand.

"In the back." Bentworth nodded, squinting at her.

She said a silent prayer that she wouldn't offend anyone and then got to her feet. "I'm afraid some of you are under a few misconceptions. I teach the A.R. class. I know with absolute certainty that none of those students is a criminal. These boys have learning problems and may have been in trouble a time or two, but that hardly constitutes the definition of a criminal. They're just kids trying to catch up so they can graduate. And another little thing—I'm also the person who was allegedly beaten and almost died. Well, that's obviously false. As you can see, I'm fine. I think if you're voting on something, you ought to get the facts before you—"

Bang! Bentworth's gavel crashed down on the desk. Nicole's gasp of surprise matched that of the audience.

"That's enough, Ms. Weston. This is a forum for our community association members, not the general public. You don't belong here." He looked at a woman sitting beside him taking notes. "Please strike Ms. Weston's statements from the minutes." Then he addressed the group. "I'm sorry, I didn't realize the error. Let's move on."

"She's here with me," Cam interjected. "And I *am* part of this community."

Nicole's nerves ignited. She shoved back her chair to get out and heard it scrape across the tiled floor. All heads turned to see the commotion as she kneed the chair aside and marched toward the door.

Cam followed, catching her arm on the way out. She stopped, adrenaline pumping hard.

"I'm really sorry about that," Cam said. "I wouldn't have asked you to come if I'd known."

Her face flamed, but not because of him. The narrow-mindedness of those people incensed her. It was no different from what she'd encountered all her life with her mother.

"It's not your fault, Cam. You only tried to help. But I doubt anyone can change the attitudes of people whose minds are so small they can't squeeze in an ounce of compassion." She paced the sidewalk outside the door.

"If one of *their* kids had a learning problem, I'm sure they'd be singing a different tune. God only knows what they'd think if they knew that the woman teaching their first-graders had a mother with schizophrenia."

She whirled around—and saw the woman in the flowered dress, listening to every word. Mrs. Sipowitz.

Oh, God.

"C'mon," Cam said. "Let's go home."

She stopped him. "No, you should stay," she said quietly. "You and Michael live here and I don't. There's no point in putting yourself on the chopping block just because—"

He shushed her with a finger to her lips. "I have a few things to say to that group myself, but I'm not going to let you walk home alone."

"It's okay. Nothing's happened lately. I think it's pretty safe and—"

"Forget it."

He took her hand and they walked in silence. But she

could feel the anger coursing through him. She was angry, too, but at herself as much as Bentworth and his cronies. She worried all the way home that she'd screwed up any chance to help the kids who were counting on her.

"What if they cut the program? What will the kids do? What will I do if they fire me?"

"Why don't we cross those bridges when—and if—we get to them," Cam said in his usual understated way.

We. That sounded so good.

At home, Nicole went to her room to prepare Dylan's assignment, and immersing herself in the project, she was able to put her own problems aside—however momentarily. There'd been a message from Jenny's caseworker—just a request to call back on Monday morning. Nothing she could do about it now, but…

She always felt better when she stopped thinking about herself and concentrated on others. Her own brand of therapy. And fortunately, it worked.

A half hour later, she went to the kitchen and found Cameron filling a couple of glasses with her favorite chardonnay.

He handed her one. "I've got an idea on how to forget all that meeting stuff."

She smiled and raised her glass to his. "I can't wait to hear it."

"Good." He turned her around and holding her hand, walked her into the den where the lights were low. He flicked on a CD and when the music started, she recognized the song. "You interested in a slow dance with a cowboy?"

She pulled in a ragged breath. As he reached out and drew her into his strong arms, she said, "Right now, I can't think of anything I'd like more."

As they moved slowly to the music, he touched a warm

hand to her collarbone and flicked the thin strap of her shirt off her shoulder. "I can," he drawled, and after a few seconds, he added, "That is, if I can get you out of these heavy clothes."

She raised her arms. "Be my guest."

A blissful hour later, she snuggled into Cam's arms and slept. But not for long. She awoke horribly anxious and in a sweat, thinking about the caseworker's call. The woman would've left a message if the placement had been approved, so it had to be something else. But Nicole couldn't imagine what.

To keep from waking Cam, she went to the guest room to sleep. He planned to work with his crew in the morning and there was no reason he shouldn't get a good night's rest just because she was jittery.

Despite her brief respite, she couldn't seem to shake off the problems plaguing her—her mom's placement, Dylan's situation and the meeting tonight. She couldn't stop thinking about the look on Mrs. Sipowitz's face when she heard Nicole say her mother was mentally ill.

That outburst was going to come back and haunt her; she just knew it. She decided right then that she had to talk with Roy first thing Monday morning. She wasn't sure what she'd say, but she couldn't postpone it.

The rest of the night, sleep came in fits and starts, and she woke every hour on the hour. Each short stretch of sleep was filled with wild dreams that came in a series of fast frames. In some, she was standing separate from the rest of the world and looking in; in others she was in the midst of it all.

Vignettes came and went. People from all parts of her life flitted in and out—Cameron and Michael, Jenny, her class at school, Risa and Dylan, the police, faceless doctors all lined up in their white coats, their arms holding her mother down. And then, the next thing she knew, they were examining *her.* Then she was standing there, all alone, gripped by panic, shaking with fright. And she was falling and falling and falling and flames shot up from far below and she knew she'd descended into the fiery pit of hell.

But in the next instant, she was walking and then running, and it was hazy. Through the silvery mist, she saw Mrs. Nelson sitting at the table in her own kitchen. Then the image slipped away and morphed into the sparsely furnished one-room apartment where Nicole and her mother had once lived.

Her mommy was there, face creamy white and flowers in her long red hair that swirled and flowed out like a mermaid's. Her mommy was beautiful and as she watched in awe, her mommy's hair suddenly turned into tentacles, her face contorted, and she growled and snapped and snarled at Nicole, who was ten years old again. They both lunged for the door, Nicole racing to get there before her mommy did.

Reaching it first, Nicole whirled around and slammed her back flat against the rough wood. With skinny legs splayed and arms outstretched, she braced herself, fists pressed hard into the doorjamb on each side.

Please. Oh, please, get here soon, she prayed, watching her mommy steal forward. Nicole pressed her fists harder and harder against the doorjamb until her knuckles were white and her muscles quivered.

"No, Mommy! No. You can't go." At Nicole's outburst, stark terror filled her mommy's big gray eyes, and she crouched in the middle of the room like an animal. Then Mommy sprang at Nicole, tearing at her arms, clawing at the knob trying to open the door and get away.

"No, Mommy. No!" Nicole shrieked. "You'll get hurt out there."

Three loud thuds rattled the door and echoed through the bare room. Her mom flew into the corner, cowering with her arms wrapped over her head.

They came. Thank God they came. Nicole sucked in a deep breath and swiped at the tears running down her cheeks.

With wild eyes, her mother sat up and glaring at Nicole, she rocked back and forth and began to chant, "Alabaster. Satan. Lucifer! Devil's child," and she repeated the words over and over until they all ran together in a jumble Nicole couldn't understand. Then Mommy started groaning and making awful, terrible noises in her throat. "Ohhhh. Mmmmm. Ohhhh."

Bang, bang. The knocking echoed again. Nicole bit her bottom lip and trying not to cry, she slid sideways and inched open the door. She stared into the steely eyes of a white-uniformed man. Beside him stood a lady, also in white, and two more white-coated men behind with a table on wheels—just like that television show.

The people looked past Nicole, eyeing her mom. Nicole's stomach lurched. Oh, no! She shouldn't have called? But the doctors said it would be okay, that it was best for her mom.

She searched their faces. Had she done the right thing? Had she? "That's my mom. Please be careful," Nicole pleaded, her voice trembling, her small body shaking.

"What's her name?" the steely-eyed man demanded.

"J-Jenny," Nicole whispered. "Jenny Weston. But please be careful. She's scared." Nicole was scared, too, and her heart beat so hard it practically crashed through her chest. But she didn't know what else to do. She just didn't. Nobody told her what to do.

She let them in and then darted to her mommy's side, dropping to her knees. She reached out to hug her because that's what Mommy always did when Nicole was sick or scared.

"It's okay, Mommy. They're going to help you."

Jenny's eyes went wild. She shrieked and jumped to her feet, knocking Nicole backward onto her butt. The men bolted toward her mom and flattened her against the wall.

The two men stayed there holding her mommy while the fat lady groped in her bag and drew out a long silver needle and a small bottle.

Mommy's eyes went wide with terror, her face as white as chalk. She hit at the men, her arms and legs flailing like a puppet's, but they kept holding on to her—harder and harder.

Nicole's horror fixed her to the spot. She couldn't move, she couldn't speak. "It wasn't her f-fault. Sh-she didn't mean to do it," Nicole finally stammered, but no one heard her.

"Noooo!" her mommy shrieked. "Don't. Please, no, it's poison. I'll die," she cried. "I'll die. I'll die."

She hurt so much for her mommy, but all she could do was stand there and watch.

The nurse stalked closer, needle in hand.

"Please. Please, no. Please!" Jenny screamed as she thrashed against the men.

The nurse's face hardened. "Come on now. We're here to help you." She nodded to the men and said, "Get her ready."

"Murderers!" Jenny shrieked. "Poison. Get away."

Oh, oh, oh. Nicole pressed against the wall. She shouldn't have called. The people were so cold. They didn't care about her mom—not like she did. Angry tears

stung the backs of her eyes. ''Don't hurt her! Please b
careful. Please don't hurt her.''

Nicole stifled a sob. She had to be brave so her momm
wouldn't see she was scared. Biting her knuckles, sh
crept closer, but the nurse sharply motioned her back.

''Please don't hurt her,'' Nicole whimpered. ''It's oka
Mommy. It's okay. They're going to help you.''

Just as she said the words, her mother's balled fists sh
out, pummeling the burly man's face again and again.

He grunted, grabbed her mommy's frail body in a tigh
locked grip against his big chest, whipped her around an
threw her, facedown, onto the hard table on wheels. The
he leaned himself across her back. A whoosh of air wa
expelled from her mom's lungs and she moaned.

''You'll feel better after this,'' the nurse said quietl
moving to stand in front of the table while she lowere
the long, silver needle into the bottle.

Her mommy screeched, a piercing, unending wail. Ni
cole cupped her hands over her ears.

''Please. No. No, no, no,'' her mommy begged, cranin
her neck to see Nicole. ''It hurts. It hurts too much. Don'
let them kill me. Please, please, please don't let them ki
me.''

Nicole brought the back of her hand against her teet
Fiery tears blazed from her eyes and spilled down he
cheeks. Her chest hurt so much she thought it would spl
right down the middle.

It was her fault they were here. Her fault Mommy wa
so afraid. Mommy would hate her. But she'd only wante
to make things better, to help her.

''Relax, Mrs. Weston,'' the nurse soothed. ''Sto
thrashing around or it'll hurt even more.''

But her mommy struggled and fought until her breath
ing came in gurgles from the bottom of her throa

and when the nurse plunged in the needle, Nicole's anguished cries were as loud as her mom's.

Low, wretched sobs tore from her throat and tears streamed down her cheeks as she watched them wrap her mommy in a funny-looking blanket and strap her down.

Nicole clutched her stomach as they took her mommy away. A sour, acrid taste filled the back of her throat.

She had to puke.

And then she had to go to school.

"NICOLE. NICOLE." A faint voice, someone calling her, cool hands on her hot shoulders. Her eyes flew open. She bolted upright, heart hammering violently in her chest.

"Nicole, are you okay?"

Cameron was sitting next to her on sweat-drenched sheets. A *dream.* Only a dream.

But as real as the day she'd lived it.

"Damn. You had me worried. I thought someone had broken into the house or something."

She sagged back against the pillow.

"Are you sick?"

"No, it was…just a nightmare. One I've had before."

He reached up to trace a fingertip across her forehead, gently lifting the hair from her face, and then his hand came down to rest on her cheek. His touch calmed her.

"You had me worried," he whispered.

She drew his hand from her face to her mouth, tenderly kissing his fingers. "Sorry."

He pulled her into his arms and she nestled against him. He was steady and solid, and she needed him so much. He seemed to understand that and held her as if he'd never let go.

While still holding her, he glanced around the sparsely

decorated guest room, then brought his questioning gaze to hers.

"You like this bedroom better? We can switch here."

"No. But I couldn't sleep and didn't want to disturb you with all my tossing and turning."

A wicked gleam shone in his eyes. "I have a great remedy for insomnia, you know."

"I didn't want to wear you out," she teased back, feeling more uplifted by the moment. She managed a smile.

"Ah, but three times is the charm."

Now she really smiled. "So they say. And I'll probably need some of your remedy when I get home tonight. Right now, I have got to get ready for school. The Saturday class, remember? No one's kicked me out yet."

"They'll have to answer to me if they do." He held up a fist and gave her one of his lopsided grins. "I need to head out, too, but now I'll be thinking about that remedy all day." He stood up and went to the door, giving her an outrageous wink.

She loved him so much it hurt.

He was wearing a pair of low-riding, hacked-off sweatpants and nothing else. Just looking at him made her want to take him up on his offer right this minute, but she had to exercise *some* semblance of good sense.

As he left the room, her thoughts went directly to the problems she had to deal with today—among them, the phone call from last night.

And each situation, old or new, brought home the reality that, eventually, she had to face. She and Cam couldn't remain friends and lovers without commitment forever. Life just didn't work that way and she already felt in over her head.

No matter how much Cam said he understood and accepted things as they were, she knew that down deep he wanted more. For Michael if no other reason. Wouldn't being ''friends'' without commitment affect Michael? What message would that give the child? Not to mention, if she persisted in going this route, she was keeping Cam from finding a real mother for his son.

God, what if Michael had been at home and heard her scream? How could she ever explain that to a six-year-old?

Lord, she needed to think. She had a decision to make before this whole thing got totally out of hand.

AFTER A QUIET DINNER on Sunday, Nicole excused herself to take a shower. When she'd called the caseworker yesterday, she'd discovered the placement had been denied a second time.

As she listened, she'd felt as if she'd been whacked in the stomach with a baseball bat. The slim thread of hope she'd clung to had snapped. She'd have to start the process all over again. She hadn't told Cam yet and planned to do so after Michael was in bed.

Bone weary, she padded slowly down the hall to the shower, her shoulders sagging. She was so tired. Tired of trying so damned hard and having it all turn to crap in the end.

She simply couldn't think about it right now. She'd think about it later tonight, when she was alone for a few hours and no one could see her deep disappointment. When no one could see her cry.

Nicole came out of the shower hearing voices at the door. Two voices, one louder than the other, but she couldn't make out the conversation. Curious, she tied her robe and wandered down the hall to see who was there, but before she reached the entry, Cam had shut the door.

''What was that all about?''

"Nothing." Cam dismissed the incident with a wave of his hand.

"Nothing?"

Their eyes met. Cam's expression closed, but not before she caught the flash of guilt. Was he keeping something from her?

He'd always been a terrible liar. But he offered no further explanation, merely excusing himself to get Michael off to bed. Harry and Sharon had brought him home so close to dinner, they hadn't had much time together.

And though Cam usually invited her in to say goodnight to Michael, he didn't ask her to join him tonight. He said he and Michael had something to discuss.

Fine. She'd been battling her own demons ever since she'd heard about the application denial. Even though the caseworker had told her she'd try again, the futility of it overwhelmed her.

How many more residential facilities were there? What would happen to her mom if they couldn't find one to take her?

Leaving Jenny in the hospital wasn't an option. But if her mother was discharged with no place to go, Nicole would have to take her home. The thought was depressing.

She'd always worked with her mother's psychiatrists and clinical team to create a workable outpatient treatment plan, but it had never been successful.

Jenny hated taking medication and when she didn't, she deteriorated. Psychotic episodes were frequent, she'd disappear and they'd find her wandering the streets, hungry and homeless, a victim for whoever wanted to exploit her.

Working full-time plus, Nicole didn't know how she'd manage if Jenny had to move in with her—as she probably would. She didn't have the resources or expertise to care for her mom on her own. Even the disability checks weren't enough to ensure proper care while Nicole was at work. But there might not be any choice.

And she hated herself for wishing there was—hated herself for wishing she didn't have to do this anymore.

Oh, she knew it was common for family members to go through guilt and recriminations, but knowing it didn't change a thing. This was her mother.

She squeezed her eyes shut and prayed the next application would get approved. But she couldn't shake the foreboding that coursed through her.

So deep in thought was she that a soft knock on the front door took her by surprise. In fact, she wasn't even sure it was a knock at all. She went into the foyer and saw that someone had slipped an envelope under the door.

Oh, God. Not again.

She shuddered. The thought of someone stalking her here, at this house with a small child inside, sent an icy chill up her spine. Dammit all! If someone wanted to threaten *her,* that was one thing, but she wasn't going to let it spill over onto Michael or Cam. Furious, she jerked open the door to catch whoever was there.

But all she saw was Bentworth picking up something on the sidewalk. He glanced at her and then from side to side before slamming the door behind him.

She reached down and snatched up the large envelope at her feet. It was only something from the homeowner's association. Relief seeped through her. She stood for a moment, letting her anxiety subside, but even so, she knew she had a decision to make.

She turned the paper to read a sticky note on the front that said, *Mr. Colter. Enclosed is the copy of the petition, statistics and other information you asked for. Please review, sign and return to me ASAP.*

CHAPTER FOURTEEN

CAM LEANED OVER, tucked in Michael's blanket and sat at his side. Yawning, Michael said, "How come Nicole can't come in? I like it when she's here, too."

"Because I've got something to ask you, and I don't want her to hear. That's why." Michael had obviously gotten used to having both of them tuck him in and read to him at night.

"*Then* can she come in?"

"Well, maybe, but I need to talk with her. If you're still awake after that, sure, she can come in."

"What do ya wanna ask me?"

"Well, I guess I know how much you like Nicole, and I really like her, too. That's—"

"Are you going to marry her, Dad?" Michael burst out. "Are ya? Are ya?"

"That's sort of what I wanted to ask you. How would you feel if I said I was thinking about it?"

"Would she be my mom then?" The boy beamed.

"If I asked her to marry me and she said yes, then she'd be your stepmom."

His face fell, and his bottom lip jutted out. After a second, his eyes rounded and with hope in his voice, he said, "But I could *call* her my mom, couldn't I? Because I don't have one anymore."

Cam winced at the longing in his son's voice. "I'm sure she'd like that. But remember, this is all just in the hinking stages, son. So don't go saying anything about it o anyone. Not even Nicole. Okay? Because lots of other hings have to happen first. This is a big secret just be-ween you and me."

"Yeah. You need to get a 'gagement ring first. Right?"

Cam laughed, then gave his son a hug until he squealed. 'Da-ad!" Michael pushed him away, his laughter subsid-ng. "Guys don't hug. Just moms and girlfriends and boy-riends."

"Sorry, but I know for a fact that dads hug their kids once in a while, too. So don't go getting all grown-up on ne yet."

Michael settled down. "Okay. Maybe you can do it once in a while, but not in front of my friends."

"You got it."

It didn't take two minutes for the boy to drop off to sleep after that.

Cam was glad they'd talked. His fears about bringing another person into Michael's life had been dispelled in an instant. He'd seen the easy rapport between his son and Nicole, and when she was around, Michael seemed like a different kid. His acceptance of a possible marriage between Nicole and his dad had given Cam the emotional reinforcement he needed to really think about a future for the three of them. He'd had his doubts. Not only about himself, but also about Michael.

If it didn't work out, Michael would experience the loss as much as he. Maybe more so, since he'd been through such hell with his mother.

Tough for a kid, he thought, to have other people de-ciding who will or won't be in your life.

As Michael's father, it was his responsibility to protect his son, and that responsibility was precisely why he'd never involved Michael in any of his previous relationships. It wouldn't be fair to allow his son to grow attache to someone if that person wasn't going to be around i the future.

He'd veered from that course twice, first with Gen That hadn't been a serious relationship and had sneake up on him before he realized the effect it could have o Michael. But then he'd done the same thing with Nicole— when he *was* fully aware. Hell, he realized he wouldn have brought Nicole into his house if he hadn't wante them to be together. Because, as Michael's teacher, sh could have helped his son without any personal or soci interaction between him and Nicole.

He had to admit that almost from the moment he'd see her again, he'd imagined what the future might hold i things worked out. He'd imagined the three of them livin in this house, being a family. Maybe they'd even adop some children. The house was certainly large enough fo more.

But somewhere deep inside, he hadn't been able to ge rid of that niggling doubt—the uncertainty created because Nicole hadn't trusted him enough to tell him th truth. He'd spent ten years believing a lie.

Even so, somewhere along the line, he'd let down hi guard and realized just how deeply he loved her. An since they'd talked about the past, he'd come to recogniz his own part in their breakup.

She'd lied and kept the truth from him, but he'd bee too prideful to ask her what had gone wrong. Instead, he' chosen to take it personally. He'd probably done that lot back then—blaming his problems on everyone bu himself.

But there was another question he had to answer befor he could think of a future with Nicole. Though he coul accept a life without more children of his own, there were other considerations.

He'd be a liar if he said he never wondered what life would be like if Nicole were to end up like her mother—even if it happened gradually. He'd talked with her mom's caseworker and discovered that the illness usually exhibited itself in males from about eighteen up, and later in women, around twenty-five and up. The most startling thing he'd learned was the prevalence of mental illness in general. He'd also learned that schizophrenia is experienced by more than two million people in the U.S., not including the homeless or those in prison or institutions.

But he was in love with *Nicole.* Not with a statistic.

His gaze drifted back to his son, angelic in sleep. The boy's thick blond hair swooped into careless bangs across his forehead, long lashes almost as light as his hair curled against smooth pink cheeks. Like his mother, Cam guessed, though he hardly remembered what she looked like.

He'd wondered more than once why Michael's mother hadn't told him about their son—and why she'd never hit him up for money. Particularly since her drug habit must have made her desperate for money. He didn't even know if she'd been on drugs while she was pregnant. If so, had Michael been affected? He didn't seem to be, but she was gone, and Cam might never know for sure.

That thought set off other memories and, just like that, he had an answer to his other question. He knew exactly what he'd do if Nicole got sick. He'd love her, just as he would Michael.

He slipped gently off the bed, treading softly to the door, and went out. It was time he and Nicole talked.

She wasn't in the family room, and assuming she'd gone into the bathroom or kitchen for a minute, he stretched out on the leather sofa and waited for her to return.

He looked across the room, catching sight of the overstuffed easy chair where Nicole always sat while correcting her papers. The three of them spent the first part of each evening as a family here; after that, when Michael was asleep, it was just the two of them. Sometimes they snuggled quietly, and at other times, they simply talked.

In two weeks, they'd fallen into the comfortable pattern of two people confident in the feeling of rightness between them. Just the way he'd envisioned it so many years before. His spirits lifted at the thought.

This was even better than he'd imagined. Waiting, he rubbed his chin. Where the heck was she? He had a sharp urge to share his emotions with her and to talk about the future. *Their* future.

They were both older, wiser, and not afraid of the truth. Sure, he remembered what she'd said the first night they'd made love, but that was before they'd achieved the level of comfort and certainty with which they'd been living. Together they could face anything.

Excited, he sprang from the couch.

When he didn't find her in the kitchen, he went to her bedroom and tapped lightly on the door. "Nic?"

Nothing.

Ear to the door, he listened for movement inside. A sliver of light shone from underneath. Moments passed and he rapped again. "Nic, are you in there?" When there was still no answer, he slowly twisted the knob and eased open the door.

Nicole stood grim-faced before him, suitcase in hand. Speechless, he stared, shifting his eyes from her face to the bag and back again. "What's that for?" he finally managed.

"I'm going home, Cam."

"What...why?" His earlier elation crashed.

"It's time. I really need to go."

He reached out to pull her to him, but her body was unyielding. "Nic, what is it? What's wrong?" He held her at arm's length. "If something's wrong, you need to tell me. We can work it out."

Lips compressed and still holding the suitcase, she nodded to indicate a pile of papers on the dresser. He knew what it was. The information Bentworth had supplied—and the petition. Bentworth had wanted him to sign it when he was here less than an hour ago. He'd refused and they'd had words. Cam had never read the statistics and brochures Bentworth had brought him several weeks ago—to Bentworth's barely disguised fury. He must have dropped off new copies of everything.

"It's not what you think," Cam said quietly.

"Why is that here?"

"Initially I told Bentworth I'd look at it, but that was a few weeks ago. I didn't say I'd sign. In fact, I said I wouldn't." He paused, shaking his head. "Nic, after you were assaulted, I wanted to kill whoever was responsible. Bentworth came over spouting statistics and information and I thought I should at least look at the stuff. Statistics on recidivism and how many kids get worse instead of better. I was worried for Michael's safety, too. So I said I'd read it. That's all. I don't know why he brought it back without my asking."

He stepped flush against the door. "The only reason I agreed to read it in the first place is that I'm concerned about the safety of the two people who mean more to me than anything in the world. Concerned for the two people I love most."

Her amber eyes flashed. ‘‘That’s the same logic *they* used.’’

‘‘They?’’

‘‘Yes. That’s what Bentworth’s group was advocating Friday night.’’

He felt as if he’d been punched in the gut. ‘‘You *know* me, Nicole. You know who I am and what I stand for. I can’t believe you’re including me with people like that.’’

‘‘I’m not including you with anyone. I just think… Well, it doesn’t matter anymore.’’

Cam stiffened. ‘‘I didn’t sign anything and I don’t intend to.’’

‘‘It really doesn’t matter, Cam. I can’t blame you for your concern. I’m concerned myself and it’s made me realize how impossible this is. Now, please, I need to go home.’’

He stepped aside. If she wanted to leave, fine. If she wanted to twist his motives around, nothing he said was going to change her mind.

But before she left, he said, ‘‘If you think about this at all—’’ He paused, his mouth dry. ‘‘Remember that all I’ve ever wanted to do is protect those I love. That’s the truth.’’ His voice broke. ‘‘Remember that, Nicole.’’

Looking at him, she believed him. And she understood. How could she not? But she couldn’t dismiss the underlying significance of those words.

Cam was worried about his son’s safety. How would he feel if he ever had to cope with anything threatening Michael’s safety—and in his own house? If she was there, it could happen.

Despair settled in the very core of her. She bit her lower lip, fighting back tears as the awful knowledge twisted inside.

‘‘My mother’s application was rejected again. I may

need to bring her home with me, which means I need to make plans. I can't stay here anymore, Cam. It's not good for any of us in the long run. Please tell Michael goodbye for me,'' she said, her voice barely audible.

''Tell him I'll talk with him the first chance I get.''

THE LONGEST NIGHT of her life followed the worst day she'd ever had. All night she'd questioned herself over and over. Had she done the right thing? Had she cut off their relationship soon enough? She countered her doubts with all the reasons she believed her departure was truly the wisest choice. Even so, no matter what she told herself, she was miserable.

Cam and Michael would adjust. She wasn't so sure about herself. But then, her feelings weren't an important part of this equation. She'd accepted that a long time ago.

Cam had come back into her life—and she'd let him. She'd known what could happen, and despite that knowledge, she'd let it go too far. Just as she'd done ten years ago. She had no one to blame but herself.

Would she never learn?

Probably not where Cam was concerned. Maybe *that* was the reality she had to accept instead of trying to deny it every step of the way. She had to get on with her life and let him get on with his. She just hoped she hadn't hurt both him and Michael in the process.

The next day at school, Michael wouldn't even talk to her except to answer the questions she asked in class. When she did get a chance to talk to him, all she could do was ensure that he understood it had simply been time for her to go home. That it didn't have anything to do with him.

They'd told him in the beginning that she'd be staying only until the work on her condo was finished, so she didn't understand his very pointed anger. She decided to give it the rest of the day and if nothing changed, she'd have to call Cam tonight. She hated to do it, but she owed him that.

She picked up a note on her desk. It was from Roy asking that she meet with him during lunch. The energy drained from her limbs and it was all she could do to carry on with the class. She knew exactly what the meeting was about and she might as well kiss any thoughts of a permanent contract goodbye.

When lunchtime arrived, Josie, her aide, escorted the children to lunch. Nicole walked with the class partway and then headed toward the administrative office for the dreaded meeting with Roy.

No one was at the reception desk, so she slipped into the waiting area, rapped lightly on Roy's door and entered. Standing with the door at her back, she wondered if she should bother explaining or just let him fire her without a fight. That would be cowardly. Her A.R. students deserved to be defended.

"Sit down, Nicole. This won't take long."

Right. As she walked forward to sit in the chair off to the side, he steepled his chubby hands, his expression grim.

He was going to fire her. She knew it.

"There's no easy way to say this, Nicole, except to simply tell you that I'm extremely sorry."

She nodded. "I understand. No point in drawing it out. I do have a couple of things I'd like to say, however, and I hope you'll give me that opportunity."

"I'd be happy to listen. But first, let me say that I've been so preoccupied with doing what I thought I needed to do from an administrative perspective, I've forgotten who it is we're serving. We serve the public, which includes our students—*all* our students."

What? If he was going to tell her she wasn't serving her students, she'd…she'd—

He continued. "Unfortunately, I'd lost sight of that when some members of the community uh, made their opinions about the A.R. program known—and, well, let's just say I thought I could please everyone. The meeting on Friday night was a wake-up call for me, and listening to you make a case for your students, I realized that what I'd been doing was wrong. Not to mention impossible. Trying to appease everyone never works, and I don't know why I thought I could. When the community association couldn't get the petition off the ground and the board voted this morning to keep the program at Barton for the rest of the year, I knew how wrong I'd been. And the worst part was that I felt relieved."

"Keep…the…program?" Dumbstruck, Nicole could barely get the words out. "They decided to keep the program?"

"At least for the rest of this year. After that, we'll assess its outcome and go from there."

She brought her fingers to her mouth and broke into a huge smile. "Ohmigosh! That's *wonderful.* Really wonderful. The students deserve this chance and it means a lot to me, too. Thank you so much."

Roy gave a grimace. "Don't thank me. I don't deserve it. When I said I was relieved, it was because the decision had been taken out of my hands. I've spent the past two days thinking about that—and how far I've veered from being the educator I wanted to be. I'd like to apologize for my wife, too. She told me about the conversation she overheard between you and Mr. Colter, and…I'm afraid she told some other people. I'm sorry about that."

A knot formed dead center in her stomach. She took a breath, and with it came a strange sensation. She was *glad* he knew. She no longer had to worry about his finding out. "No apology necessary. It took a lot of guts to admit what you just did."

If she hadn't respected him for anything else, she had to respect him for that. Good grief, his own wife was one of the people pressuring him. That had to be tough.

But Nicole's sympathy for Roy was overshadowed by her excitement that the program would continue.

"I also want to offer you a contract for the fall. We need more teachers like you. However, I still need to talk with Mrs. Jessup to straighten out some things. I'd appreciate it if you don't say anything to anyone until the contracts come out. I just wanted you to know."

A few seconds ago, she'd thought she couldn't be more ecstatic, but she was wrong. Everything she'd hoped for concerning her career was about to come true and she was practically in a state of shock. "I won't. Is Mrs. Jessup better now? For some reason I thought she wasn't well enough to come back."

He shook his head. "No, there were other reasons she left. But don't worry, I'm just dealing with procedure. I'll get that contract for you."

Nicole left Roy's office so light-headed she thought she might float all the way back to her room. She hadn't felt this *happy* since...since she'd been with Cam and Michael.

In her classroom after lunch, she found Michael sporting an attitude as big as he was, and within the hour, he'd pestered so many classmates, she had to make him sit by himself. When the day ended, she went to talk with him, but he'd bolted almost before the final bell. She wasn't sure she should follow. He might need time alone.

Arriving at her apartment, she was welcomed by some more good news. Her mother's application had received approval from a brand-new facility and all Nicole had to do was check it out to see if she liked the place. Risa attributed all her recent good fortune to some alignment of the moon and stars.

Well, whatever it was, she didn't care, and when Risa said she'd go with her to see the facility, they left immediately.

"Turn on this street." Risa, studying the map, nudged Nicole with an elbow. "Turn right. Okay, it's down the next block."

Nicole's stomach fluttered as they drove closer, and she prayed that this would be the one.

"Over there. That's it. Thirty-seven twenty-four."

Nicole stopped the car by the curb, got out and headed up the walkway with Risa at her side. She rang the doorbell, taking a deep breath.

This was a huge step for her mom. It had been a long time since Jenny had been outside the hospital for more than half a day, and Nicole had to make sure the facility was right for her.

A chubby middle-aged lady with gray hair answered the door. She introduced herself as Lena Olson, the residential director, and proudly showed Nicole and Risa around. The house wasn't fancy, but it was large, clean and cheery.

Jenny would be the first resident, Lena Olson said, and three others would come within the month. They screened carefully, so everyone would be compatible. There were four resident bedrooms and one for staff.

When Nicole entered the last bedroom, she knew it was perfect for her mom. The room wasn't huge, but spacious enough, and decorated in a pink-and-white floral pattern with white wicker furniture. It reminded her of the spring flower garden they'd planted in California.

Lord. She hadn't thought about that for the longest time. Her mom had been so proud of that garden. She'd even helped Nicole plant her own little corner with both vegetables and flowers and then taught her how to tend it. Jenny had been happy then, Nicole remembered.

"We have one television," Lena said, "and two bathrooms that will be shared. We offer a life-skills program and our residents participate in household chores, cooking and other tasks to the extent they can. Our goal is to make this house a home and assist our family members to be as self-sufficient as possible."

Nicole glanced around again, noticing fresh flowers on the kitchen table. Yes, Jenny would like it here. She was sure of it.

When they'd finished with the tour, Lena offered them a cup of tea. "I'm a master's degree R.N. I also have an M.S.W. with a focus in clinical care, and it's my job to screen staff, ensure adequate supervision, medication monitoring and regular visits by the physician," she said with a smile. "We're licensed by the state. I take my responsibilities seriously and I do a good job. If you ever have any complaints, you bring them directly to me and I'll take care of them."

Nicole didn't doubt that for a minute and was comforted not only by the woman's professionalism, but also by her sensitivity and nurturing manner. It was exactly the feeling she needed to ease her mind.

Now if she just knew what to do about Michael.

If she just knew what to do about the rest of her life—and her feelings for Cam.

CHAPTER FIFTEEN

BY THE END OF THE WEEK, Michael's behavior had improved. He was playing more with some of the boys in class and seemed to accept her as his teacher and nothing more. A good sign, she believed. Children bounced back quickly.

She found it tough to stay focused, however, and far too often caught herself longing for what she couldn't have. The only solution was to immerse herself in her work. Work kept her sane, kept her from descending into feelings of hopelessness and self-pity. Work was exactly what she had planned when she arrived home early on Friday.

She made a sandwich and brought it to the table to eat while preparing new assignments for Dylan. Just as she pulled up a chair, the phone rang. At Maria's halting hello, dread shot through Nicole. Maria had *never* called her before.

"I don't know what to do, Miss Weston. So I call you."

"What is it, Maria?"

The housekeeper's explanation came in a rapid-fire combination of English and Spanish.

"I cannot reach Mr. Colter. There's a fire and Michael is very upset and crying."

Nicole's stomach plummeted. "Where's Michael?

Where's the fire? Did you call 911? Are you out of the house?''

''It's not in the house and the fire trucks are there already,'' Maria stammered. ''The boy is okay but he's scared. He ask for you.''

''I'm on my way.'' Nicole slammed down the phone. Maria hadn't given her any details; it was enough that Michael needed her. She flew down the stairs, climbed into her car and drove the speed limit, her pulse racing as fast as the vehicle.

Reaching the intersection near the turn to Cam's, she saw a black plume of smoke rising to meet the sky.

Oh, Lord. If Michael's hurt… But no, Maria had said they were both safe. *Stay calm.*

When Maria called, Nicole had imagined the worst, that something had happened to Cameron or Michael, and it was as if the floor had suddenly dropped out from under her. At that moment, she knew—she wasn't only in love with Cam, she had also formed an inextricable bond with Michael.

She loved the little guy as much as if he were her own.

She hit the brakes at the intersection where a police officer stood in the middle, directing traffic away from where she wanted to turn. Lowering the window, she called out, ''I need to go down that street.''

He barreled toward her. ''You can't go that way, ma'am.''

''But I have to!'' she cried. ''I need to know if…if my family's okay.''

''No one's been hurt, ma'am. Your family's fine.''

A horn blared behind her. Then another, until the cacophony drowned out what the officer was saying.

He bent down. ''You need to move, ma'am. That way!'' He pointed to the left.

Damn. She obeyed, but raced down the first street she came to, winding her way through the labyrinth of residential streets, many of which ended in culs-de-sac.

When she finally reached Cam's place and got out of her car, Maria bolted from the house to meet her. Smoke stung Nicole's eyes and burned her nostrils.

Between the heat of the day and the fire, she felt as if she'd stepped into an inferno. Through the haze, she saw several neighbors gathered in clusters on the corner, heads bobbing, gesturing in the direction where the smoke was thickest.

"The fire's over there," Maria said, pointing away from them. "But the wind blew the smoke this way."

"Where's Michael?" Nicole charged through the open garage door. Maria followed her into the kitchen where they stopped at the island. The acrid fumes had penetrated inside the house, as well.

"He's in his room. I got him calmed down a little, but he's still scared. He won't tell me what happened."

"What do you mean?"

"When he came home from school, his clothes were all dirty, his nose bloodied and his pants ripped," Maria explained.

"What does that have to do with the fire? I thought he was upset about the fire."

On the verge of tears, Maria talked more slowly now, making a concentrated effort to separate English from Spanish.

"He came home from school that way. You know, all dirty." She wrung her hands. "He said he was in a fight on the playground. And then before I got him cleaned up, we heard the sirens and the fire trucks came. I saw the smoke out the window, so we went outside to see. All the neighbors were coming out and then everyone tried to figure out where the fire was.'' She pointed westward.

''I was talking to my friend Vera Foster. She works for Mr. and Mrs. Davis, and I asked if anyone was hurt and then...'' Her voice wobbled. ''Michael went to stand with some children he knew, and I thought it was okay. But when I looked again they were all fighting and the two big boys were on top of him. By the time I could help—''

Tears filled Maria's eyes. She hiccuped, then brought a wadded handkerchief to her lips. ''It was my fault. I wasn't watching him. And now Mr. Cameron is going to be very mad at me.''

Nicole placed a hand on the older woman's shoulder. ''But Michael's okay—right?''

Maria nodded.

''I'll go see him,'' she said and hurried toward the boy's room. Poor Maria. She felt responsible.

Knocking lightly on the closed door, Nicole wondered what would provoke Michael to get into two fights in one day. ''Michael, it's Nicole. Can I come in?'' Something rustled inside, and then a small, muffled voice said, ''Okay.''

He was on his bed, face turned to the wall. She sank onto the edge of the mattress and touched his back. Even though Maria had said he was okay, she'd imagined all kinds of things and was filled with relief to see that his injuries weren't serious.

''You all right, Michael?'' she asked, then stroked his shoulders. ''Can I help?'' When he didn't answer right away, she leaned closer. ''Whatever happened, Michael, it's okay. You can tell me if you want to. And if you don't want to tell me, that's okay, too.''

She didn't press, but continued to rub his shoulders.

Shortly afterward, Michael pulled himself to a sitting position with his knees drawn to his chest.

"Oww—" Nicole winced when she saw his eye. She lifted his chin with two fingers to assess the damage. "You're going to have quite a shiner there."

Michael looked down, his dirty cheeks marked with tears.

"Bet the other guy looks worse," she teased.

Fighting a tiny grin, he said, "My dad's gonna be mad. *Real* mad."

"Well..." Nicole said, "All little boys get into fights now and then."

She gave him a quick squeeze. Maria had been more alarmed than necessary. A boys' fight was par for the course. A black eye, while not terrific, was preferable to the other injuries that could have occurred.

"Wanna tell me about it?"

He shook his head, and his flaxen bangs swayed across his forehead.

"Okay. Just remember, I'm available. Any time you want to talk. Got that?"

Michael nodded, then leaned into her. Swallowing a lump in her throat, she put both arms around him, pulling him tight against her chest. Lord, she'd missed him. She'd missed both of them so much.

"I guess you never want to come back now, huh?"

Nicole drew back to hold him at arm's length and stared incredulously at him. "Whatever are you talking about, Michael?"

The boy bit his lower lip and his chin quivered. He sniffled again before dragging his shirtsleeve across his face, smearing the dirt even more. "You'll think I'm too much of a bother to come back now."

Flabbergasted, Nicole could only sputter. "Michael!

How could you think such a thing? I *love* you, silly kid. How could you ever believe I thought you were a bother?"

Blinking, Michael shrugged. "You went away."

Her heart sank at his words. *His mother had gone away, too.* She hadn't forgotten, she just didn't know Michael had become as attached to her as she had to him.

She hugged him again, rocking him in her arms. "I *didn't* go because of you, Michael. I had other reasons. Reasons between me and your dad. It wasn't you. Not you at all. Besides," she said, attempting to change the subject. "Remember I told you I have a home of my own? I had to go back to take care of some things. I bet your dad told you that, too, didn't he?"

He nodded. Then he raised his eyes to the door behind her.

Nicole turned. Cameron stood in the doorway, his face ashen and drawn. "What's going on?"

Nicole gently released Michael and the boy crossed his arms over his chest again. His eyes narrowed defiantly. Cameron looked at Nicole.

"Maria called me because she couldn't reach you. I came right away." She rumpled Michael's hair. "But it seems things are fine."

"Oh, really?" Cam came forward. "Let me see that eye."

Michael turned away from his father. "It's okay. It doesn't hurt."

Nicole watched the exchange. She'd never seen Michael act like this with his dad. And Cam seemed equally disturbed, as if something else was bothering him.

His face was pallid, dark circles ringed his eyes, and he looked as if he hadn't slept in days.

Seeing his son's resistance, Cam said, "Okay, kid. We

can talk later.'' He stepped out the door and motioned for Nicole to join him. ''Can I see you for a minute?''

Nicole gave Michael one last squeeze, reminding him he could call her anytime he wanted to talk. She picked up a piece of paper and a crayon from his table and scribbled her home number on it. ''Here,'' she whispered, slipping the paper into the boy's shirt pocket. ''Call me whenever you want.'' Then she got up and followed Cam out the door.

Cam asked her to go into the den. He followed and shut the door behind him.

Something was dreadfully wrong; she saw it in his eyes. And the problem wasn't just Michael's behavior of a moment ago.

He spoke first, but seemed to have trouble saying whatever he needed to say. ''Nic—'' He stopped, took a breath, then moved closer to her and began again. ''Nic, I have bad news.''

''What's wrong?''

''Something happened at the school.'' He moved forward another step and placed his hands on her upper arms, his eyes dark with concern.

She stiffened, dread rising within her. ''What?''

''The fire. It was at the school. In the portable.''

Her stomach dropped. ''How...badly?''

''Destroyed. The building burned to the ground.''

''Oh, no.'' She touched her fingertips to her lips.

He reached for her, but she stepped back. The uncertainty in his eyes was more telling than his words.

''That's not all, is it?''

''No.'' He stared at the floor. ''The police think Dylan was involved.''

She fought back a flash of anger and tried to keep her voice even. ''That figures. That really figures.''

"Someone saw him at the scene," he said bluntly.

"So? So what? He goes to school there. He was probably dropping off lessons for me." Realizing what she'd just said, she added, "He's a student and has every right to be there. They've got to have more proof than that."

Cam shook his head, as if the verdict was in and there was nothing he could say to make it any easier for her. "I'm just reporting what I heard."

"So, *who* saw him?" Her head began to throb.

"I don't know. I didn't hear any more than what I told you."

"Well, the whole thing's absurd! What reason could Dylan possibly have for doing something like that?"

"Some people think his record speaks for itself."

"And those people are wrong! Dead wrong."

Cam came forward and took her hands in his. "I'm sorry Nic. I hate to be the bearer of bad news. I know how much the program means to you."

She bit her lip. Ignoring his comment, she said, "Maybe I can get the school to let me use a different room. Maybe—"

"I'm sure they'll come up with some solution. Maybe a new school with better facilities. I've heard charter schools are popping up all over."

She pulled away. "Yes," she said bitterly. "I guess that makes everything okay. As long as the program isn't at Barton. Right?"

Cam straightened. "Nicole, don't do this."

"I'm not doing anything." She met his eyes. "But *someone* is, and no one really cares if they find out who. Not the police, not the people in this neighborhood, not even you, Cam."

Without warning, he grabbed her shoulders. Startled by the contact, she tried to jerk away. He loosened his grip but still held her firmly, his mouth thin, his anger barely contained as he spoke through clenched jaws.

"Dammit, Nicole! It's not as simple as someone wanting the program or not. Don't you see what you're doing? *You* have a cause and it's related to lifelong feelings of yours. You can't blame other people who want to protect their own. For me, that includes both you and Michael."

"And why do you think I need your protection? What's going to happen to me?"

"I don't know what *might* happen." He let out an exasperated breath. "That's just the point. But based on what's *been* happening, I'm worried. I'm worried about you. I'm worried about my son. When you were attacked, I—" His voice wavered.

He let his hands drop. "When you were attacked and Dylan disappeared, it seemed obvious the two events were connected. And now, with a witness seeing him at the fire when he hasn't been seen anytime since then, I'd say that's fairly damning evidence, wouldn't you? At least that's what the police think and they're the experts."

"And you agree."

"I don't agree or disagree. If I think Michael's safety could be at risk, if I think *your* safety is at risk—and God knows it is—I'm going to look for solutions. Am I supposed to say and do nothing? That's impossible! I'm no different from you, Nicole. I want to protect those I love. You can't fault me for that."

She couldn't. But it didn't change the real problem. "No, I can't. But just once, you could put your pride aside and trust *my* judgment. I'm the one who knows the boy. Why can't you trust my judgment?"

Cam shifted his weight and crossed his arms over his chest. A muscle twitched under his right eye. "Because trust is a two-way street, Nicole. How can I trust you if you don't trust me? How can I trust your judgment when you don't trust it yourself?"

"What're you talking about?"

"Why didn't you tell me about your mom all those years ago? Why were you willing to give up everything we had together? You were afraid, weren't you? So afraid, you tossed away our relationship rather than be honest with me—rather than trust me to love you anyway. If your judgment was so sound, you would've known you could trust me with your life."

He stared at her as if seeing her for the first time. "No, you didn't hide it from me because of some noble concern about my feelings. You didn't want me—or anyone else—to know." He shook his head. "Don't be so quick to judge others' motives when your own are no purer than anyone else's. Good God, Nicole, if you can't trust the man who loves you, how can you expect trust from him in return?"

Nicole staggered back as if she'd been hit. It took a moment for her to find words, but when she did, she said quietly, succinctly, "You're right. I was hiding things from myself as well as you. But I was nineteen, Cam. And I learned that I was wrong. You're an adult and you're still doing what you did back then."

He scowled.

"Look around you. Is this what you really want? What's the *real* reason you're living in Phoenix? What are you running away from? You've created a perfect little environment for you and Michael, but unfortunately you did it by denying everything that was important to you. I don't know what happened between you and your brothers. To my mind, though, nothing's as important as family. But then I guess you probably take that for granted and you can discard it if you want." She gestured wildly.

"What's all of this for Cam? So Michael can grow up with the likes of Bentworth as a role model? I can't believe you think that's a better choice rather than being with his family and people who *really* care."

He flinched, and she couldn't tell if he was angry or hurt.

"My family has nothing to do with you and me," he muttered.

"You're wrong about that. Very wrong." And the fact that he didn't know it made it even worse. If he could leave his family, the people he'd loved all his life, that easily, well...

Any other words she might've had dried up in her mouth. She didn't know if he understood at all. The only thing she knew for sure was that there was no solution.

There had never been one.

A bone-deep hopelessness filled her and, as she turned and walked out of Cam's house, Cam's life, she knew she was walking out forever.

CHAPTER SIXTEEN

CAM WATCHED as Nicole disappeared from his view. Her words echoed in his head. Was she right? Was he running away? But what did that have to do with their relationship? Why was she so concerned about his rift with his brothers? What did that have to do with anything? Or his wanting to protect her and Michael?

Wearily, he dropped the curtain and headed back to Michael's room. He rapped lightly on the bedroom door.

"Go away!" Michael's angry words met him before he stepped inside.

"I'm your father and I want to talk with you, Michael."

"I don't want to talk to you."

Cameron swallowed his hurt and his anger, remembering how he'd desperately wanted to stand up to his own parents, how he wanted them to listen, how he wanted their acceptance for who he was, not what they wanted him to be. And they'd given him that, he realized. He just didn't know it at the time.

"Well, then, even more reason for us to talk." He entered the room.

Michael was standing by the window, but he rounded angrily on his dad. "It's your fault," he shouted.

Cam stopped at the end of the bed. "Okay. And if you'll tell me exactly what's my fault, we'll see what we can do to fix it."

"It's your fault she's not coming back." Michael made no attempt to disguise his rage.

"My fault, huh? Well, if it's any consolation, I didn't want Nicole to leave." He moved forward to get Michael to look at him, but the boy stared defiantly in the other direction. He was a stubborn kid, stubborn as his old man, sometimes.

"She said you did."

"Did what?" He shook his head, more confused than ever.

"She said there were reasons between you and her."

Cam crouched, balancing himself with one hand on the window ledge. "You mean the reasons she left? She said they were between me and her?"

Nodding, Michael folded his arms tightly across his chest.

"And the kids all said so, too."

The kids? "Whoa... Wait a minute. What kids said what?"

"The kids at school. Jimmy Bentworth said I was a...a bastard and I'd never get a mother. So I punched him." He pointed to his ripped pants. "We got in a fight."

This was getting more complicated by the minute. Michael thought *he* was the reason Nicole had left. That much he understood. But the school stuff? "You know what that word means?"

"No. But I know it's bad."

"Well, don't worry about it. Only dumb kids who don't know any smarter words talk like that." He placed a hand on his son's shoulder, directing him to the red beanbag chair nearby. Then he maneuvered himself into it and pulled Michael onto his lap. "Okay, son. Let's get to the bottom of this. I'm a little confused, so let's start from the beginning."

The boy's arms remained locked.

''Let's start with why you think it's my fault Nicole left. Okay?''

Michael's lips pursed, as if he wasn't going to give his father the satisfaction.

''Please, Michael. I really want to know, and I can't fix anything if I don't know what the problem is.''

Michael finally began, and the words poured out. ''She said it was something *you* did and it wasn't because of me. And after school when we were waiting for the bus Jimmy said you didn't want her here, either. So I punched him, again.''

He rubbed his eye with a knuckle, apparently reminded of his own battle scars. ''But it was true, 'cause I heard you guys arguing, and that's when she went away.''

''Okay, let's back up a minute. Why would Jimmy say something like that? How would he know anything without talking to me?''

''He said you signed a paper for his dad to keep her and those bad kids away from our neighborhood.''

Ho, boy. Cam released another exasperated sigh and sank back into the beanbag. Michael slid off his lap to stand beside him, eyes shiny with tears.

''It's not true, is it, Dad? They said she was bad and she wanted to bring bad people here. They said all the other parents signed a paper to keep her away and you signed it, too. That's not true, is it?''

Cam's hopes sank. Why was everything so damn complicated? Didn't people ever just fall in love, marry and live happy, straightforward lives? ''I never signed a paper to keep Nicole away. I never signed a paper at all. But I would have if I truly believed it might protect you.'' Damn. That was the truth. He'd do just about anything to protect those he loved. Was that wrong? He honestly didn't know.

Michael looked confused. ''But aren't you mad 'cause I got in fights? Are you gonna send me away?''

''Send you away? Don't be ridiculous! Absolutely nothing you do would make me send you away. We're family and you're stuck with me, kid. Like it or not.''

If he thought his reassurance would make Michael happy, he was wrong. The boy's eyes widened with doubt. ''But Uncle Jack and Uncle Rans are family, and you don't see them anymore or even talk to them 'cause you're mad at them.''

Michael's words slammed into him. For the first time, Cam realized the inherent truth in the old adage, *actions speak louder than words.* Michael was a little boy caught in the middle of things he couldn't possibly understand. All the child knew was that Nicole, the only real mother figure he'd ever had, was gone, and he thought his own father was to blame. And he thought his father would send him away, just like he'd disowned his family when he got mad at them.

In light of that, the other problems seemed minor. He was faced again with the same issues he'd dealt with all his life. The same things kids everywhere deal with. He'd been stupid to think he could prevent any of it. Moving away hadn't solved a thing. All he'd succeeded in doing was isolating the two of them from friends and family.

How ironic. He'd used the pretext of protecting Michael to run away from his family and his own problems. And now it was all coming back to haunt him. Cam reached over and gave his son a hug.

''Okay, I can see how you'd think that. But with adults, sometimes things get really complicated. I might be mad at your uncles but I still care about them.'' He realized

the truth as he said it. "And they still care about me. A
for you, all I can say is you're my son, Michael, and n
matter how mad I get, I'll never send you away. And I'
not mad at you for fighting, either. I hope you punche
him a good one."

Michael's eyes lit and a crooked smile formed. "I did
I punched him really, really hard. I bet he's got a big o
shiner."

Cam's chest filled with love, and his mind raced for
solution. Finally he said, "I don't want you to worry any
more. I'm going to take care of things. I want Nicole t
be with us as much as you do, and I'll just have to figur
out a way so she is."

He hugged Michael again. He didn't know how, o
even *if,* he could set things right, but he'd be damned i
he'd leave things hanging the way he did before. They'
already wasted ten years. Ten years he and Nicole coul
have been together.

He'd let it all go because of his damned pride. Becaus
he wouldn't give in to anyone, because he couldn't brin
himself to ask, because he couldn't, *wouldn't,* let peopl
think they'd got the best of him.

And what had it gotten him?

He peered deep into Michael's eyes. "You up for help
ing me?"

"You mean it, Dad?" Michael's voice rang with ex
citement. "Can you get her to come back? Can you marr
her and get me a mom?"

"No guarantees, champ. But between the two of us, w
can give it our best shot. How's that sound?"

Michael's whoop of glee and a high five between the
sealed their pact.

ON MONDAY, Nicole was sitting at her desk after schoo
deep in thought, when the phone rang. Kara, the admin

istrative assistant, said, "You have a message to call a Mrs. Nelson."

Nicole pinched the bridge of her nose. "Did she say it was important?"

"No. She sounded a little frantic, but wouldn't tell me a thing."

"Okay. Thanks. I'll try to call her. *Maybe she's heard from Dylan. Maybe he's home.* She hoped so.

Hanging up, she looked for the number and called. No answer. Waiting, Nicole ran through the events leading up to Dylan's disappearance, just as she'd done so many times before. No matter what she thought of, some things didn't gel. She tried to remember the details from the night of the assault, tried to remember everything that had happened from the first incident to the last.

If the person who assaulted her was the same person who'd left the note in the drawer, and he'd come back to leave another message, he might've been in the room when she arrived. It was possible she'd frightened him, and fearing recognition, he'd attacked her.

Since no one knew she was going to be there, that was logical. It was also what the police had concluded as the most likely scenario. Which went along with the fact that Risa had seen the man place her carefully on the concrete instead of dropping her. That implied thought of some kind.

Too bizarre. Nothing about this whole debacle made any sense. But who set the fire? She couldn't even hazard a guess. It could've been the same person who'd vandalized the place—or even someone else, who wanted the police to think it was the same person.

Thank goodness Roy had been supportive after the fire

and had made space in the main building for the A.R. program to finish out the year.

She tried Mrs. Nelson's number. Still no answer. She glanced at her watch. It was nearly five. Okay, new plan. She'd go home, and call from there.

Risa met Nicole at her door the minute she arrived and handed over some mail that had been mistakenly put into her box. While Nicole searched her backpack for the keys, Risa said she had something to tell her but didn't have time right then. If Nicole planned to stay up for a while, she'd pop in later.

"Okay, I'm gone," Risa said. "Got an appointment."

Nicole said goodbye, went in and set down her pack, then tucked the mail under her arm while she locked the door. As she walked into the living room, she glanced at the letters. One was a white envelope with her name and address written in what looked like chicken scratches—and no return address. She immediately got a queasy feeling.

Refusing to give in to fear, she tore open the envelope. It was from Mrs. Nelson. *Thank you for everything you've done for us. We're leaving. I don't see any other way. I won't let them put him in jail again. No matter what. I'm sorry your time was wasted on us.*

What a strange note. And the fact that she'd written the letter, mailed it and then called today told Nicole she was desperate. But interestingly, the note implied that Mrs. Nelson knew where Dylan was. Why else would she worry that he'd go to jail again? Nicole needed to set her straight. Without evidence the police couldn't arrest him.

Nicole flipped through her address book for the number and punched it in. Five rings and no answer. She tried again and again, and finally, she heard a click.

"Mrs. Nelson, it's Nicole Weston." A commotion on

the other end muffled the woman's response. "I'm sorry. I didn't hear what you said."

"I'm not going to let them put him in jail."

"Is Dylan there with you?"

More commotion—and banging—loud enough for Nicole to hear over the phone. "What's going on?" Another loud bang, then a thud, as if the phone had been dropped. More voices. Shouting. More banging.

"Go away! I have a gun."

"Mrs. Nelson!" Nicole yelled into the receiver. To no avail. Nicole hung up, then flew out the door, passing Risa as she ran to her car.

"What's going on?" Risa asked. "Want me to come with you? My appointment just canceled."

"C'mon, get in. I'll tell you on the way."

Risa followed, no questions asked, and slid into the front seat next to Nicole. "Where are we going?"

"Mrs. Nelson's." Nicole shoved the key into the ignition, started the car and gunned to the exit. When traffic cleared, she peeled out, tires screaming. "Dylan must be there with her, that's all I can figure. I heard a lot of commotion and I heard her say she has a gun."

"You gotta be kidding! A helpless little old lady like her has a gun? I can't imagine."

"She's not a helpless old lady. Okay, old maybe, but she's very capable—and determined." Feeling helpless herself, Nicole shook her head. "Something's going on. That note was ominous. Like a 'goodbye forever' kind of thing. I don't like the sound of it at all, and I've got to help if I can. I just hope it isn't too late."

Turning the corner of Mrs. Nelson's street, they found a throng of people blocking the way. Nicole parked the car, they both got out and hurried, shoulder to shoulder, toward the house.

A squad car was parked across the street and Nicole could see two officers sitting inside the vehicle. A small circle of people stood behind, watching them.

Nicole stopped briefly to ask one of the bystanders what was happening. ''Some woman's in there,'' a thick-necked teen in a black T-shirt said. ''The police want to take her kid out, but she says he ain't going nowhere.''

Nicole pushed forward and Risa followed. ''You're gonna get us both killed, Nicole! C'mon, this is *not* one of your better ideas. It's getting dark and I don't like being here and you can't do anything, anyway.''

Reaching the squad car, Nicole recognized the officer in the driver's seat. ''Detective Arnette,'' she said. ''What's going on?''

''We have a situation, Ms. Weston.'' He glanced at Risa and smiled. ''It's best if both you and Ms. Beaumont stay back behind us.''

''I'm a good friend of Mrs. Nelson's. Maybe I can help?''

''Mrs. Nelson, her nephew and son are inside. She's refused to let us talk to either her nephew or her son and says she's armed.''

Nicole felt a moment of fresh panic. Mrs. Nelson had sounded distraught fifteen minutes ago on the phone, but she'd never imagined something like this.

During the drive over, a million thoughts had raced through Nicole's head. The woman was sick, she was worried about what would happen to her son when she was gone, she wanted desperately to help Dylan, because Dylan had promised to take care of her son, and if Dylan went to jail, there would be no one to see to Roland's care.

''What's she done?''

''Nothing yet. And we want to keep it that way.''

"But why are you still here if she's done nothing?"

"We're waiting on a search warrant so we can go in. ɔr your own safety, you need to move back now."

Oh, God. If they went in… "I—I don't understand. If ɹe's done nothing, why would you need to go in?"

Arnette looked at Risa and back to Nicole. He glanced his partner, who was on the phone. Arnette spoke softly. We believe there's evidence inside and we want to talk her nephew about it."

"I think I can help," Nicole persisted. "I *know* Mrs. elson. In fact, I just spoke with her and I think she'd sten to me. I don't believe she has a gun. Did you see ?"

Arnette shook his head. The other officer hung up the hone and said, "It'll be a while on the warrant and Kelso an't get through. She's not picking up."

"She'll talk to me. I know she will. Can you tell her rough your microphone that *I'm* going to call her on the hone?"

Arnette looked at her as if she were crazy.

"If you ask and she doesn't respond, you've lost nothıg. And if she hasn't committed any crime, I don't think ou can keep me from talking to her, can you?"

He frowned and raised the microphone. "Mrs. Nelson, have a Ms. Nicole Weston out here, and she'd like to lk to you. She's going to call you on the phone and vould like you to pick up." He reached for his cell phone, ut Nicole shook her head.

"Thanks, I have my own." Turning her back on him, ícole quickly pulled out her cell and punched the redial utton, since Mrs. Nelson's number was the last one she'd alled, back at the school. Thankful when she heard the lick—and before she even heard a voice on the other

end—Nicole said, "Mrs. Nelson! Please don't do an
thing. I can help you."

"I know what I need to do," the woman said flatly

"Can I come in? Please? Just to talk, and then I'll lea
if you want me to. Please? I really think I can help a
then the police might go away."

Silence. Then, "Okay."

Nicole looked at Arnette. "She says it's okay for
to come in." She didn't wait for a response, but dart
across the street, calling to Risa as she did, "I'll be back

She heard the officers protest behind her, but kept
running and just as she reached the house, the do
creaked open.

Nicole slipped inside. It was midnight-dark except
a tiny puddle of light leaking under the front door fro
the streetlamps outside. As her eyes adjusted to the di
ness, she saw Mrs. Nelson's silhouette, her back agai
the frame of the front window.

When the woman drew the shade aside to peer o
more light seeped in around the edges. "I'm not going
let them take him away." Mrs. Nelson's voice was ca
and even, not the least bit quavery as it had been wh
they'd talked earlier.

The telephone rang.

Okay. She was inside. Now what? Nicole scanned t
room, and Mrs. Nelson answered her unspoken questio
"He's in the bedroom with Roland."

The phone continued to ring. "Can you answer it on
and tell them I'm okay and that we're talking? Or let
do it?"

Slowly, Mrs. Nelson put the phone to her ear. "I'
talking with Ms. Weston. She's fine. Now leave
alone."

She hung up and immediately the phone started rin

g again—until the older woman yanked the cord from e wall.

Nicole's thoughts raced as fast as the adrenaline cours-g through her veins. What could she say? What *should* ie say? What would make Mrs. Nelson let the police at ast talk to Dylan? Arnette said they only wanted to talk him, and if the police had to force their way in, things ould only get worse. Much worse.

''Mrs. Nelson. We know Dylan hasn't done anything, why are you hiding him? Aren't you making more ouble for him by doing this?''

The older woman reached forward for the shade pull, id the canvas snapped upward. Suddenly floodlights lared through the lace-curtained window.

Mrs. Nelson seemed unaware of the painfully bright ghts—unaware or uncaring. ''Dylan's always had trou-le. Just like Roland. It never mattered what I did, Roland lways had trouble.'' Her tone was defeated, resigned.

How many times had *she* felt the same way—that noth-ig she could do would ever change things? Mrs. Nelson 'as terminally ill, she had a son who needed care, and a ephew who'd help her if he had the chance.

And he *would* have a chance if he had the right people n his side. But could she convince Mrs. Nelson of that? 'icole was afraid the woman couldn't take any more, that ie wanted to end their problems, once and for all. Her wn, Roland's and Dylan's.

''I can help,'' she said to the woman. ''But I can't do nything unless you're willing to help me.'' The words imbled out fast.

''They put Roland in jail before when it wasn't his ault. He only did what those other boys told him to do nd they kept him a long time before they found out he idn't belong there. No one cared about him in that jail.

No one cared that he was beat up and attacked by th
other men.'' She shook her fist. ''I'll be damned if I
that happen to him again.''

Good grief! All this time she'd thought Mrs. Nels
was talking about Dylan, not Roland. ''Dylan is the o
they want to see, Mrs. Nelson. And he can clear eve
thing up very quickly.''

In the glaring light, she saw Mrs. Nelson reach tow
a small table and pick up what appeared to be a g
Nicole gasped when the older woman raised it to the w
dow.

''I told them I had a gun,'' she said quietly.

Fear spurted through Nicole. Fear for them all.

''Once the police go away, Dylan will be able
leave,'' Mrs. Nelson said.

''And Roland? If the police take you in because of th
what'll happen to him?''

''No one's going to take me or Roland anywhere.''

''Mrs. Nelson, *please* let me help you. I know the le
system.'' She realized that if she didn't convince t
woman to give up right away, the police might do so
thing unnecessary once they got their search warrant.
they did, Mrs. Nelson might very well carry out her thre

''The police only want to *question* Dylan,'' she s
again. ''No one has any evidence that he's done anythi
wrong.''

''That's what they said before about Roland.'' M
Nelson folded her arms over her chest, the gun s
clenched in one hand.

''It won't happen again. I know a good attorney. Som
one who helped me with my mother.''

''Dylan's been guilty from the day that school was va
dalized. He's been tried and convicted in all their min
Now someone says they saw him at the fire.''

"Who told you that?" Nicole asked, stalling for time.

"The officer who came to the door."

"Did he tell you *who* said it? Who actually saw Dylan t the scene of the fire?" Cam was right; eyewitness tesmony was a damning indictment. For the first time, she ad a flash of doubt. God, she hoped she hadn't been vrong about Dylan.

"He didn't say. But it's a flat-out lie."

Nicole's other questions loomed large. Where had Dyan been all this time? Why did he disappear in the first lace?

"Dylan didn't want to make trouble for me and Roand," Mrs. Nelson said, although Nicole hadn't yet sked. "He knew how upset Roland gets about the police nd any talk about jail."

"When did he return?"

She saw the silver head bobble slightly, the tremors vident again. "Two days ago. I wouldn't let him go novhere then, because I knew they'd arrest him. When the olice came today, I wouldn't let them in."

"How did they find out he was here?"

"I don't know. Someone told them, I guess." She lifted he gun upward, waving it in the air. "They know I have his."

Who knew Dylan was there? And where did Mrs. Nelon get the gun? Nicole was almost afraid to ask, hoping t wasn't Dylan's. "Where did you get it?"

"I bought it. For protection. In this neighborhood veryone needs protection. Now I need to protect my oys." She paused, and Nicole could see the rigid deterination on her face.

She'd seen that expression before. On her own mother's ace. *Fight or flight,* she remembered from a psychology

class. Mrs. Nelson had the look of a mother ready to pr
tect her offspring in whatever way she could.

"Please put down the gun, Mrs. Nelson. I truly think
can help Dylan. Roland, too."

The old woman lifted her chin, eyes narrowin
"How?"

"For one, I can get Dylan a good attorney." Her co
lege friend Ainsley Jennings had handled things when h
mom was picked up by the police, and even if Ainsle
couldn't help, she'd know other attorneys who did p
bono work.

After all this, she suspected both Dylan and Mrs. Ne
son might need a good attorney. But she didn't want
confuse the issue or add to the problems at hand.

"I've worked with many people to get help for m
mother, who needs constant supervision and medical car
and I know I can help you find a good home for Rolan
when he needs it, as he eventually will. Roland deserv
a chance, Mrs. Nelson. Both boys do, and I'll help i
whatever way I can. But I'll need *your* help, too. Pleas
Mrs. Nelson, for their sake."

The woman appeared to be thinking about it, weighin
her choices. "Dylan will have a chance this way," Nico
pressed. "If he runs, he'll have no chance whatsoeve
He'll spend the rest of his life running. Or in jail. H
won't be able to get a good job, he won't have a futu
at all. He's such a bright boy with so much potential, an
he deserves a chance to achieve it. Don't you think *h*
should be the one to decide?"

A long moment passed before Mrs. Nelson laid the gu
on the table. Nicole didn't move a muscle, still afraid sh
might cause her to do something rash. She spoke softl
"If Dylan has a good attorney when the police questio
him, it might not go any further. The attorney will re

esent him and advise him. And he'll probably be allowed
o go back home right away.''

Nicole tried to think of other arguments that might convince the woman to believe Dylan would be safe if he gave himself up. ''If Dylan told the police where he was during the fire, it would help immensely.''

''Dylan won't tell you where he was. I know that. Maybe his friend, the boy who dropped him off, will tell you.''

''Who dropped him off?''

''That boy with the white car. I don't know his name.''

She wasn't talking about Aaron, Justin or Mitchell. None had cars that she knew of. If she could find out who it was, she might learn where he'd been staying; if he'd been with this other person when the fire occurred, he'd be in the clear.

''I'd like to talk with Dylan. If he says no, I'll leave.''

After a moment's thought, Mrs. Nelson signaled her agreement with a wave of her hand. ''Go into the bedroom. I don't want Roland out here where he can see what's going on. If Dylan leaves, Roland will follow. He'll start carrying on something awful if he sees the police.''

A huge sigh of relief escaped Nicole's lungs. She didn't know if talking to Dylan would even work, but she had to try. She'd still have to convince the boy that surrendering to the police was the right thing to do.

Mrs. Nelson pointed toward the archway and to the left, still maintaining her vigil at the window. ''Please try not to scare Roland. Okay? Tell him you're here to help him and Dylan.''

Don't scare her. It's okay, Mommy. They're here to help you. She hoped she could do a better job this time.

As Nicole was about to step into the hall, a man's voice

boomed from outside. Red and white lights flashed. Sl
froze in her tracks.

"Ms. Weston, this is Detective Arnette. Please answ
me, Ms. Weston."

As she turned, Mrs. Nelson grabbed for the gun.

Nicole's adrenaline surged. She glanced around, to
stock of the situation and held on to her calm.

"Mrs. Nelson," she said quietly. "I need to tell the
I'm okay. If they think I'm in danger…well, they mig
do something that wouldn't be good for any of us. Som
thing that would for sure scare Roland."

Mrs. Nelson reached over, slid the window up a fe
inches with one hand, and motioned to Nicole. "C
ahead. Tell 'em you're okay."

Nicole walked slowly and carefully. Any quick moti
might lead either the police or Mrs. Nelson to mistake h
intentions. Standing opposite the woman on the other si
of the window, Nicole crouched to be heard through t
small opening.

"This is Nicole Weston. I'm fine. We just need a litt
more time," Nicole called back as best she could, h
vocal cords still not healed completely. "Soon." Sh
peered out the corner of the window but was blinded b
all the flashing lights.

"Five minutes, Ms. Weston. You've got five minutes.

Nicole faced Mrs. Nelson. "I'll be careful not to sca
Roland," she promised.

CHAPTER SEVENTEEN

CAM BARRELED THROUGH the crowd, fear knotting his gut. Risa had called in the middle of his workout and he'd dashed out the door, not sure what was going on except that Nicole was in trouble.

To make matters worse, he'd never been in this part of town before and had difficulty finding the place. When he did, he still wasn't sure where to go.

Risa had been vague, her message unclear because of static on the line. He saw her standing directly behind an officer who was holding a crowd at bay.

"Risa!" She turned, her eyes searching, and spotted him. She tugged on the officer's sleeve. The man listened, looked at Cam, and then gestured for the other officers to let him through.

"Where's Nicole?"

Risa pointed to the house. "She's in there trying to get her student and his aunt to come out. The old lady's got a gun."

Panic shot through him. "How in God's name did she get in there? Who let that happen?"

The officer told both of them to move back with the rest of the crowd.

"She went in before the SWAT team arrived. Nicole figured she could get them to come out, but then these guys showed up and all hell broke loose."

"What do they plan to do?" Cam asked, knowing Risa

didn't have an answer any more than he did. But watching the group of men in their black clothes surround the house, he knew things could go from bad to worse. And every second she was in that house, she was in danger. The reality of that sent a jolt of fear directly to his heart.

He swung around, fists clenched. He wanted to punch something, smash something, find some way to release the terror inside him and the anger at his inability to do anything but watch this nightmare unfold. Nicole's life was in jeopardy and he was totally impotent to help her.

As the time passed, minutes seemed like hours. They watched and waited. Others were watching and waiting, too—but it meant something different to them. They didn't know any of the people inside.

He did, and if anything happened to Nicole… Oh, Lord.

Their last confrontation flashed through his head, just as it had dozens of times since. Nicole's betrayed expression was indelibly etched in his mind and a swell of pain, greater than anything he'd felt before, lodged deep in his chest.

Risa chewed one piece of gum after another and finally sank down on a boulder near the boulevard. After what seemed an interminable time, Cam saw a TV crew arrive and noticed Arnette in animated discussion with two of the SWAT team officers. One of them lifted the microphone again.

"This is Officer Jensen. Ms. Weston, I understand you have a cell phone. Please call me at this number so I'll know you're okay." The officer rattled off the number and seconds later put a phone to his ear.

Cam beckoned to Risa and she came over. Standing at his shoulder, she whispered, "That Jensen guy is one of those experts. I heard them talking about tear gas."

Cam clenched and unclenched his fists, his helplessness

frightening, the waiting more awful than anything he'd ever experienced.

He stared at the door, willing Nicole out and into the safety of his arms. And with each second that passed, the tumult of fear inside him was magnified a thousandfold.

Then—as if his wish had been miraculously granted—he saw the door open slightly. Risa latched on to his arm. A hand clutching a piece of white fabric was thrust through the opening. Someone tossed out a gun.

Detective Arnette motioned his men back. "Okay, please come out, one by one, with your arms over your heads. It's just a precaution. We don't want anyone to get hurt."

AT THE POLICE STATION, each of them sat at a separate officer's desk. Nicole had told Mrs. Nelson, Dylan and Roland to say nothing until the attorney arrived. In order to get Roland to leave the house without panicking, they had to tell him they were playing a game.

She stared through the plate glass window watching Cam pace the hall like an anxious father-to-be. How did *he* get involved in this?

Seeing Risa come in, Nicole knew. Risa's eyes filled with relief when she saw Nicole. Detective Arnette allowed her inside the squad room. "God, Nicole, I was so *worried* with you in that house!" She threw her arms around Nicole and held her in a long hug.

The uncharacteristic physical display of emotions caught Nicole off guard. She'd been so intent on helping Mrs. Nelson, she hadn't considered that her friend might be worried about *her*.

"Cam's really upset, in case you didn't notice," Risa said. "Guess you figured out I called him, huh?"

Risa wrinkled her nose—her way of asking if she'd

done the right thing. ''I know you guys haven't been getting along so well, but I wouldn't have felt right if I didn't let him know. I mean, what if something awful had happened while you were in there, and—''

''It's okay, Risa. I'll talk to him. What about my car?''

''You took the keys, so it's still back there. This nice officer gave me a ride and he said he'd take me home, too.'' She glanced at Arnette. ''He said you'd have to make a statement or something.''

Nicole nodded. ''I'll see you later.'' Risa gave her another quick hug and then disappeared.

Nicole glanced at Dylan, surly and brooding as he sat at Arnette's gray metal desk. He didn't want to be here, and she knew he didn't trust that everything would work out. But he'd done as Nicole had asked so his aunt wouldn't get into further trouble or get hurt doing something stupid.

While still in the house, Nicole had contacted her friend, Ainsley Jennings, who was on her way. Ainsley was a good attorney and would do her best for them. Paying her, however, was another story.

As she waited for Ainsley, her eyes were drawn back to Cameron. She'd so wanted to rush into his arms, but knew it was a bad idea, the result of her own weakness and fear.

While they waited, another officer took Roland and Mrs. Nelson into a different room; Dylan was led off somewhere else. Arnette had allowed Roland to stay with his mother, and Mrs. Nelson was grateful for that.

Ainsley arrived soon after. She immediately questioned Nicole and then went to talk with Mrs. Nelson and with Dylan. A while later, Nicole took a break to go to the ladies' room, and when she returned, Ainsley and Cam were deep in conversation.

The lawyer had agreed to represent Mrs. Nelson, her son and Dylan, and with Ainsley at her side, Nicole went in and gave her own statement. After that, Ainsley said there was nothing to do except get the evidence they needed. She was adamant that Nicole should not be further involved.

"But what'll happen to them? Can they go home? What about bail? What if they need money?"

"Don't worry," the attorney assured Nicole as she guided her to the door. "Everything's taken care of, money included," she said nodding toward Cam. "Now go home and be good to yourself. You look awful."

Cam was paying Ainsley? What a generous gesture. But this wasn't his responsibility, and she hoped he wasn't doing it because of her. When he hurried toward her, Nicole suddenly found herself at a loss for words. She wanted more than anything to feel the comfort of his strong arms. Cam must've known; he immediately put an arm around her shoulders.

"Cam. I—I'll see that the money is reimbursed somehow."

"Like hell. That's my decision, not yours. Now c'mon, I'll drive you home." He walked her to the door.

Just before they reached it, a man, apparently a plainclothes detective, stopped them. "Excuse me. Can you please wait a minute?"

The man waved Arnette over and the two went off to one side to talk. When they were finished, Arnette walked back to Nicole and Cam, his expression grim. He held out a hand and on his palm lay a slender silver chain.

Nicole's fingers automatically went to her neck. "My chain?"

"Is it?" Officer Arnette looked disappointed, but Nicole didn't know why. She was grateful someone had found her necklace.

"Can you identify it?"

"Of course." Nicole lifted the delicate chain between two fingers and before she turned over the small silver circle attached to the fastener, she answered, "It'll say 'To Jenny.' That's my mother's name. My grandparents gave it to her, and she gave it to me on my tenth birthday. It means a lot to me. Who found it? And where?"

Officer Arnette hedged. Then he sighed and nodded toward the office, where Ainsley remained with Dylan. "He had it."

Nicole felt as if she'd been poleaxed. She curled her fingers around the necklace. "I—I don't understand."

Arnette squared his shoulders. "It doesn't look good." He put out a hand for the necklace. "We'll have to keep it for a while. It's material evidence."

Nicole clasped the silver chain tightly. It was obvious they thought Dylan's possession of the necklace was as good as a confession. But just because he had it didn't mean he was guilty of anything. She *knew* he wasn't the one who'd assaulted her. So how did he get it?

"I must've lost it when I was visiting Mrs. Nelson," she said.

"I'm sure his attorney will be talking with you about all of that," Arnette said. He gently removed the chain from Nicole's grasp, strode to where the other detective stood and handed over the necklace. After that, he came back and offered to have someone give Nicole a ride to her car.

"I'll do it," Cam said.

An overwhelming weariness numbed Nicole's senses. A weak "Thank you" was all she could manage.

They rode in silence until they neared Nicole's car. "I

know this isn't a good time,'' Cam murmured, ''but I'd like to talk, Nicole.''

''You're right,'' she said softly. ''It's not a good time.''

''Then I'll call later and we'll find a time. Okay?''

''Okay.''

''I WAS SO WORRIED, Mr. Colter.'' Maria was flushed, as if embarrassed by her own concern. ''It was on all the news, and everyone was so worried about Ms. Weston. I didn't say anything to young Michael or let him hear about it. I thought he might get too upset.''

''That's good. Thank you, Maria. Nicole's okay.'' His stomach roiled as he said the words. ''I was worried, too. But everything's under control now.''

He knew Maria was waiting for a better explanation, but he was incapable of providing one. There was too much he didn't know, didn't understand.

Only after knowing Nicole was okay had he allowed himself to feel angry at her. Risa hadn't given any details, except that Mrs. Nelson had holed up in her house with her son and nephew and Nicole was foolish enough to go over and somehow get in to talk to them.

Granted, she'd been successful, but what if Mrs. Nelson had lost it, or the police had?

Every time he thought about it, an indescribable combination of fear and anger tore through him. Dammit! Nicole consistently put everyone ahead of herself, never considering what might happen to her, or how the people who cared about her would feel if something did.

He yanked his damp sweatshirt over his head, headed into the half bath near the kitchen and splashed cold water on his face. Back in the kitchen, he leaned against the island and slammed a fist on the countertop.

He couldn't get rid of the...the what? The panic? Terror? Pain? Loss? Grief? He'd felt every one of those emotions when he'd realized he could lose her—really lose her.

Maria came in, filled a copper teakettle with water, flipped on a stove burner and then slid a large earthenware mug in front of him.

"I'll need more than tea to be able to sleep tonight, Maria."

The older woman smiled and continued with her task. She wiped a spot from the stove top with a corner of her apron, her eyes fixed on the teapot as she waited for the water to boil. "Your brother called," she told him. "He saw the story on the news about Ms. Weston and he was worried, too. He asked that you call him back as soon as you can."

Cam looked at the clock.

"He said it didn't matter what time it was."

"Thanks. I will in a bit." He didn't feel like talking or explaining anything right now. Yet he knew he should.

Okay. Might as well do it. He reached for the cordless phone and punched in the number. No answer. He got up and grabbed a beer, then wandered into the living room. Seeing movement outside, he stopped in front of the window and saw Bentworth and his son returning home.

The man cast a suspicious glance around his property before lowering the garage door; his son did the same. The boy would turn out just like his father, Cam mused, remembering what Nicole had asked him.

He stared outside long after Bentworth had shut the door. Because suddenly he knew what Nicole had meant when she asked if he really thought this was the better place to raise his son.

The relationship Cam had with Michael was no different from the one between Bentworth and his son. Both men would pass on their prejudices to their children. And by taking Michael away from the family, by protecting Michael from his own bad experiences, he was telling his son that when things got tough, it was okay to run. Avoid your problems at all costs.

He shifted from one foot to the other. Ironically, he'd done exactly what he'd accused Nicole of doing. He'd run away.

All he'd wanted was a fresh start somewhere people didn't know his background, somewhere Michael wouldn't be stigmatized because of his father's reputation or heritage.

His stomach knotted as he remembered the taunts and name-calling. But was that *really* it? Had he really left to protect Michael? Or was he, as Nicole had suggested, punishing his brothers and using Michael as his excuse?

He sank to the couch and punched the pillow in self-disgust. He wasn't protecting Michael; he was protecting himself.

Even family wasn't as important to him as his damnable pride. How the hell could Nicole expect him to do anything different in *their* relationship if things got tough between them? How could Michael?

He wiped a hand over his face and closed his eyes. How far he'd come from what he really wanted.

And there was only one person with the power to change that.

He spent some time making a plan and then, with an urgency he hadn't felt before, went to the phone and punched the redial button. Harry was his link to the family, and more than anything, he needed to reconnect—whether Nicole was in his life or not.

"Harry, what's happening?"

"Cam?" Harry sounded half-asleep.

"I know it's late, but Maria said you wanted me to call no matter what time it was."

"Yeah, we were real worried. Is Nicole okay? You okay?"

"Nicole's fine," he assured Harry. They exchanged quick pleasantries, then Cam launched into the story, telling Harry everything that had happened.

He started at the beginning, describing his reluctance to get involved with Nicole again, Nicole's reason for breaking it off, his need to protect Michael and Nicole after the attack—and his stupidity.

When he finished, he felt as if a massive weight had been removed from his shoulders. He'd tried so hard to control the outcome of everything in his life that he hadn't recognized the burden he'd been carrying. He told Harry about his tentative plans, for which he needed Harry's advice and help.

At first, Harry was speechless, then he was completely enthusiastic, ready to go the distance, just as he'd been when Cam had needed him after their mother's death. Cam realized right then that he'd deprived *all* his brothers of their dreams, including Harry. Dreams of carrying on their father's legacy.

When they finished talking, Cam made phone calls to his attorney and his accountant. He had other people to talk to, but he wanted to do that in person. He just hoped Jack and Ransom weren't going to be as bullheaded as he'd been.

After his last call, he was wide-awake and exhilarated. He'd taken positive steps toward changing the things he could. The others, he'd have to continue to pursue—or learn to let go, however difficult it might be.

That included his relationship with Nicole. But first he

resolved to do something he hadn't had the courage to do before....

ON FRIDAY AFTERNOON, even though Nicole hadn't planned on it, she ended up in front of Mrs. Nelson's house, debating whether or not to knock. Her determination to help won out over her good judgment. She wanted to let Mrs. Nelson know she'd be there for her and would assist her in securing a future placement for Roland if that turned out to be necessary.

She couldn't stop thinking about Dylan. She still felt there was something missing in the equation. Determined to find out what it was, she knocked a couple of times and waited. The weathered door creaked open just enough so she could see Mrs. Nelson on the other side.

"It's Nicole, Mrs. Nelson."

"What is it?" The woman's voice wavered.

"I came by to see if I can do anything. May I come in for a minute?"

Chains rustled across the door before it opened. Mrs. Nelson blocked Nicole's entry. "Ms. Jennings said I shouldn't talk to anyone but her."

"It's okay," Nicole said. "I don't want to talk about the case, only about how I can help you and Roland once all this is over."

The woman let Nicole in, then shuffled toward the kitchen, her shoulders hunched forward, her slippers dusting the floor as she went.

"Might not be any need for anyone's help when it's over," she said, pulling out a chair.

Nicole had been happy to hear from Ainsley that Mrs. Nelson had been released and that Roland had gone home with her. Apparently the police, on a tip that Dylan was at his aunt's house, had gone out to talk with him. Mrs.

Nelson had refused to let them in and told them she ha
a gun. But since she had a license for the gun and hadn'
actually threatened anyone, she hadn't broken the law an
couldn't be held.

Dylan, unfortunately, had been arrested for violating hi
probation and would remain in detention pending a hear
ing. Dylan had said he'd found the necklace outside hi
aunt's house, and since the police had no proof otherwise
Ainsley didn't think it would go any further.

He denied being at the school when the fire broke ou
and said the person who'd identified him was a liar
Ainsley believed the police were holding Dylan whil
they tried to get other evidence against him—and mayb
persuade the person who claimed he'd seen Dylan at th
fire to positively identify him.

Nicole sat beside Mrs. Nelson at the table. After school
she'd changed into a pair of khaki shorts, tank top an
sandals because of the heat, and her bare legs stuck in
stantly to the vinyl chair. All Mrs. Nelson had in her hom
was an old swamp cooler, the kind that circulated wate
to cool the air and was used before air-conditioning be
came common.

"I'm sorry about the way things turned out. I know
there's an explanation, and you've got an excellent attor
ney who'll do the best she can for Dylan."

The older woman leaned forward. "I tried to do every
thing right with Roland, but nothing worked. Now I don'
know what to do."

"That's why I came over. I told you before that I'
help you find a placement for Roland when he needs i
and I want you to know I still intend to do that."

Mrs. Nelson reached out a trembling hand and laid i
over Nicole's. "Thank you, Ms. Weston. You're a ver

thoughtful and caring person. Your mother must be very proud of you.''

Nicole managed a smile. Barely.

''Come with me,'' Mrs. Nelson said as she pushed to her feet.

Nicole followed the woman into the same bedroom where she'd met with Dylan.

Roland was sitting in a chair staring at the television and when Mrs. Nelson shut off the set, he said, ''I want to watch the cartoons.''

''I'll turn it on again after you tell this nice lady why Dylan took your silver necklace.''

His necklace?

Roland's eyes grew wide. ''Dylan said I had to give it back. I did a bad thing. He said I hurt the lady and that was bad. I didn't mean to, but when I tried to help her, she screamed and hurt my ears. I didn't want Dylan to get mad at me.''

Mrs. Nelson smiled, flicked on the television and said, ''Okay. Now you can go back to your cartoons, sweetheart.''

At the mention of the necklace, Nicole had found herself speechless. She still couldn't believe what she'd heard. She followed Mrs. Nelson into the kitchen again, her mind spinning.

''Dylan's protecting Roland,'' Mrs. Nelson said. ''He won't say anything because he knows they could put Roland away, and he knows how scared Roland is of the police and of being locked up.''

Nicole shook her head. ''I'm sorry, but I'm really confused. Was Roland saying that *he* was in my classroom and he was the one who...who hurt me? And that he took the necklace?''

Mrs. Nelson nodded.

"But *how?* How did he get there? How did he get in?"

"I think you better talk to the lawyer lady about all that. I just wanted you to know it wasn't Dylan, because you always helped him and you're so nice to us."

She smiled at the woman's thoughtfulness. "I appreciate that and, for what it's worth, I never believed for a second that Dylan was involved in anything, even if he had the necklace. I *would* like to talk with Ms. Jennings, but I don't think she'll talk to me about the case unless you tell her it's okay. Can you do that?"

Mrs. Nelson nodded.

An hour and a half later, Nicole left Ainsley's office and drove home. Her friend was taking care of the legal end of Dylan's case and there was nothing more for Nicole to do.

Risa was waiting for her when she arrived home, and they went into Nicole's condo together.

"So what happened? You said you had good news."

"Well, a little good and some not so good. I went to Mrs. Nelson's to see what I could do to help her arrange some kind of care for Roland. That's when Mrs. Nelson told me Roland was the one who had my necklace, not Dylan."

Risa's eyes widened as they walked into the kitchen.

"Yeah. Weird, huh? According to Ainsley, Dylan had gone to the school with a camera to watch for vandals and catch them in the act. He knew the police suspected him and thought that was the only way he could prove it *wasn't* him. Roland decided to follow Dylan, who then decided it would be quicker to take his cousin along than to bring him back home. When they reached the school, Dylan found the door ajar and went in. Roland did, too. The lights were out, and it was obvious someone had been in the building and maybe still was. Dylan parked Roland n a spot near the door, told him not to make a sound, and then he went off to check.''

Nicole stopped for a breath and hurried to the fridge, pulling out two bottles of mineral water. She gave one to Risa and they sat down at the kitchen table.

''So then what?''

''That's when I came in, and although I left the door ajar, a draft slammed it shut. Roland was watching, noticed I couldn't get the door open and came to help. But since Dylan had told him to be very quiet, that's what he was trying to do. He reached in front of me to open the door and that's when I screamed. He got scared, grabbed me and covered my mouth because he didn't want Dylan to think he'd disobeyed. Then because he knew I wanted to leave, he opened the door and took me outside.''

Risa teetered on the edge of her seat and grabbed her water bottle for a long swig.

''When Dylan heard the scream, he came running and by then Roland was outside and I'd passed out. He told Roland to put me down. That's when you came around and started screaming, too.''

''This is too bizarre.''

''And that's not all.'' Nicole finished her water. ''It was dark. Dylan didn't know it was me, and seeing you, he figured you'd call for help. He also knew Roland would freak if he saw the police. Since Dylan was standing behind Roland and you hadn't seen him, he whisked his cousin off in the other direction, where they ran into a kid Dylan knew. The friend gave them a ride and when they dropped Roland off, Dylan learned the police were looking for him again. That's when he decided to leave, because if he wasn't there, he wouldn't have to tell the police what his cousin had done and Roland wouldn't get into trouble.''

Risa shook her head and held up a hand. "Hold it. I'r
lost. Why would Roland get in trouble if it was all
mishap?"

"Roland was arrested before for something he wa
goaded into doing by some kids, and because he was a
adult, and because he was scared and swung at the officer
who tried to arrest him, the police held him in jail—unti
they discovered he had a disability, or rather, diminishe
capacity. He wasn't incarcerated for long, but long enoug
to be attacked and beaten up."

"That's horrible! Wouldn't they send a person wit
problems like his somewhere other than jail?"

"Unfortunately not. It happens all the time because th
police can't always tell the person has a problem. Believ
me, I know all about that."

"Your mother?"

Nicole nodded. "And in Roland's case, he wouldn'
talk to them because he was too scared, and the polic
didn't know a thing about him until his mother reporte
him missing. Dylan didn't know what might happen t
Roland—just that he couldn't handle jail again, couldn'
even handle police questioning. And since his aunt wa
sick, he didn't want to burden her with more bad news
So he took the necklace from Roland and told him not t
say a word to anyone. Dylan figured as long as he staye
away, he wouldn't have to lie to the police and no on
would know Roland was involved. He also hoped the po
lice would find the real vandals, and when they did, he'
be in the clear."

"So, the attack wasn't really an attack, after all, an
Dylan *wasn't* involved."

"Right. And I can't tell you how relieved I was to hea
that. Now you can quit worrying about me."

"Still doesn't explain the stuff with your classroom, th

notes and the fire. Could Dylan have been involved in any of those?''

''Of course not! Ainsley has a theory that all the incidents were the work of one party and plans to follow up on it with the police, but she wouldn't tell me any more.''

''I bet the perp has something against the school.''

Nicole narrowed her gaze at Risa. ''Perp? Have you been reading mystery novels? I've never known you to have any interest in that kind of thing.''

''Yeah.'' Risa grinned. ''I've been doing a little reading. One of my customers is in the law enforcement field and I need to keep up, you know. Make small talk and all that.''

Risa's guilty expression gave her away. ''Really? You sure it's not a little more than just keeping up?''

Her friend shrugged. ''Well, yeah. Maybe. But it's too soon to tell.''

With a smile she couldn't hide, Nicole said, ''Good. I've been a little worried about you.''

''Oh, no, you don't! You worry about all those other people. I don't want *anyone* worrying about me.''

Laughing, Nicole acquiesced, ''Okay. I won't worry about you and vice versa. Okay?''

''We're cool.'' Risa gave her a thumbs-up.

''Back on topic,'' Nicole went on, ''it makes sense that the vandalism and notes were the work of the same person. It's logical to think the fire was, too, and it seems obvious the acts were carried out by someone who has a grudge against the school. Why else destroy school property?''

''And the notes to you? The one delivered to your house?''

''Something to throw the police off? Make it look like

one of my students? I don't know. But I'd barely been at the school a week when it happened."

"Except for the A.R. class. You started with that earlier."

"Right. I did." Nicole thought about Dennis Caruso, the angry kid who'd left her class almost before it had begun. He had something against the school. She also remembered the community meeting in Cam's neighborhood. It wasn't the first time she'd thought some of those people might be that vindictive. Bentworth, Mrs. Sipowitz, a few others. But she'd been careful not to ascribe motives based on past behavior, because that was exactly what *they'd* done when they blamed her students. She wasn't going to turn into one of *them.*

Risa said, "And everyone thought the attack was part of it."

"But—" Nicole stopped, thinking as she spoke. "We know differently. However, the perp—" she grinned at Risa "—wouldn't know that we know." As if a light had gone off in her head, she remembered something her friend had said early on. *Look near, not far.* It made sense. It made the utmost sense.

"And you know what else?" Nicole's body literally hummed with excitement.

Risa frowned. "I'm not sure I want to hear this."

"I think I've figured out who the guilty party might be, and since *he* doesn't know what *we* know, maybe I can talk to him, get him to slip up and—"

"Oh-h, no. Stop right there." Risa raised her hand in a time-out signal. "If you've figured all this out, don't you think the police can, too? Don't you think they've questioned everyone even remotely connected with the school?"

Nicole pushed away from the table. "I'm aware of all

hat. I'm also aware that with Dylan in custody, they won't look any farther."

For once, Risa didn't have a ready answer. Finally she said, "They have to follow procedure."

"I know they do. But I don't."

CHAPTER EIGHTEEN

ON MONDAY AFTER SCHOOL, Nicole kept watch till all staff had gone and then went to the office and rifled through the files. A–B–C. Ah, there it was. Caruso. Dennis Caruso's little brother attended Barton. She scribbled the address and phone number on a piece of paper and shoved it in the pocket of her tan linen blazer.

"What're you doing there?" a harsh male voice boomed from behind her.

Nicole's nerves shattered. She swung around, her heart pounding in her throat. "Oh—" Relief filled her when she saw it was just the janitor. "Bob! Good grief, you scared the daylights out of me."

He scowled. "You're not supposed to be in here, are you?"

"It's okay. I just had to get some information on one of my students."

"You better watch out for those boys. You could get hurt."

Where had she heard that before? "Thanks for your concern, Bob, but I know them well. They wouldn't hurt anyone."

"The police don't think so."

"Really?" She moved away from the file cabinet and looked at him. "And what do you know about that?"

He shrugged, and she noticed how unkempt he was.

She hadn't paid that much attention before, but she saw he definitely needed a bath.

"The police, they talked to me," he said. "I told them what I know. I'm here a lot, and I see things."

And maybe he'd seen someone before or after the vandalism, before or after the fire. If so, she hadn't heard anything about it.

"I'm sure you do. You're here quite a bit, aren't you? You've worked here a long time, and I'll bet you know most of the kids who've gone through this place, too."

"Ten years, I've been around. Just like Mrs. Jessup, the teacher you took over for."

"Really. She was here that long, huh?"

"She was a good teacher. Treated me real nice."

"I'm sure she was. I'm sorry she's ill, even though that's why they hired me for the rest of the year."

Bob moved toward her and at the same time, Nicole took a step closer to the door. She smelled alcohol and she was getting an uncomfortable feeling from the man. But Bob had always seemed a decent person, and she shouldn't be having thoughts like that just because he was a little disheveled.

Still, he made her nervous and she'd never felt that way about him before.

She remembered the assault, how she'd pushed away her fears because she'd thought it was her imagination. But it hadn't been. It was real. Just like this felt real. She pulled in a breath.

"She wasn't sick," he muttered. "They made her leave. But she'll be back next year."

Odd. How could Roy offer Nicole a contract if Mrs. Jessup was coming back? And how did Bob know the teacher was coming back when Roy didn't? "That's nice. I'm glad to hear it."

He frowned and stepped toward her, and the closer he came, the stronger the scent of alcohol on his breath. "You're not going to teach here next year," he said. It wasn't a question.

Standing with a desk between them, she worked her way around to the other side, near the door. "No, I don't think I will. I don't really feel safe because of everything that's happened."

A grin lifted a corner of his thin lips. "Yeah, I don't think it's safe, either. I told the police that."

He told the police? Was Bob the one who'd placed Dylan at the scene? He was here more than anyone, here when no one else was, so it would follow that people might believe he'd seen someone if he said he had. And he carried keys for all the rooms, could go in and out at will when no one was around.

Could write things on desks or leave notes or… A sudden cold fear snatched her breath away. She didn't like where her thoughts were going, and worse, she wasn't sure if she could trust her instincts.

But she had to know. She squared her shoulders and said, "I'm so glad to hear that. So, did you see anyone the night of the fire? I bet if you can identify him, the police will pick him up and put him in jail. And since Mrs. Jessup's coming back, things will be normal around here again."

"That's right. You think you're pretty smart, don't you?"

Her mouth fell open. She gripped the back of the chair in front of her. "Excuse me? I don't know what you mea—"

"You think you've got it figured out, don't you? That I did it all to get Mrs. Jessup back here." His eyes narrowed. "And you're right."

She couldn't believe it...had never even suspected. "You did all that to scare me away? Or get even?"

"Both, I guess. But now, you and me, we've got a bigger problem." He took a step toward her.

She took a step back. "I—I won't say anything. And like I said, I'm leaving the school."

"That's might nice of you. But y'know, it doesn't jibe with what I heard. I told you I hear things, didn't I?" He lurched toward her.

She spun around, bolted for the door, and ran smack into someone standing there. Stumbling back, Cam caught her by the arms.

"Whoa, there. Where are you going in such a hurry, Nicole?" He held his position in the doorway and pulled out his cell phone.

She released her breath and slipped around to his side and under the protection of his arm. "I think we should leave."

Cam's eyes were pinned on Bob, who seemed frozen in place. "Not before the police get here."

CAM KNOCKED and waited for Nicole to answer her door. He'd gone to the school last night to talk to her and had come in on her conversation with Bob. After the police had arrested the janitor, they discovered he'd been the perpetrator of everything except the assault on Nicole. He'd wanted the other teacher back because he was in love with her and she'd been let go for what he believed was an invalid reason. In fact, she'd been dismissed because she'd neglected her job. Rather than firing her, the principal had let her take a leave of absence to find another job. When she wanted to come back instead of resigning, he'd told her no and Bob had taken things into his own hands.

Nicole had been happy to hear it wasn't Bentworth and his community, but she felt bad for concluding that it was Dennis Caruso. She'd vowed to help him if she could. She'd also told Cam what Roland had done and that Dylan had been covering for him.

When all of that was over, Nicole had agreed with Cam that they should talk, she and Cam, but not right then.

So here he was again, and this time he was going to do it. He wanted her to know exactly where he stood before he left town.

He loved her. But love alone wouldn't work. She had to trust him, too. A man couldn't live without trust; it was as simple as that.

"Hi," he said when she opened the door.

"Hi. C'mon in." They went to the couch together, and he sat down next to her. After a quiet moment, he forged ahead.

He took her hand in his and without preamble, said, "I love you, Nicole. I have since the beginning. I know this might not be the best time to tell you certain things, but I'm afraid if I don't do it now, I won't have another chance."

He cleared his throat. "You were right about me, right about everything, even when you said I was running away. I took that to heart, examined my life and made a few decisions. The most significant one is that Michael and I are moving back to the ranch as soon as school is out. I've got the house up for sale, I've hired a manager to run the Phoenix office and plan to come down a few times a week. I may sell it eventually, but I haven't decided yet. I still have lots of things to work out, but nothing insurmountable."

"You're leaving?"

He hoped the disappointment in her eyes was a positive sign. "I'm going to build a new house on the ranch."

"Cam, that's wonderful. But it isn't necessary for you to explain to me—"

"Yes, it is. It's completely necessary. Because I know now that my inability to open up was part of the reason our relationship didn't work ten years ago. I'd expected everything to go as *I* planned and never confided in you the way I should have. Maybe then you would've confided in me, too." He shook his head. "I guess I only wanted you to see the good stuff so you'd continue to think I was this great guy. But I wasn't and I'm not."

"Cam, don't! It won't change anything."

"I need to do this, Nicole, so humor me."

She just looked at him with those beautiful amber eyes. Eyes that might regard him with disgust when he'd finished. But this time he was going to get it all out, no matter how hard that was.

"Remember lunch at Sam's, when I told you about my life after we split?"

She nodded.

"Well, there didn't seem to be any point in discussing all the details about my marriage and about Michael's mother, but there is now."

She rose to her feet. "Cam, why do thi—"

"It's important to me that you know, that's why. I want you to know *me*—the real me." He took her hands and pulled her down beside him again. "My marriage was a brief one, two months to be exact. But my wife was not Michael's mother."

Her expression stilled, her eyes wide with surprise.

"I was still upset over our split when my dad died. I decided I needed a break and took a trip to California and ended up staying. My mom died not long after, and I guess I went off the deep end for a few months with booze and…well, I was a mess. I didn't care about much and I lived pretty recklessly."

He wiped his hands on his thighs, took a breath and went on. "During that time, I met Michael's mother in a bar. We had a couple of encounters, and both times I'd had way more to drink than I should've. I didn't know anything about her, not where she worked or where she lived. I did discover she was heavily into drugs and we parted ways after two very hazy days and nights. The first I heard about Michael was last year. His mother had died and he'd been in a few different foster homes until they finally located me. My name was on the birth certificate as the father." He took in another long breath.

"Cam, really, you don't need to tell me all this."

"Her name was Melissa," he went on because he *needed* to tell her whether she wanted him to or not. "Hell, I don't even know if I knew her name at the time."

He dropped his gaze. "Social Services tried to find her family, Michael's family, without success."

He rubbed the back of his neck where it was tight, then rolled his head from side to side. Nicole was quiet now, but he knew she must be wondering where he was going with all this. He wasn't quite sure, either, and dammit, he hadn't known it would be so hard.

But if it made the slightest difference to their relationship, he had to see it through. He leaped to his feet and shoved a hand through his hair.

"The whole point of this is that I love Michael. I don't know what the future will bring for him. I don't know if his mother used drugs when she was pregnant. I don't know if there might be medical problems because of that or anything else. Hell, I don't even know if he's really my kid. But I don't care. I love him. I intend to raise him, and if there's something in his family background or...if any genetic problems arise, we'll deal with it. I'll still love him and care for him. Always."

He turned to face her. "Life is a risk, Nicole, and you never know what's going to happen. People aren't disposable. You don't stop loving someone if that person gets sick or disabled."

Nicole knew what he was saying, but it didn't seem to her that he practiced what he preached. "What about your brothers, Cam? What did they do that was so terrible that you'd leave and never speak to them again? What could possibly be so awful that you'd abandon your family?"

"That's the thing, Nicole. I know what it looks like to you, but life isn't that black-and-white. Relationships aren't that simple. I was wrong to move away for the reasons I did. I used Michael as an excuse to do so. But even then, I never stopped loving my brothers. They know it and I know it. Thanks to you, I've realized the importance of bridging that gap sooner than I might otherwise have. Because of you, I learned how wrong I was. I swallowed my pride and called both Jack and Ransom. We got together, and that's when I learned—" He stopped to breathe.

"All these years, I blamed my brothers for not telling me my mother was sick, and now I've learned that *she* was the one who didn't want to tell me and made them swear they wouldn't. She wanted me to remember her as she was. I can't tell you how it makes me feel to know I've lost so much time with them because of this...this misunderstanding. But that's not the point. The point is that if they'd ever needed me, I'd have been there in an instant and vice versa. Even though we weren't on good terms, we know that about each other. We know that no matter how angry or bullheaded or far apart we might be, we'll come through for each other in the end. Because w have that faith, that bond, that kind of trust.''

All she could do was nod. She had no experience wit family like that. Nothing to compare it to. She wishe with all her heart that she had.

''I thought *we* had that kind of relationship, Nicole. really did. And what hurts the most is knowing you don' believe in me. You don't trust in my love.''

He stopped in the doorway, his hands clenched at hi sides. ''But regardless, who I love is up to me. It's no your decision. And I love you, Nicole, so much I ach with it. I honestly believe you love me, too. But if yo don't trust that I'll love you even if you're not perfec even if we have ups and downs and fall out over whatever then there's nothing I can do to convince you. And wouldn't want to. Because without trust, all the love i the world isn't enough.''

He stood for a moment and she knew he was waitin for a response. But she couldn't let him think the wron thing. She just couldn't. Maybe he wouldn't thank her fo it, but in her heart of hearts, she knew it was best for al of them.

She wished it wasn't so.

He shook his head and went on. ''When school's out we'll be leaving. If, before then, you think about wha I've said... If you think about what we could have to- gether...here or in Patterson or both... If you think you could trust me enough—''

He stopped and blew out a stream of air. ''Well...you know where I'll be.''

She couldn't speak and after a moment, he muttered, ''Yeah... Okay, I've said what I needed to say.''

And then he closed the door. He was gone.

FOR TWO WEEKS, Cam's words reverberated in Nicole's head, and even tonight, as she sat in the fifth row of the small high school auditorium waiting for the graduation program to start, she couldn't stop hearing them. *Without trust, all the love in the world isn't enough.*

She had desperately wanted things to be different. She'd thought about it from every angle, but every time she considered the ramifications, she came to the same conclusion. Nothing had changed.

A child's voice in front returned her to the moment. More families entered, some with small children, some with grandparents and friends. She smiled at the woman who sat next to her and then scanned the line of graduates for her A.R. students, eager to see their expressions.

Remembering the exhilaration she'd felt when she finally graduated, she hoped they'd feel even a little of the same.

She glanced around the room full of bright-eyed students, hopeful and ready to face the world and all its challenges.

There. She saw them now. Dylan, Justin, Aaron and Mitchell. They stood together, a little apart from the rest of their graduating class, waiting for their names to be called. For them, she'd worn her victory dress, the same red sheath she'd donned when she received her own degree. She sat ramrod straight, so proud of her students' accomplishments. Proud that she'd played even a small part in their success.

Waiting for these four students to graduate was a feeling unlike any other, a moment of triumph. *This*—this, she'd realized, was her calling. She knew that now. These were the students she was meant to teach.

Maybe this was the twist of fate Risa always talked about. If she hadn't taken on the class just to get over the financial hump, she never would've known where she could do the most good.

While Sipowitz had offered her a contract for the first grade, and she loved small children dearly, she knew she wasn't going to sign. She'd already met with a charter school principal about taking on another At Risk class or two and been assured she'd have a job, perhaps even full-time. New schools and classes like hers were gaining popularity in other parts of the city and throughout the state. She could continue teaching A.R. part-time as she was doing now, or work full-time, whichever would better fit her schedule while she completed her master's in secondary education.

But despite all that, the void inside her continued to grow, and worsened with the knowledge that it would always be there. She was not only alone, she was lonely. Her time with Cam and Michael had only magnified her awareness of what she was missing.

She listened as the main speaker droned on. He'd weathered some of his own storms, he said, but had become stronger for it. Not a unique thought; she'd heard it time and again. What doesn't kill you makes you stronger.

Well…she'd had a lifetime of storms to weather, and she wasn't so sure the analogy fit in her case.

"Some of you may go on to be politicians, judges or university professors…."

She listened to the speech in a detached sort of way, and had the oddest sensation that she was floating around the periphery somewhere, above the crowd, a watcher of life rather than a participant.

Since the day Cam was at her place, she'd thought deeply about what he'd said. She didn't trust in his love, he'd claimed. But that wasn't it at all.

To her, wanting the best for the people you cared about

was what love really signified. If loving her meant Cam had to forgo a family of his own or that he might have to spend the rest of his life looking after her if she got sick—or Jenny, if it came to that—what would that be like for him? For his business? And for Michael? She couldn't imagine Michael going through what she had as a child. No child should have to.

She'd thought about Cam's choice. Was it really up to him to decide? What made her think *she* should make that decision for him? How could he make a decision when he had no idea what it meant?

She didn't know the answers.

She looked at the students in front of her. So full of hope. So full of promise.

"Some of you may go on to be politicians, some judges..." the speaker's words rang in her head. "No one can predict what the future will hold. No one knows if there'll even be a future. But you must plan for it anyway. Why? Because..."

He continued talking, but as if on instant replay, those last few lines started playing over and over in her head. And suddenly...the words took on a whole new meaning. "No one can predict what the future will hold. No one knows if there'll even be a future..."

In that one swift moment, she realized with absolute clarity that *her* future was no more certain or uncertain than that of any other person sitting there. She glanced around her at the students and their families, their parents, some young, some old, some disabled, some not even there. They'd all started out with many of the same hopes and dreams.

A tiny kernel of hope grew inside her as the speaker finished and she watched each graduate accept his or her hard-earned diploma amid the cheers and applause of friends and relatives. Not one of the students, not one person in this roomful of people, had a guarantee for the future. None of them knew if they'd get sick, go on to have families or succeed in their professions.

Oh, Lord. Cam was so right. She'd cut herself off because of that uncertainty. Because of her fears, she'd destroyed her future—their future.

A dull pain of regret settled deep inside her.

Then she heard Dylan's name. And just that quickly, her pain switched to happiness, happiness for him, and it filled her completely. This was his moment. His wonderful moment and she had to forget her stupid self-pity and pay attention.

Most of the students in the regular graduating class had accepted their diplomas as a matter of course and returned to their seats. But when it came his turn, Dylan stopped at the podium and whispered something to the speaker, who nodded and then said to the audience, "We have a special request tonight from a young man who has a few words to say. I think it most appropriate that he do so." The speaker stepped to the side.

Dylan's hands were shaking, but he held his diploma tightly. "I'm not very good at this..." He gave the front-row audience a big smile and doing that seemed to pull him together. "My three fellow graduates and I have someone to thank for getting us here." He looked at Nicole.

"I know this piece of paper isn't a big deal to most people, but it is to all of us. I didn't think I'd ever get a diploma. No one in my family ever did. In fact, no one in my whole life ever believed in me, except two people. My aunt and my teacher, Ms. Weston.

"Ms. Weston believed in me when no one else did—no other teacher, no judge, no social worker. She taught me that a person can do more than he thinks if he's willing to try. But the really hard part is you've got to *want* it enough to try—even if you fail. Because it's the trying that shows what kind of person you are.''

Applause rang out.

He cleared his throat, directed his gaze to the full graduating class and went on. ''I don't know what the rest of you guys are going to do with your future, but I'm going to spend mine doing whatever I can to earn the belief Ms. Weston had in me. And I just hope you're all lucky enough, sometime, somewhere, to have a person like her walk through your life.''

Tears rolled unchecked down Nicole's cheeks, and amid a rain of applause, she clapped, too. She clapped for Dylan and because that was the most wonderful, heartfelt speech she'd ever heard.

Then Justin, Mitchell and Aaron joined Dylan at the podium. Aaron handed something to Dylan. ''This isn't much,'' Dylan said, ''but it comes from our hearts.''

Mitchell punched Dylan on the arm and said, ''Just give it to her, man.''

''We want to present this, our own special Teacher of the Year award, to Ms. Weston. Because no one deserves it more.''

Waves of applause echoed throughout the room. Voices called for her to get up and go onstage. Blindly, she worked her way to the end of the aisle and then up the stairs. Just as she reached the top and stepped onto the platform, loud cheers and whistles reverberated in the auditorium. She turned to see a flurry of balloons rising like multicolored bubbles in the air.

And then—midway down the rows of seats, she saw them—Michael perched on Cam's shoulders and waving a banner that said ''Way to go, Teacher of the Year!''

More tears welled up as she saw Roy Sipowitz and several teachers and aides from the elementary school, Harry, Sharon and the children, Mrs. Nelson and Roland, and Risa with— Oh, good heavens…Detective Arnette?

Cam slid Michael down from his shoulders and leaned down to talk to someone beside him.

Her mother.

Jenny sat next to Cam and on her other side sat Lena Olson and her mom's caseworker. Touched beyond belief, Nicole let the tears stream down her cheeks—tears of happiness instead of hopelessness, tears of immense love—and she wanted to run over to hug them all.

She accepted the award from Dylan, a single bronzed rose, and all she could do was blubber, "Thank you. I'm so proud of all of you," and then she hugged each one of them.

She left the stage and somehow sat through the rest of the program, eager to see the people who'd come to support her. And while she waited, between her pride and elation she reflected on the truth she hadn't been willing to face. Cam was right, and Dylan's speech had pounded it home.

She'd taken the easy way out. She'd done what she'd accused Cam of doing. Instead of confronting her fears, she'd run away.

She hadn't even been willing to try. She'd trusted others, but she hadn't trusted him. And she finally understood why. Because no one else wanted what he did. He wanted her to trust him with her heart.

And the most incredibly stupid part of all was that she loved him. And he knew it. He loved her and she knew it. But she hadn't been willing to commit herself unless she could be sure his love would never die. The irony was that she of all people knew there could be no guarantees.

All she could do was trust him. And she wanted more han anything to tell him she did.

When the audience began to disperse, she started mov-ng toward Cam and the others, but on the way came doubt. Just because Cam had attended the graduation didn't mean anything else had changed. It didn't mean he still felt the same about her or was willing to try a second time. He'd gone back to Patterson and probably— *No!*

Dammit, she was doing it again. Doubting his love. Two weeks ago, he'd told her how he felt about her, and tonight he was there. That *had* to mean something. And even if it didn't, even if all he wanted now was friendship, she had to tell him what was in her heart.

After the ceremony, her students whisked her off for a graduation party at the condo clubhouse Risa had reserved for the occasion. They'd all been in on the planning, including Cam who'd had the food catered and plotted with Risa to arrange for her mother to come.

Lena Olson stayed by Jenny's side, but after a short time, she told Nicole they were leaving because Jenny was getting tired. Nicole bent to give her mom a long hug. "I'm so glad you came. It meant so much to me."

"She's very proud of you," the nurse said.

Nicole looked up, tears spilling from her eyes. "Thanks for saying that, Lena. I hope she is, because I love her very much."

"Well, it's true. She told me so."

Nicole did a double take.

"She doesn't say much, but we understand each other."

Nicole grinned and waved goodbye. Jenny looked almost radiant, and even though she hadn't said a word, Nicole believed she was as proud of her daughter as any mother could be. Best of all, Nicole knew her mom was in good hands.

After that, Nicole joined the party, making the rounds to talk to everyone who'd come.

Cam had hired two musicians who played soft music in the background, and she felt downright giddy with happiness. Harry apologized and said he'd only been concerned about his brother getting hurt again but had soon discovered—with Sharon's help—that he was acting like a jerk. Cam, who'd discarded his suit jacket and tie, came to stand by Nicole as she talked with Harry.

"I probably deserved every bad thought you had about me, Harry," Nicole said.

Cam interjected, "I doubt that. And I'm glad to hear my little brother admit he was wrong."

"I *was* wrong," Harry said. "And I do admit it. How can I have anything but the utmost admiration for the woman who got my bullheaded brother to come back to the ranch and admit *he* was wrong about certain things."

They all laughed, and Sharon, wearing a pink silk dress that matched both her daughters', sidled over. "I was hoping you'd be coming to the ranch, too, Nicole. You know, they do have schools in Patterson."

"The same kinds of classes you're teaching now," Harry added. "Kids everywhere need help."

Nicole's cheeks warmed. She didn't know what to say because none of that mattered if Cam didn't want her there.

Apparently noticing Nicole's discomfort, Sharon said, "Okay, let's not put the lady on the spot." She went on to praise the wonderful ceremony, congratulated Nicole again on her award and then attempted to corral the children who ran in circles around them all, including Maria, who was keeping one eye on Michael, and Ainsley, who was deep in conversation with Mitchell, Aaron and Justin.

Risa dragged her date over and explained that until the investigation had been completed, she couldn't talk about seeing Andy, Detective Andrew Arnette. When Andy left to get drinks, Risa said, "Hey, I take my own advice. Love when it comes is better than no love at all. Even if it's only for a little while."

Nicole thought about Risa's words for a long time. Her friend was right. She was *so* damned right. But a person had to be wise enough to act on it.

Later, filled with as many warm and wonderful feelings as she'd ever had, Nicole was standing to one side, watching Dylan talk with Harry, when Cam came to stand beside her. He draped one arm around her shoulders. "The boy talks like a politician, doesn't he? Maybe that's his calling."

"Maybe so. He was eloquent." She turned to face Cam. "Thanks for helping arrange all this."

"You didn't think we'd let this occasion slip by, did you?" He shrugged. "What are friends for?"

Friends. Were they back to that? She smiled. It didn't matter if that was all he wanted now; she needed to tell him how she felt. She needed to take that step, regardless. "You were right, you know. Everything you said was right." She breathed deeply, astonished that admitting it seemed to free something inside her.

"The point wasn't to be right."

"I know. But I want you to know how I feel, even if all you want is to be...well, be friends. Or...whatever."

He looked at her incredulously, then whisked her around the corner and outside to the Spanish-tiled patio, where a fountain trickled fresh water onto stones at its base and the sweet scent of feathery cassia filled the air.

Surrounded by wispy queen palms, oleanders and bougainvillea, Cam said, "Friends? You think I want to be *friends?* I love you, Nicole. I've loved you for ten years. I wanted to marry you then, and I still do. I want to spend the rest of my life with you for better or—" he threw up his hands "—whatever."

His hands came down onto her shoulders and pulling her closer, he brought his gaze to hers. "You said you want to tell me how you feel, and I want to know. Do you love me, Nicole? Because if you do, this isn't going to end, not here, not next week or next month. I'll keep asking you to marry me until you say yes. And the only way I'll go away and never bother you again is if you tell me you don't love me." He stopped for a second, and then with a huge smile, said, "But you know what? If you tell me that, I won't believe it."

She broke into a wide smile of her own and started laughing. Such a serious moment, and she wanted to laugh. Such a happy moment, and she wanted to cry. Her eyes were overflowing with tears again. Oh, Lord. She was a mess.

"I feel so silly. I was going to ask if I could see Michael once in a while."

"You can see me all the time if you'll be my mom!" Michael piped up from somewhere behind a palm tree.

"Sorry, kid. She's got to be a wife first. And I've got dibs on that." He winked at Michael, gave him a thumbs-up, and said under his breath, "I think we're making progress. Now shoo."

Michael scampered away and Cam turned to Nicole again. He stepped closer and in a hushed voice, said, "Maybe you haven't missed me enough yet?"

All she could hear was their breathing. "I've missed you more than you can possibly imagine," she whispered.

"I'm always going to love you, Nicole."

She gazed into his eyes and, in their depths, saw everything she needed to see. "I'm going to hold you to that, cowboy."

"I was hoping you'd say that."

The sounds around them stilled, the guests faded into the background, and she was aware only of him…and the music floating softly on the air. Still looking deep into her eyes, Cam reached out to her and in a voice low and husky with love, he said, "Want to slow dance with a cowboy?"

Without a word, she drifted into his arms and together they swayed to the music, barely moving, dancing the way they had so many years before.

This was where she was meant to be. In Cam's arms—slow dancing—for whatever time they had.

"Say you'll marry me," Cam whispered in her ear.

She had no doubts now, no reservations at all. "Yes. I'll marry you, Cam. Because I'm always going to love you. For better or whatever."

Facts about mental illness:

- One in four people worldwide have a mental or neu
rological disorder at some point in their lives.
- 450 million people currently suffer from such cond
tions, placing mental disorders among the leading cause
of ill health and disability throughout the world.
- Treatments are available, but nearly two-thirds of th
people with a known mental disorder never seek hel
from a health professional.
- Stigma, discrimination and neglect can prevent care an
treatment from reaching people with mental disorders.

Mental illnesses can affect persons of any age, race, re
ligion or income, and are not the result of personal weak
ness, lack of character or poor upbringing. They are dis
orders of the brain that disrupt a person's thinking
feeling, moods and ability to relate to others. These brai
disorders are treatable. Just as a diabetic takes insulin
most people with serious mental illness need medicatio
to help control symptoms. Supportive counseling, self
help groups, housing, vocational rehabilitation, income as
sistance and other community services can also provide
support and stability.

Preceding information from the National Alliance for the Mentally Ill, 1-800-950-6264/TDD 703-516-7277, Web site http://www.nami.org and the Arizona Alliance for the Mentally Ill, http://www.aami.org.

C'mon back home to Crystal Creek with a BRAND-NEW anthology from

bestselling authors

Vicki Lewis Thompson
Cathy Gillen Thacker
Bethany Campbell

Return to Crystal Creek

Nothing much has changed in Crystal Creek... till now!

The mysterious Nick Belyle has shown up in town, and what he's up to is anyone's guess. But one thing is certain. Something big is going down in Crystal Creek, and folks aren't going to rest till they find out what the future holds.

Look for this exciting anthology, on-sale in July 2002.

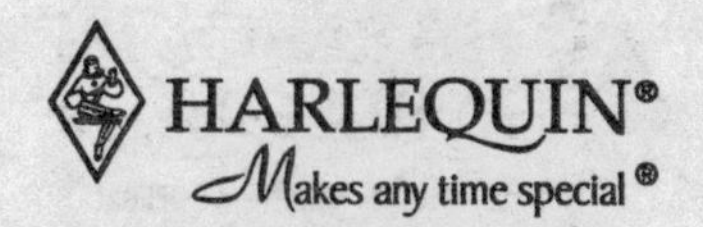

Visit us at www.eHarlequin.com

PHRTCC